Jane Davis lives in Surrey w...
She has enjoyed writing as ...
years while pursuing a succe...
Latterly, her hobby has increas... ... and she
has now given up her full-tim... job to dedicate more
time to it. *Half-truths & White Lies* is her first novel.

For further information visit the author's website at
www.jane-davis.co.uk

70003918209X

HALF-TRUTHS & WHITE LIES

Jane Davis

BLACK SWAN

TRANSWORLD PUBLISHERS
61–63 Uxbridge Road, London W5 5SA
A Random House Group Company
www.rbooks.co.uk

HALF-TRUTHS & WHITE LIES
A BLACK SWAN BOOK: 9780552775700

First publication in Great Britain
Black Swan edition published 2009

Copyright © Jane Davis 2009

Jane Davis has asserted her right under the Copyright, Designs and
Patents Act 1988 to be identified as the author of this work.

This book is a work of fiction and, except in the case of historical fact, any
resemblance to actual persons, living or dead, is purely coincidental.

A CIP catalogue record for this book
is available from the British Library.

This book is sold subject to the condition that it shall not,
by way of trade or otherwise, be lent, resold, hired out,
or otherwise circulated without the publisher's prior
consent in any form of binding or cover other than that
in which it is published and without a similar condition,
including this condition, being imposed on the
subsequent purchaser.

Addresses for Random House Group Ltd companies outside the UK
can be found at: www.randomhouse.co.uk
The Random House Group Ltd Reg. No. 954009

The Random House Group Limited supports The Forest Stewardship
Council (FSC), the leading international forest certification organisation.
All our titles that are printed on Greenpeace approved FSC certified paper
carry the FSC logo. Our paper procurement policy can be found at
www.rbooks.co.uk/environment

Typeset in 11/13pt Giovanni Book by
Falcon Oast Graphic Art Ltd.
Printed in the UK by CPI Cox & Wyman, Reading, RG1 8EX.

2 4 6 8 10 9 7 5 3 1

For Maureen, whose story telling was an inspiration.
See you on the other side.

Acknowledgements

Thanks are owed to many people, but there are some who are worthy of particular mention: to all at the *Daily Mail* and Transworld Publishers for this wonderful opportunity, especially Francesca Liversidge; to my agent, Teresa Chris, for your guidance; to those who read the early drafts including Daniel and Gillian Davis (truly the best hosts in all of Scotland), my fabulous sisters, Anne Clinton and Louise Davis; to Charlotte Martin, Bernie Barthram and Sarah Marshall; to Amanda Osborne and Delia Porter – your friendship means the world to me; to Dad, who broke the habit of a lifetime and didn't read the last page first; to Mum who refused to read it until it was in print; to Jean Porter for tea in china cups and words of wisdom; to Rosemary Williams for helping to remind me who I am; to Helen Williams (no relation) for keeping me sane and being an inspiration; and to William, Timothy, Dexter, Lara and 'Mimi', for making me smile on the bad days. But most of all, thank you to Matt for saying you would read it if I would write it, for your unfailing support and unquestioning faith in me – and for not even flinching when I handed my notice in at work: you are my rock.

'I never saw any good that came out of telling the truth.'
John Dryden

'Three may keep a secret, if two of them are dead.'
Benjamin Franklin

Part One

Andrea's Story

Chapter One

Is it possible to tell the difference between a dream and a premonition? Or is a premonition just a dream that life later adds meaning to, so that we convince ourselves that we have the power to see into the future?

My family lived with my mother's mother who, it was whispered, could change the course of history with the use of a simple phrase, so concepts such as these do not seem so very extraordinary to me. Although she was oblivious to the extent of her powers, Nana's sentences that began 'Mark my words' were the kiss of death. She thought that she just had the uncanny knack of always being right.

'Mark my words! That boy will never amount to anything.' She would cast her opinions carelessly, and a future of misfortune and underachievement would now be a certainty for her poor victim rather than a vague possibility.

When she aimed her comments at one of us, we were quick to cross our fingers for luck, the traditional family method of preventing her from sealing our fates.

'Mark my words, Andrea, you're going to regret having seconds later,' she scolded when I insisted on another spoonful of shepherd's pie. 'You won't have any room for rice pudding.' As I had to sit and watch the others eat my favourite dessert, she couldn't resist raising her eyebrows and saying, 'What did I tell you?'

As a child, I had a recurring dream. In that dream I was falling in a rolling motion, gathering momentum all the way. The green of the grass, the brown of the earth and the blue of the sky became blurred, but provided clues of which way was up and which was down. Eventually, I would have to close my eyes when dizzying nausea overtook me.

I associated that dream with a heady feeling of excitement and anticipation in the pit of my stomach. The point where the familiar meets the unfamiliar; the solid ground of the gentle slope giving way to the sheer drop.

I felt drawn to activities that induced that feeling. Somersaults, cartwheels, spinning in circles; being blindfolded at the start of a party game; rolling down grassy, daisy-speckled banks, arms folded over my chest. Sliding down slopes on tea-trays in the fresh snow; riding the big wheel when the fair came to town. Handstands on the side of the swimming pool, legs hovering aloft, waiting for the moment when the water reaches up to swallow you. I would jump into my father's arms from a height, safe in the knowledge that he was there to catch me. The pause at the top of the slide before letting go translated into the hesitation at the top of the ski slope before digging in the poles and pushing off. On my first holiday alone, I tried bungee jumping from a suspension bridge.

'That girl has no inbuilt sense of fear,' was Nana's reaction. 'She doesn't know when to stop. Mark my words, she'll come a cropper.'

'Weren't you scared of falling?' My mother, a vertigo sufferer, asked with genuine wonderment when I showed her the photos.

'It's the feeling of falling I enjoy,' I tried to explain. 'It's the only thing that makes you feel free.'

'Oh, I couldn't.' She shuddered. 'I'd be the one standing at the top refusing to jump.'

'It's not the fall you want to worry about, love,' my father joked. 'It's landing that'll kill you.'

'Oh, Tom!' Nana tutted, convinced that others were capable of bringing bad luck into the house.

It seemed to me that my parents had always played it safe. Semi-detached in suburbia, room enough for me and, because she couldn't cope on her own, for Nana. Nine to five. Fish-and-chip takeaway on a Friday. Sunday roast. Ford Escort. Two weeks' holiday in the same hotel in Spain every summer. God knows they deserved it. The truth is that I had long since outgrown the safety of the semi but, like so many of my generation, I lacked the means to buy a property of my own and the inclination to rough it in the sort of bed-sit that my wages would have afforded. I led a charmed life, although I would have taken great offence at anyone who suggested as much.

Our very average family was illustrated by a family tree that I had drawn as part of a school project at the age of eleven. It hung in the hall among family photographs, something that I passed several times every day and took little notice of, but I would have been embarrassed to admit that it was my handiwork. I can remember being criticized very harshly by my teacher for failing to make an entry for my paternal grandfather.

'But my daddy didn't have a father,' I protested, repeating what he had told me over the years. (I enjoyed this small piece of information – as I grew older it was the only thing that made me think that there might be a story behind my family that was actually worth hearing.)

'Of course he had a father,' the teacher insisted. 'Everybody has a father.'

When I asked my father about this, he told me that my diagram was one hundred per cent accurate and that he was more than happy with it.

'Who does she think she is?' he asked with genuine annoyance. 'You would think that I would know if I had a father or not.' I knew better than to push him any further on the subject. I could twist him around my little finger, but there were certain subjects that were simply not up for discussion. 'My mother loved me enough for two,' was all he would say. This did not prevent him discussing the matter with my teacher. I was humiliated to learn that he had paid a visit to the school and told her that neither he nor his family would be forced to fit into whatever outgrown idea of a family they had in mind.

'But what did you say?' I asked miserably, trying to prepare myself for whatever sarcastic comments might pass my way.

'Nothing for you to worry about. I simply told her that I may not want to be a tree and that I can be a twig, a bush or a herbaceous border if I chose.'

'You didn't!' I squealed.

'Now I come to think of it, I shouldn't have stopped there. I might like to be a family triangle, or a family rhomboid or a family flow chart. Or even a family Venn diagram.'

'A Venn diagram?' I was horrified.

He sketched a series of three interlinking circles for me. 'Yes, that works just fine. That's Mummy, that's you and that's me. You can tell Miss Whateverhernameis that from now on we will be a Venn diagram.'

'Andrea, don't listen to him, love,' my mother sighed. 'Tom, she's just trying to teach them about where they have come from. This isn't personal.'

'They should be trying to teach children to think, not to stick ridiculous labels on people.'

You can guess who won that debate by the fact that the family tree found its way into a frame and on to the wall.

'This is nice, isn't it?' my mother would habitually say as we settled round the dining-room table for Sunday lunch. The question was serious enough, and she looked around the table searching, almost as if she expected someone else to appear, sometimes

17

challenging us to disagree, checking that we were all satisfied with our individual lots. Occasionally, I felt that she was trying to convince herself that this was what she worked so hard for every week. The chance to have her family around the table and share a home-cooked meal. It seemed such a small reward. I knew that I could never be satisfied with the life that she had settled for.

'Smashing, love,' my father replied as he carved. 'You've done us proud again.'

'Oh, yes,' Nana would agree, frowning at the pink centre of the meat and the crispness of the vegetables, which were not to her taste. Steamed, for goodness' sake! 'The roasties look marvellous. Done to a "t".'

My mother beamed at this, the ultimate compliment. 'You must have taught me well, Mum.'

It was the same routines that I found so tedious at times that made us feel safe, made it possible for us to go out into the world, to be who we were and do our own things. Without those routines, for that one meal of the week when the television was turned off, we didn't always have enough to say to each other. My father would comment, 'It must be good, love, it's all gone quiet. You could hear a pin drop in here.' It was in the silences that my mother would take the time to look at us in turn and smile. 'This is nice, isn't it?'

And then it all changed. All the routines were taken away, and I can hardly believe that I miss them the most.

To celebrate my parents' twenty-fifth wedding

anniversary, my father surprised my mother by arranging a weekend away. He had let me in on the secret, of course. I was needed to stay at home to look after Nana, otherwise he wouldn't have put it past my mother to refuse to go. Or to want to take Nana with them. But he had planned for that.

He kept one surprise even from me. That Friday evening he arrived home from work in an open-topped Austin-Healey 3000, sleek in black and chrome with red leather seats. Only two red leather seats. It had been a dream of his to own one, a dream which had been whittled away gradually and demoted to a dream to drive one. Even so, the grin on his face told me that it was not a disappointment, although the luggage I had so carefully planned had to be downsized to fit in the boot.

'One hundred and fifty brake horse power.' He rubbed his hands together.

My mother became a teenager again when she saw the car. Any reservations that she might have dreamt up at the thought of being whisked off at a moment's notice were quelled. Normally, she wouldn't have even contemplated the idea of a weekend away before completing a full inventory of the freezer to ensure that there were enough single-sized portions of homemade cottage pie to feed Nana and me for a good few weeks.

'I wonder . . .' She paused outside, tapping a finger against the side of her mouth and narrowing her eyes. Then she turned and ran into the house.

'Laura!' My father called after her. 'We've got to get

going. The traffic on the motorway is going to be chocka. Oh, it's no good.' He looked momentarily deflated. 'Once she's got an idea in her head . . .'

'Ta-da!' She appeared wearing a pair of red sling-backs that looked as if they had seen far better days under her jeans and clutching a red dress, which she was trying unsuccessfully to fit into her handbag.

It seems that those shoes had much the same effect on my father as the car had done on my mother, and he looked ten years younger as he opened the car door for her. 'Your lucky shoes! Now you're talking.'

I stood at the end of the path to watch my parents disappear down the road, their eyes aglow, hands touching thighs and laps, feeling that I was intruding. Feeling strangely parental. Shouting, 'Keep your eyes on the road!'

Nana knocked that out of me quickly enough by commenting, 'Mark my words, that thing looks like a death trap.'

The news came about four hours later, delivered by two policemen who arrived on the doorstep just as I was about to go to bed. It was without any outward sign of emotion that I heard that my parents had been driving in the middle lane of the M6 when a foreign lorry driver had pulled out and clipped the edge of their car, sending it into a spin. In all likelihood, the car would have been too low on the road for the lorry driver to see in his mirrors. My mother had been at the wheel. She tried to correct the unfamiliar vehicle but veered to the left at speed, crashing through the barrier before the car rolled down the bank. There was talk that her red sling-backs had become caught in the pedals, causing her to lose control. At that point, there was quite a steep drop and the car would have bounced before rolling several times, giving alternate views of steel, lights and sky. Steel, lights and sky. My mother wouldn't have seen much of the blurred view or felt the nauseous feeling of anticipation in her stomach for long. She was decapitated, possibly as early as the first roll of the car, her body thrown clear of the wreckage, fuelling speculation that she hadn't been wearing a seatbelt. My father's neck was broken, but witnesses say he was still alive in his position trapped upside down under the vehicle, facing my mother's head, where it had come to rest in the ditch.

'Oh, my love,' he was heard to say, 'I always said it's not the fall that'll kill you.'

Chapter Two

Every child has an adult in their lives that they call 'uncle' even though he is not a relative. A man who hides his loose change down the back of the sofa for you to find. A man who lets you ride on his back around the living room and tickle him relentlessly. A man who brings your father home late smelling of beer. A man who pretends to steal your nose and hides it in his clenched fist. Who makes you count his fingers forwards and backwards to see if he still has the full set. A man who seems to keep the pockets of his work suit full of sweets. Mine was Uncle Pete, my father's best friend, a crumpled, lovable mess of a man.

It was Uncle Pete I called the morning after that terrible news. Before I had the courage to tell Nana, who had been fast asleep throughout, I needed to experiment saying the words out loud. Killed in a car crash. Shoes caught in the pedals. Both killed. No seatbelt. Staring at her head. Hit by a decapitated lorry. Dead red sling-backs.

For a long time I stared at the phone, hoping it would

ring, willing it to be him. Car rolled down the bank. 'Dial,' I instructed my hand. 'Dial now.' Rolled several times. Falling makes you feel free. I made a couple of false starts, hanging up before he answered. M6. Still alive when they found him. The time before last, I ended the call as soon as he picked up the receiver, unable to speak. Lost control. Rolled over and over. Ended up in a foreign ditch. It's not the fall that'll kill you, love. Red lorry, yellow lorry. Red lorry, yellow lorry.

I took a deep breath and rang again. *Answer! Why don't you answer?*

'Look, who is this?' he answered gruffly. 'This is the fifth time. I haven't got time for your games. This had better be good. '

'Uncle Pete, it's me. Andrea. I don't know how to tell you this, but there's been an accident. It's Mum and Dad. They're both . . .'

I was prepared for many things, but not for him to hang up on me. I didn't recognize the noise that escaped me as my own.

'Andrea!' Nana was calling loudly. 'Is that you? Run down the road and get us a paper. There's a love. Money's in the tin on the fridge. Have you seen my glasses?'

Escape seemed as good a plan as any. Anywhere other than the cheerful kitchen and its yellow walls and framed prints of rare breeds of pigs, bought as a set from Woolies.

On automatic pilot, I turned in the direction of the paper shop, hands in pockets, head down. As long as no one speaks to me. As long as I don't see anyone I know. I walked fast. Faster than usual. I felt myself breaking into a run. I hadn't run in years. Run for the sheer hell of it. My legs carried me further than I imagined possible before my breathing shortened to panting and I struggled to catch my breath. I ran through the pain, not looking or caring where I was going. I didn't see what made me fall, but I fell quite spectacularly, or so I hear, without putting out my hands to stop me. My chin hit the pavement and I tasted blood. That's when I stopped. Climbing frames, ski slopes and bungee jumps had not defeated me. An ordinary pavement less than a mile from home broke my jaw but saved me from the horrors of breaking the news to Nana and of formally identifying my parents' bodies. And my mother's head.

Chapter Three

I couldn't be angry with Uncle Pete when he came to visit me in hospital. Even if I'd been fuming, it would have been difficult to tell him so with very limited jaw movement, so he was completely safe.

Whenever my mother referred to Uncle Pete, she had always commented that what he needed was the love of a good woman. When I was very young, I loved him so much that I imagined that woman might one day be me. I had long since been of the opinion that what he actually needed was to lose a couple of stone, learn to iron and for a good friend to tell him to shave what little was left of his black, wiry hair into a number one (or to cut it for him when he was asleep on the sofa after one of his legendary 'working lunches'). My mother described him as an attractive young man who would have been a very good catch. I doubted that anyone who was unable to take care of himself would make a great partner, regardless of how much money he earned. Unless, of course, you were capable of winning an Oscar, partially sighted, aspiring towards sainthood or prepared for a life of domestic slavery.

That day, instead of his normal, confident amble, he shuffled into the ward, timidly asking the starched nurse for directions. His eyes seemed to have shrunk beneath puffy lids and dark circles, and at first they couldn't meet my own. His unshaven double chins were exaggerated three-fold under a bowed head.

'I didn't realize you'd been in the accident as well!' He looked shocked at my bandaged head. I found myself looking back at him, aware that I was mirroring his expression. He didn't need to explain what my parents' deaths meant to him. His face said it all.

'Fell,' I tried to explain with difficulty through my wired jaw. 'Tipped over.' I shook my head, unable to form the words I wanted to say. Two at a time was as much as I could manage. No 'r's. On an ordinary day, we would have made a joke out of that.

'Andrea's not herself today. She's got no "r"s.'

'What on earth is she going to sit on?'

As it was, I would have to build up to a sentence, let alone a conversation.

He looked confused by the sequence of events, but I could only point to my jaw, motion downwards with a hand to suggest a fall, and shrug.

'Don't try to talk. Look, I'm so sorry I let you down, ' he stumbled. 'I thought you were going to tell me you had been arrested or that you are on drugs or pregnant or something. I could have coped with any of those . . .'

There was silence between us for a while, then he sighed, closed his eyes and shuddered. 'I'm going to make it up to you. The red sling-backs. I don't suppose your mother ever told you the story of her lucky shoes?'

I raised my eyebrows and shook my sorry head. The sling-backs did not conjure up any happy memories for me. They only represented one thing; they had been instrumental in the crash that killed both of my parents. Uncle Pete must have known this. He wanted to tell me what they had meant to my mother.

'Then she didn't tell you the story of how she and your father met.'

I racked my brains and then thought this very strange.

'No? I expect they were being kind.' He reached out and covered one of my small, pale hands completely with one of his own bear-sized paws. 'You probably don't realize that I went to school with Laura,' he began. 'She was the prettiest girl in the school by far. No one came near her. And she was nice to go with it. Never underestimate the importance of being nice. Most of the girls would just ignore the boys who weren't popular or in the sports teams, but your mother would always say "hello" in the lunch queue or shout after me to wait for her if she was walking home alone. I was always secretly in love with her, but she was so far out of my league that it wasn't even worth worrying about. Your mother was a goddess.

'We lost touch for a while when she left school at sixteen. I took my A levels and went to university, while your mother went out to work. On the odd occasion I saw her, she looked so sophisticated. Those of us who stayed on at school had the chance to grow up

27

much more slowly. I felt like a child compared with her.

'After I qualified, my first job was at Atkins and Company on the local High Street, where your mother was already working as a secretary. How do you like that for a coincidence?'

Pennies were falling into place, although I had had no idea that Uncle Pete had known my mother first; he had always been my father's friend.

'It was so good to see a friendly face. And what a face! We chatted about the people we had kept in contact with from school, what they were doing, who they were going out with. She always was easy to talk to. Good company should make you feel relaxed, and she had the knack. She was dating an older fellow – can't remember his name for the life of me – but he was an electrician or something like that. He was paid cash in hand at the end of the week and I can tell you that it was better money than a trainee solicitor earned in those days. He could afford to look the part, had a car, could take her out to dinner and buy her all the things she wanted. I met him once or twice when he picked her up from work. He was a bit too flashy for my liking, but you couldn't ignore the attraction.

'When they split up, it was my shoulder she cried on. He'd been cheating on her with some other girl, the fool. It was after that that we got very close. If we were a couple of girls you'd have called us best friends, I suppose. She always told me how much she valued our friendship, which wasn't exactly what I wanted to hear. I have to admit that I hoped it would turn into something more. And it might have done if she hadn't met your father.

'One day, we were sitting in her favourite café. It had a bar by the window that faced out on to the High Street, where your mother liked to sit on a high stool and watch the world go by. She was dressed in a fitted red dress and her red sling-backs, which were new. It wasn't an outfit that just anyone could have got away with. They were her going-out clothes – not like today when young people have the money for a whole wardrobe full. You had your work clothes and, if you were lucky, you had another outfit for best. The shoes must have had a good three-inch stiletto heel on them, which she had hooked over the metal bar on the stool. She couldn't resist a glance at them every now and then. And I was aware of other people looking at her as well.

'Suddenly, your mother grabbed my arm, and pointed to a young man with shoulder-length hair, wearing a leather jacket with a picture of an eagle on the back. He was sauntering past, cool as anything. "Isn't that Tommy Fellows from the Spearheads?" she said. They were a local rock band who were just getting some recognition, and he was their lead singer. I was so desperate to impress her that I stupidly told her I knew him. "I'd love to meet him," she said, and there was nothing else for it.

'Without any idea of what I was going to say, I ran after him, caught him up – panting away – and told him that my girlfriend (yes, I actually called her my girlfriend) was dying to meet him and could he please pretend that he knew me. He looked at me like I was a madman, then he glanced over his shoulder towards the window of the café where your mother was sitting, waving at us. And that was all it took. When he saw her, his expression changed completely, "Your girlfriend, you said?" He frowned. I don't think he could move for a good minute.

'I nodded enthusiastically. "Laura Albury."

'As we reached the door of the café, he turned to me and said, "You'd better tell me your name."

'"It's Pete. Peter Churcher."

'So he ushered me through the door, patting me on the back and saying, "It's good to see you, mate. It must be . . . what?"

'"Two years."

'"Two years! And don't tell me," – he held out a hand to your mother – "you must be Laura. Pete, for once, you didn't exaggerate."

'And it was at the moment I saw them exchange looks that I realized what a stupid mistake I had made. What chance did I stand against the Tom Fellowses of this world? But it was more than that. It was obvious from the start that Tom and your mother were made for each other. And he wasn't just an idiot in a band who was happy to steal some other bloke's girlfriend. When I tried to make my excuses and leave, he followed me outside, we exchanged telephone numbers and he invited me for a beer.

' "Look," he said, "I feel weird about this," meaning the fact that I had left him alone with your mother.

'"Make sure you see her home," I said. "Her mother always makes me promise I'll see her home." I knew that the only thing that I could do was walk away.

'"I'll do that, Pete," and he gave me as warm a hand-shake as I've ever been given from someone I've just met, with Laura nodding and smiling from her bar stool. After that, she always called the red sling-backs her lucky shoes. Turns out they weren't quite as lucky as she thought.'

His eyes filled and he blew his nose noisily on a cotton handkerchief. 'Love at first sight.' He tried to smile. 'People talk about it, but I've experienced it and I've seen it. That was the effect your mother had on people. She could light up a room. And you know, as far as I know Tom never did give the game away that we didn't know each other before that day at the café. When we met up, we padded out our history a little more each time. That was how we became such great friends. We were co-conspirators even when there was no longer a cause. It was some time before I realized that Tom Fellows, even with his hair and his leathers and his front-man image, felt the need to impress Laura Albury as much as I did. It was an unspoken thing between us that he realized how much I cared for her. If he caught me looking at her for too long occasionally, he would just smile. He remembered how it felt when he couldn't take his eyes off her the first day he saw her sitting in the café window.'

Uncle Pete didn't bring chocolates or grapes as a gift. He brought me an old photograph album, leather-bound with black card pages and photo corners.

'This is for you now.' He choked, patting the cover, as if he didn't really want to let it go. 'You think your parents were middle-aged and boring. Don't try to tell me you don't. But I can assure you that they were, quite simply, magnificent. There,' he said as if talking to someone other than himself, 'I've told her now.'

Then he broke down. The hand that had trailed on the photograph album half waved, half gestured that I was not to say anything, and he left without another word. His shoulders were so hunched that I was left with the image of a headless man walking away from me.

Chapter Four

I was twenty-four when I lost both of my parents, but I discovered the people that they had been for the first time as I recovered in St Theresa's Hospital thumbing through Uncle Pete's photograph album. In that volume I saw them larking about and exchanging tender glances as lovers. They became more real to me than they ever had been, people starting out on their lives with hopes, dreams and ambitions, rather than just members of that strange species called parents. Uncle Pete had catalogued those early years so religiously, so honestly that the photos conveyed more than the words that we dared not speak. Each photo was dated and captioned in white ink. No one but a casual observer could have ignored the role that he played in their history, and I could only draw the conclusion that it wasn't just my mother he loved. The photographs of my father betrayed an amateur photographer who had spent many hours studying the lines of my father's jaw and the fall of his hair. Tom Fellows, as I discovered to my surprise, had been a very beautiful young man.

Of course I had seen photographs of my parents before. Their official wedding photographs, stiff and formal. My first birthday. Family holidays. I could track their gradual transformation through the seventies and eighties. My father's changing facial hair and collars. My mother's changing hemlines and hair colour. And at the centre of most of the family photos, me, gap-toothed and grinning, the rather surprising product of such a beautiful couple.

Although Uncle Pete's photo album showed me faces that I already knew, his photos portrayed real, living people.

Nineteen seventy-four. My mother watching my father's band play in a smoke-filled room, eyes transfixed, the light from the stage catching her face. Close-ups of my father holding the mic and singing, eyes closed, strands of hair glued to his face, beads of sweat clinging to his forehead. A photo of them both at the same venue, my father in leather, arms wrapped about my mother from behind. My mother posing coyly, one hip jutting out, bottom lip pouting, every inch the rock chick. Then, off guard, she is coiling a curl of hair around her index finger, lips slightly parted, looking abandoned in the crowd. Her guard is down and she looks more vulnerable than I have ever seen her.

Nineteen seventy-five. A trip to the seaside. My father and Uncle Pete skimming stones, a blur of movement. My mother and father paddling in the sea, silhouettes holding hands. My father splashing my mother while she tries to run away. A sequence of photos with my mother in a bikini. Deliberately hiding her face with her hands as she sees the camera. Lying on a striped towel, her face half hidden by a wide-brimmed sun hat, legs crossed. Arms wrapped around her knees, looking thoughtful. Asleep with her head resting on my father's chest. The caption is 'Laura snoring in tune'. The two of them on a bench eating fish and chips from a newspaper, a seagull perched perilously close by. Another shot of the seagull eating the abandoned bag of chips with my father, arms outstretched, about to wring the bird's neck.

Nineteen seventy-six. My mother and father arm in arm in a park, my mother in heels that were clearly not designed with walking in mind. A picnic with strawberries and champagne, my mother raises a champagne glass to the camera, my father a beer can. Heads back, laughing at a joke. Both of them sheltering under a tree, hair wet, the picnic blanket around their shoulders. My father whispering in my mother's ear, a look of surprise on her face. Both of them wet through, clothes like a second skin, wrapped around each other, kissing, the photographer forgotten.

My mother showing off an engagement ring, pointing to it, holding it up to the camera. My father's hair is noticeably shorter, but not short by any means. He has swapped his trademark T-shirt and leather jacket for a shirt.

My mother sitting in the window of a café. Is it *the* café window? Is this the outfit that she was wearing when she met my father?

35

My father's stag night. Too much beer, too few clothes. Another woman perched on his lap. Uncle Pete and my father with arms around each others' shoulders. My father trying to flag down a cab wearing his leather jacket, underwear, socks and boots. Lying on a bed, eyes closed but grinning madly, in his pants, socks and boots. Skinny ankles, hairy legs, big boots.

Colour photos! A picture of my mother being made up for her wedding day, eyes closed, face raised. A picture of her in her wedding dress wearing the red sling-backs with the caption, 'Laura's choice of shoes'. A picture of her in her wedding dress and white sandals with the caption, 'Mrs Albury's choice of shoes'. A photograph of my mother and a formidable-looking Nana, although she could only have been in her late forties. A photo of Uncle Pete pretending to catch the bouquet. A picture of my mother, her veil lifted, on Uncle Pete's arm. I already knew that Uncle Pete had given my mother away, her father having died very shortly beforehand. I have heard it said that it is a miracle they got married at all, but the wedding had been paid for in advance and money was sufficiently tight that cancelling wasn't an option.

A picture of my father looking pale outside the church, suited and booted, a cigarette in hand. A picture of him frowning at his watch. A picture of him leaning on a wall for support. Leaning on Uncle Pete for support.

A picture of an Austin-Healey 3000 with tin cans attached to the back, the significance of his final choice of car made clear.

Nineteen eighty. I had to check that a photo of a toddler shown with my mother, obviously pregnant, was me.

'She had a stillborn child,' Uncle Pete explained, clearly distraught. 'It broke her heart. I meant to take that photo out of the album, but it must have slipped my mind.' I could tell that he wanted the photograph back, so I gently removed it from the photo corners. Immediately, he covered it protectively with both hands and, as soon as he thought that I wasn't looking, he stowed it in the inside pocket of his suit.

I looked at him, frowning, for an explanation.

'She wouldn't talk about it. Never. Not to anyone.' I could tell that he was uncomfortable with the subject, turning his face away. '*Couldn't* talk about it. It was just too painful.'

I might have had a brother or a sister. My thoughts were racing.

'He would have been your brother. The son that your father was so desperate for.' He sighed heavily. 'Didn't you ever wonder why you had to spend your Saturdays polishing his car and learning the basics of mechanics?'

'Keep me quiet?' I tried to contribute through a mouth that would not yet move.

'He could have taken you to play on the swings and slides like the other dads. But then you wouldn't know when you are getting ripped off by a garage. Or the year that the Austin-Healey 3000 was launched.'

I flicked backwards through the pages to the photograph of the wedding car.

'I know what you're going to ask.' He almost allowed himself a laugh. In retrospect I should have noticed that it was tinged with bitterness. 'And yes. It was the very same car. He managed to track down the one they hired on their wedding day.'

'Romantic.' I struggled with the three syllables.

'Well, it turns out it wasn't one of Tom's better ideas!' he blurted out, his face turning red, taking me by surprise. 'The two people I loved the most in this world wiped out in an instant.'

As my eyes filled, he pawed for my hand. 'I'm sorry. I'm so sorry. I wasn't thinking.'

Chapter Five

The hospital gave me a protective atmosphere to view my new predicament from. Staff fussed round me kindly. A steady stream of cautious visitors approached my bed with their offers of 'If there's anything I can do' and updates of what was happening in the outside world. Not my world, which was somehow out of bounds, but the larger world of celebrity gossip, soaps, weather conditions and local scandals.

There were the neighbours.

'Have they given you a television, love? No! Well, you won't have seen "Corrie" for two weeks! I'd better bring you up to date.'

'Well, you may as well be in here. It's done nothing but rain.' As if the weather would have been my greatest concern.

'Now, you know that one who was on *Friends* . . . what's her name?'

'I've brought you a copy of *OK!* I know what it's like when you're in hospital. You don't have any idea what's going on: Ah, yes! The bible for the modern world. How could I have managed without it?

'I ran into Mrs B. in the post office and *she* said . . ' As if I should know who Mrs B. was or prize her opinion highly.

'Anyway, I brought you some homemade cake,' one said with a wink and a glance over her shoulder, as if smuggling contraband. 'I know you won't be eating right: Well, that's all the main food categories covered, then.

'I brought you some decent shampoo,' one well-wisher whispered, obviously concerned that I might be letting myself go to rack and ruin. 'I don't know what they have you using here: Under my bandages, my hair hadn't seen so much as a comb for a fortnight.

There were friends who came in pairs, relying on safety in numbers.

'So when you get out we'll have to get that on DVD:

'You missed a great party at Diane's: What a shame. I'm sure I would have been the life and soul.

'We're all thinking of going for a spa day at Annabelle's in April: Fantastic. I'd been losing sleep over the state of my cellulite.

There was my boss from Evans Textiles. That was one thing I inherited from my mother: her love of dress-making and clothes. She didn't think that she was good enough to make a living out of it but, with only a fraction of her talent, I had made a start designing dress patterns.

'We've only just found out what happened. Nobody

thought to let us know.' She looked momentarily embarrassed. Normally my parents would have phoned if I was going to be off. 'Now, there's no pressure but we'd love to see you back as soon as you feel you're ready. It can be good to have something to focus on at a time like this and to get back into some sort of routine.'

I should have been grateful. Believe it or not, some close friends seemed unable – or unwilling – to track me down. And there was a bloke I had been on a few dates with. Quite promising too. Unfortunately he thought that I wasn't returning his calls. He had moved on by the time I finally caught up with him. He was gutted, or so he said, but obviously not enough to have left a suitable mourning period, if you'll pardon the expression.

Then, just when I thought I couldn't face any more small talk, there was my mother's sister, Aunty Faye, in all her grief and grim reality. Two years younger than my mother, she had managed to avoid much in the way of family responsibility and now it had all landed squarely on her plate. She hadn't been able to sleep since seeing the bodies. Every time she closed her eyes. Shocking. Thank God I could remember them as they were. She had taken Nana in, although it really wasn't very convenient and she couldn't see any way of keeping her in the long term.

I had always admired Aunty Faye's independence and impulsiveness, even though my mother said she couldn't make the smallest decision on her own.

She had married a man she met on a trekking holiday in Peru and divorced him when he turned into a couch potato, as if that was a breach of contract. She kept a small, untidy flat with a minuscule kitchen because she was never in anyway. She was the sort of woman who owned a fridge magnet that said 'A tidy house is the sign of a wasted life' and used it as a mantra. She went to yoga, Pilates, reflexology, drumming and chanting to get rid of her demons, but they invariably caught up with her at the weekends when she succumbed to a few gin and tonics and a shopping habit that propped up the national economy. She also had a penchant for outrageous flirting with waiters who were young enough to be the sons that she didn't have.

She did contract work in IT because she didn't want to feel that anyone owned her or that she owed anyone anything. She always said her soul was not for sale. And now she was saddled with her ageing mother, who had always preferred Laura, the pretty one, and who never approved of anything she did.

As a teenager, Faye had developed a policy of deliberately making choices that her mother disapproved of because, even if she tried really hard, the end result was exactly the same. She was a punk when my mother looked like a fifties film star. She was artistic while my mother was practical. She borrowed money while my mother contributed to the household bills. In fact, I would learn, the only things that my mother ever did to register on my grandmother's grand scale of disapproval stemmed from her bringing home

Tom Fellows, a long-haired, leather-clad would-be rock star.

'Mark my words,' Nana had declared, denting his confidence, 'you'll never support a family on money earned with that guitar.'

While my mother was a listener, Aunty Faye was the sort of woman who would look you in the eye and ask meaningfully, 'And how are you?' before instantly launching into a monologue on all of her latest escapades. My father described her as a clockwork toy. 'Wind her up and she can entertain herself for hours.'

'So, don't wind her up then!' my mother would scold.

But he found Faye highly amusing and recognized that, despite their many differences, the sisters loved each other dearly and were fiercely loyal. Plus, he never stopped thanking his lucky stars that he got the sane one.

'It's bizarre, how two people who were brought up together can be so different,' he would confide in me. 'And neither of them is like their mother, thank the Lord. How can that be?'

But I had no experience of having sisters or brothers, alike or not. I could only enjoy his amusement.

'So, they're taking care of you?' Aunty Faye asked me. 'You know, I can't stand hospitals. Something about the smell of them. Do they clean this place properly? I mean, have you actually seen them polish the floors? You hear such dreadful things about people coming in for a routine procedure and going home with a super-bug.' She paused momentarily to sneeze, three precise sneezes, without covering her face or using a tissue. 'See what I mean? I think I'm coming down with something already. I'll have to grab some echinacea on the way home and dose myself up. It's not like I can afford to be ill at the moment. There's just too much to do. Everyone is relying on me. Not that I want Mum to get too settled in the spare room. I've explained to her that her social worker is trying to find her a permanent place, but she doesn't understand that she can't go home on her own. And it's so difficult when she can't remember where she is or what has happened when she wakes up in the morning. I don't think she's been to my place more than half a dozen times before. She can't remember where the bathroom is in the night so she's been wetting herself, and she's so embarrassed that she tries to hide the evidence in the most peculiar places. It's very difficult for me to come to terms with everything myself when she wakes up in the night and calls out for Laura. Can you imagine? And the look of disappointment she gives me when I go in and say, "It's me, Mum. I'm here now. It's Faye." It's like she resents me for being alive. But you know how difficult she can be. Where are the tissues?' And she blew her nose noisily, leaving the tissue on the side table for the hospital cleaners, with their well-known lack of regard for hygiene, to dispose of.

Actually, I had no idea how difficult Nana could be. I was the treasured only child of her much-loved elder daughter, spoilt from the moment I was born. There had been occasional undercurrents at family get-togethers, in the same way that my father and Nana didn't always see eye to eye. But who could expect people living under the same roof to get on all of the time? It just wasn't possible.

'Now that her mind is wandering, I really think she needs proper medical care. And with the best will in the world, even if I had the room, I can't afford to give up work to look after her. Actually, I don't know if we can afford it without selling her house.'

'I thought Nana sold her house years ago,' I said naively.

'Oh, my parents' house. Yes, Andrea' – Aunty Faye patted my arm – 'but you must know that she owns the lion's share of yours. You don't think your parents could have afforded it otherwise! It was on the understanding that Mum would live with your parents, so she was investing in her own future. That was how she explained it to me at the time. I think it's only right that if money is needed to look after her, it comes from the proceeds of the house. We can't let her down now.'

'I didn't know . . .' I mumbled pathetically. I had not contemplated the prospect of being homeless on top of everything else, but there was so much that I had to learn.

'Oh, but you hadn't thought of staying there?' My aunt registered surprise when she saw my face. 'You can't possibly want to be there on your own. Knocking round in a big place like that? I've no idea how much you earn, but the bills alone would cost an arm and a leg. One person wouldn't be able to keep it. No, a fresh start is what you're going to need.'

I felt completely out of my depth. 'I haven't been able to face thinking about it yet.'

'Of course.' She patted my arm absently again. 'It's far too early yet. That was tactless of me. It's just that I feel that I have to think of everything at the moment. Your grandmother. Funeral arrangements. The police. Statements. Solicitors. That dreadful man.' She brought her forehead to rest on one hand. I waited for her to elaborate, but her eyes came to rest on the photo album.

'What's this?' She helped herself without waiting to be asked.

'It's Uncle Pete's photo album. He gave it to me.'

'That dreadful man,' she repeated absently, opening the covers.

'Uncle Pete?' I asked.

'My God!' She was turning pages more rapidly now, her search becoming more frantic.

'Is anything wrong?' I was worried at the damage she was causing as I watched photos trying to escape from their mountings.

'It's like he's edited me out.' She was wide-eyed with disbelief. 'It's as if I was never there!'

It was true that although it was clear there had been more people present at several of the occasions, the photos chosen for the album had centred entirely on the three of them.

'Well, you tell me!' She thrust the album in my

direction before folding her arms. 'Where am I?'

'I'm not sure where I should be looking.' I was confused. I had studied the album carefully and was almost certain that I would have recognized a photo of my aunt if there had been one.

She gathered her possessions together, snatching at her handbag and holding on to it with both hands. 'It's like he's completely erased my memory. As if I wasn't part of it at all.'

'I'm sure it's not deliberate,' I foolishly tried to suggest.

'Don't try to pretend that he's put this together for you now as a keepsake or something!' She was buttoning her coat. 'I can even guess at the pictures that he's removed. It's like he's rewritten our history! What right does he think he has?'

She turned and left with the eyes of the entire ward following her, turning back to add, 'You'd better try and keep him out of my way at the funeral!' They all pretended to be minding their own business.

'Can you try to keep it down in here?' One of the sisters quietly tried to take my aunt's arm and direct her to the door. 'There are patients trying to rest . . .'

She was elbowed away for her efforts. 'God help him if I come face to face with him, Andrea,' was Aunty Faye's parting shot.

'He'll need it,' an elderly lady added after the door had swung shut, and there was laughter of polite relief as calm was restored.

'Family!' my neighbour joked. 'You can't choose 'em. Is that your mother?'

I shook my head and made the effort to smile. 'No.'

'Just as well, eh? That'd do your head in, non-stop like that. Does she ever stop to draw breath? You're closely related, though. I can see the likeness.'

Chapter Six

When it was time to leave the sanctuary of the hospital, I did so with the minimum of fuss. I didn't want to alienate Aunty Faye by asking Uncle Pete for a lift, even though he had been my most frequent visitor. I caught the 164 to the top of my road and approached the house from the opposite pavement, ready to walk past and round the block if I couldn't face it. I almost walked past by mistake and had to double back.

Half a dozen wilted bunches of flowers were propped up against the wall, the wording of the carefully written cards smudged by tears and rain. *Laura and Tom. Miss you. Words cannot express. Always valued your friendship. Not just a sister.* Faded rose petals looked as fragile as tissue paper. The front garden was overgrown and the glass of the door was clumsily boarded. No one had thought to tell me that there had been no option but to break in to rescue Nana, and I presumed there had been a burglary. I suppose that they didn't want me to feel guilty about having left her on her own. I half expected that my keys wouldn't work in the lock, but I didn't have trouble opening the door the first half-inch. It was only then that it became wedged against something on the inside. I launched an unsuccessful attack with my shoulder, my frustration growing by the minute, before bending down to try and reach under the door to move whatever was blocking the way.

I became aware of onlookers, neighbours who had appeared to see who was breaking the door down this time. Neighbours who were a little afraid to approach when they saw it was me.

'Out of the way,' bustled Lydia from next door but one. 'Coming through! You're no good to her just gawping. Andrea, love, you're home.' She held my hands in hers momentarily, this brassy woman I only knew in passing but had a reputation for being the local busybody. I could have buried my face in her jacket with gratitude. 'I wanted to come and see you, but I'm afraid I don't do hospitals. They give me the willies. And now this is all my fault. I've spent the last couple of weeks pushing post through the letter box so it didn't look like the house was empty. You can't be too careful, can you? There's been sacks full of the stuff. I'll get my Kevin to give you a hand. I'll just go and prise him off the sofa. You wait there. Won't be a mo.' And she took charge, nudging the bystanders away in the process and tutting, 'Haven't you lot got anything better to do than stand there catching flies?'

Returning with her reluctant son, I could see that she'd had to push him all the way. He didn't like crowds and was obviously ill at ease.

'Aren't you going to say something, Kevin?' She nudged him encouragingly.

'Andrea.' He nodded at me, keeping his eyes on the path. I was grateful that he kept it short and returned his nod, my eyes similarly averted, knowing that he would have been embarrassed by anything more.

'That's it, love,' Lydia approved, smiling and nodding.

I couldn't remember the last time I had seen Kevin. He was not keen to exchange his natural habitat for the great outdoors, although he had been known to wander as far as our house on occasion to see what my dad was up to under one of his cars. *That* he called 'goin' for a walk'.

'Tom,' he would acknowledge my father's feet, scrutinizing the vehicle.

'Kevin!' a muffled voice would respond. No need to avoid eye contact that way. 'Nice to see you out and about, mate.'

After a while, Kevin would enquire, 'Spot of trouble?'

'Just a little fine tuning. You've got to be gentle with her.'

Later still, after much nodding with arms folded in front of him, Kevin would add, 'Ah'll be off, then.'

He would wait for the reply, 'Right you are,' before shuffling away.

That he would call 'a discussion'.

'Nice walk?' Lydia would enquire on his return. Often she would have stood guard at the gate, pretending to busy herself with a cigarette or a few weeds that had strayed on to the path.

'Gonna have a sit down, Ma.'

'That's right, love.'

'He's simple, that one down the road.' Nana made her views on Kevin well known, but my dad said he admired his economy of speech and any grown man who had learned how to avoid working for a living.

'That's it, love,' Lydia encouraged, patting her son on the back. 'Now, what it needs is a nice big shove. Door's bust anyway. You can't do a lot more damage.' As an aside to me, she winked and said, 'That's what he's good for, breaking things. But he'll put them back together better than new. You'll see.'

I stood aside and mumbled through my useless jaw, 'Be my guest.'

'That still bothering you, love?' She put an arm round my shoulder. 'Don't expect you're ready for talking yet. Perfect excuse if you need one. Go on, Kevin! I expect Andrea's dying to get inside. Oh, Lordy!' She brought her spare hand up to her mouth. 'Could've put that a bit better, couldn't I? Me and my big mouth.'

And there it was. I had been dreading the prospect of an empty hall, an empty house. Instead, there was a cluster of neighbours, too timid to approach me and yet feeling that they should be there, and a mountain of post. I was bustled into the kitchen by Lydia who thought that a cup of tea was just the thing for it. It was black tea as the milk turned out to be well past its sell-by date and the consistency of porridge.

'I'll have that,' she enthused, after seeing me recoil.

'Make you some nice scones to go with our next cuppa. Waste not, want not.'

Never criticize a busybody. The thing about busybodies is that they are interested. They sort the junk mail from the post, they organize, they clean, they shop and they cook. They have a friend who owes them a favour who can come round and fix the lock at a moment's notice. All this without being asked. They do not pity, but they are deeply aware of your feelings and generous with their hugs. They do not stand and gawp, worrying that what comes out of their mouths is not precisely the right thing to say. In fact, Lydia could talk a fine line in drivel, but she was aware of that too.

'I'll stop if you want to think, but thinking's never got me anywhere. And it's not good for you at a time like this. You can tell me to leg it anytime you like.'

She talked. I stood and stared at the piles of post that had swiftly been sorted by size and content the moment the kettle was on.

'Bet you didn't realize you had so many friends. Those are for the bin, that's your business end, those are letters and those are the cards.' She pointed to various piles.

'How can you tell?'

'Years of practice,' she shrugged. 'Do you know, when I was a lass, many's a time when I would steam open a letter, have a look and then stick down the envelope so you wouldn't know any different. Quite an art to it. But if you need to know what's in your school report before your parents, you get the hang of it pretty quick, I can tell you.' Her laugh turned into a terrible bout of

53

smoker's cough and she thumped her chest with a clenched fist. 'They don't teach you that in school! So what shall we start with?' She tagged the question on to the end of the story so innocently that I almost answered automatically. 'I can imagine all of those people' – she tapped the table next to the pile of hand-written envelopes – 'dragging theirselves out to the shops and rummaging through the sympathies' section for half an hour, getting their knickers in a twist about which one to buy, then dragging theirselves home again and sitting there with a cup of tea, fretting for an eternity over what to write. Feeling like it's the individual words that are that important.' She paused and I wondered if she had some words of wisdom to add. 'Me?' She scraped back her chair and stood up. 'I thought I'd make you a nice brew instead. And we did all right, didn't we, love? See! I'm going to get Kevin's tea now.' She switched on the radio ('Bit of company for you') and looked around her as if she had forgotten something. 'That lad's a genius but he can burn a salad left to his own devices. You're very welcome or I can nip back later on if you need anything.'

'No.' I tried to sound convincing. 'I think I need to spend the first night here on my own.'

'That's right, love.' She patted my arm. 'I'll pop round in the morning then. Before I go and do for my ladies.'

As I followed her to the front door, she turned and said, 'You know, it's funny. I don't think we've ever had a proper chat before. Isn't it strange that you can live a few doors away and not get to know someone? It wasn't like that when I was growing up around here. Neighbours could count on each other. That's what made me decide to come back home after my Bill died. When your world falls apart you need to be close to family. I expected it to be exactly the same, that was my mistake. Not all change is for the best, you know. Anyway, love, you know where I am. Don't be a stranger.' She plodded down the corridor, and just when I thought she was gone I heard her mutter quietly, as if she was struggling to get the words out, 'I'm sorry for your troubles.'

Then, for the first time in my life, I knew what it was like to be alone.

Chapter Seven

When you lose someone, there is an expectation for quite a while that you will get over it. That, in time, things will get easier. That's what you have always been told. The first night will be the worst. There is a vague hope that the funeral will bring some sort of closure. That the first anniversary will be the most painful. Maybe once Christmas is out of the way.

As time passes, it gradually dawns on you that this feeling is not temporary. Doctors are happy to sign medical certificates with a flourish. You are offered sleeping pills, counselling and anti-depressants, but it doesn't feel as if they should be the answer. Something has changed permanently and you have to get used to this new reality, a whole new perspective. Possibly, an entirely new way of living. The loss becomes a part of who you are and, in time, as you begin to accept that, it seems only right. There is a chance that the people you knew before will not fit into your new life. It is not that you think of them any differently. It has more to do with the way that they look at you with pity in their eyes. The nervous way they approach you. The way that they call with forecasts of their good intentions, but when it actually comes down to it, it's easier for them to go to the pub with a new friend rather than cry into a mug of tea with an old one. The things that they don't say rather than the things they do. And it has to be said that I wasn't a good host to those people who dared to come near me. To tell the truth, I was far happier to be left alone with my memories than to confront all of the todays and tomorrows that were queuing up endlessly just outside the front door, complete with its brand-new five-lever mortise deadlock: Kevin's addition to what he considered to be the extremely lax approach to security taken by the so-called professionals. It was easy to sit in the centre of the sofa and imagine that my mother was in the kitchen trusting Delia to let her into the secret of what it was you were supposed to do with the celeriac you bought in Tesco in a fit of enthusiasm, while my dad was lovingly tinkering with his latest acquisition out the front. His desirable wrecks, he called them. There were days when I could swear I saw the fleeting movement of a skirt through a half-opened door, heard the clanging of a wrench being dropped. The memory of the senses is a powerful tool. Sounds that I had always thought were man-made turned out to be the sounds that the house itself made. It had a voice of its own. The central heating firing up early in the morning. The staircase creaking as the house warmed up and relaxed. The wind singing through the chimney. The clatter of the letter box when the postman visited, which sent me running down the stairs to see if we – if I – was being burgled.

Sometimes, my parents' absence seemed more powerful than their presence. Sometimes I could have sworn they were still there.

Chapter Eight

Between Aunty Faye and Social Services, it had been decreed that Nana had taken complete leave of her senses.

'In some cases, a shock like this can accelerate the ageing process,' was one of their favourite theories. Alzheimer's was the word that was being tried on for size. And, one way or another, they were determined to make it fit. Like the ugly sisters with Cinderella's glass slipper. Then they could give her a label and they would know exactly what to do with her.

There is no doubt that her inability to recall the accident from one day to the next was causing Aunty Faye a great deal of distress. 'She doesn't want to remember. She's doesn't want to remember *anything*.'

But it had to be more than that. If there was the option of choosing not to remember, I would have taken it. As, I'm sure, would Aunty Faye, who had gladly accepted the mountain of sleeping pills that her doctor had offered. If I slept, there were a few moments of peace on waking before I was struck by the stillness of the house and questioned the reason for it. Then, of course, it dawned on me, and I pulled the duvet over my head to shut the facts out. Nana had always called out for one thing or another as soon as she woke up. The first thing that I would hear was 'Laura do this' or 'Laura, fetch me that'. It was far more reliable than an alarm clock, as was my father's retort, 'Legs fallen off in the night, have they, Brenda? Sorry to hear that.'

'Nana.' I approached her single bed in Aunty Faye's spare room cautiously. 'It's me. Andrea.'

She looked at me sideways, and then gestured to the chair beside her. Even confined to bed like an invalid, Nana had a neatness about her. Her short grey hair still looked as fresh as when she returned from her weekly shampoo and set, and she gathered the duvet around her small frame as she propped herself up. I noticed her nails had been painted in a dark plum shade and suspected Aunty Faye's work. It was not her usual colour and it looked wrong.

'Well, of course it's you. Good Lord, child, what've you done to yourself?' She clutched me by the elbow, pulling me towards her. 'You never had your mother's looks but you could take a bit more care with your appearance. Mark my words, you don't want to end up on your own like that other one.'

I was a little taken aback by her bluntness. I knew she was capable of it, but I had never been her target before. 'I broke my jaw,' I explained.

'What did you want to do that for? Here! Have they let you back in the house? They tell me there's a problem with it. What's happened to it? Are the mice back again?'

'There are no mice, Nana.'

'Is it the boiler? It hasn't been the same since your dad tried to mend it. Just because he can change a set of spark plugs, he thinks he can do anything with a spanner.'

'The boiler's fine.'

'Why won't they let me home then?' she implored, then lowered her voice: 'I don't like it here. They're keeping me cooped up. Faye's got some strange ideas about cooking. Everything's out of a packet or done in the microwave. I haven't had a square meal in a fortnight.'

'I can hear you, Mum,' came a voice from the living room. 'I'm not deaf, you know. Just got the word "mug" printed across my forehead.'

'Shut the door,' Nana mouthed, looking even more frantic about her predicament. I complied. 'I can't do a thing without them checking up on me. I'm not allowed to flush when I go to the toilet because they want to see the colour of it. They take notes about everything I say. I can't leave the flat. Am I too hot, am I too cold? You don't think I'm ill, do you? I don't feel ill. Feel my head!' She grabbed my hand and pressed it to her forehead.

'Do you remember what happened to Mum and Dad, Nana?' I tried to say softly.

'Do I remember?' She became short with me and folded her arms. 'Of course I remember. They gave away my grandchild.'

'I'm your grandchild.' I was taken aback. I was her only grandchild. Thoroughly spoilt, too.

'I hope you're not going to treat me like an imbecile too, Andrea.' She was most put out and sounded like her normal self for a moment. 'The one after you. They gave away my grandson. And *you're* worried about *my* memory! I thought I could rely on you to be on my side. Now let's stop this stuff and nonsense, have a cup of tea and then you can take me home.'

'Are you talking about the stillborn baby?' I repeated what Uncle Pete had told me.

'Is that what they told you?' she sneered, before making a cradle shape in front of her. 'I held that boy in my own arms. In my own arms.' Then she started humming softly and smiling, a lullaby for the child that only she could see. 'We'll all be going home soon,' she cooed. 'All going home soon.'

'I'm afraid we can't do that.' I lowered my eyes, not knowing how I would respond to the challenge that would inevitably follow.

'Why on earth not?' She bordered on the aggressive. 'It's my house just as much as it is yours. In fact, I'm sure a lawyer would say it's almost all mine.' It seemed that there was some truth in what Aunty Faye had told me.

I hadn't wanted to lie to her. I had avoided telling her the news before and I felt that it was only right that I should make it up to her. But I honestly believed that if I had told her, she would have been distressed, and what was the point for the sake of a few short hours before she forgot again? 'You were almost right

62

about the mice.' I avoided her gaze. 'It's rats this time.'

'I knew it!' Nana seemed triumphant. 'Finally! I knew I could get the truth out of you. You've never been very good at lying.'

Returning to the living room to report back to my aunt, I sat down heavily and sighed, probably louder than I had intended.

'Well,' she asked without taking her eye off the paper she was reading, 'what's your verdict?'

'She *sounds* like Nana,' I ventured cautiously and then paused.

'But . . .' She motioned diagonally with her left hand, sweeping it away from her face.

I shrugged hopelessly and mimicked her hand movement.

'So you'll support me in finding a place for her?'

One innocent question. I knew everything that it would mean for both Nana and me. All of her hopes of living in her own home in her old age dashed. The sale of the only home that I could remember. But more than that, it felt as if I was betraying my memories of my parents. And yet I knew that it was unreasonable to expect Aunty Faye to look after Nana in the long term. Given the choice, I had to admit that I didn't want to care for Nana at home on my own, even if it meant keeping my treasured memories. I betrayed them all with a nod, swallowing the words that I could not bring myself to say.

'Good girl.' Aunty Faye's voice had no trace of emotion in it. 'It's going to work out for the best. For everyone.'

Chapter Nine

Nervously, I pushed open my parents' bedroom door against the heavy pile of the carpet. The room, usually ordered with almost military precision, was as my mother had left it after hunting for the red sling-backs. The doors of the fitted wardrobes that lined the far wall were open, shoes and handbags spilling out. I sat on the edge of the bed waiting for a little courage. As I sighed, I breathed in my mother's favourite perfume, Jasmine, still lingering. It was as if I suffered a further loss later when the trace of perfume faded and the room started to smell differently.

I was starting the slow process of packing away my memories so that I could put them somewhere safe until I was in a fit state to deal with them. There had been no shortage of offers to help me box up my parents' belongings, but I had said a firm 'No, thank you' to a nervous Uncle Pete and a relieved Aunty Faye. It felt wrong to be disturbing anything at all, but I didn't want to be rushed or be carried along with someone else's agenda.

I stood on the edge of the bed to reach the top cupboards where the suitcases were kept. I resisted the temptation to trampoline, but had a vivid memory of jumping on my parents' bed and laughing my socks off as my father pretended that my feeble jumps were propelling him into the air. A good pull brought the cases crashing down to the floor followed closely by me, thrown off balance by their weightlessness. *It's not the fall that'll kill you.* The luggage labels from last year's holiday were still attached. I hadn't gone – too old for family holidays – but Nana had joined them.

'Our little threesome,' she had joked, tucking her hand into the crook of my mother's elbow, while my dad pulled faces behind her back.

'Isn't it enough that we share our house with her?' I had heard his hushed voice through the door as I crept across the landing after a night out.

'She might not be here next year,' my mother replied.

'What are you talking about? The woman's indestructible. She'll outlive the lot of us.'

It was clearly a bone of contention between them. There was no question of who had won that particular quarrel. And yet Dad had come home referring to Nana as his gambling buddy. It seems that they found common ground when they discovered a local casino and tried their hands at the tables. It was my mother who was the lemon in the end.

My only plan was to pack away things that I wanted to keep and to put the rest in bin liners to take to Oxfam. Simple, you would have thought. But every one of my father's shirts seemed to hold a memory. As a little girl, I always helped him pick a shirt and tie to go with his work suit. Sometimes my mother would attempt to veto my choices, but my father would go along with exactly what I had laid out on the bed for him. It was a question of solidarity between us. Naturally, I was biased towards the ties that I had bought him as presents, complete with cartoon characters or corny slogans. 'Best Dad in the World'. Essential for creating the right impression in a business meeting.

Pairs of shoes conjured up an image of him sitting on the back step of the kitchen, all of his shoe-cleaning equipment laid out in a neat row in the required order on a piece of newspaper. He enjoyed the challenge of making an old pair of shoes look shiny and new almost as much as he enjoyed polishing the chrome of a bike or a car. This was a serious business to him. If you think of a doctor preparing for major surgery, you will get the picture. My father had a deep respect for tools of any sort and cared for them lovingly. Nothing was put away dirty or untidily. Everything had to be just so, exactly as he would need it the next time. When I wanted to 'help', he would allow me to pass him the right piece of cleaning equipment at the right time while he would whistle to me. I learned to whistle sitting next to my father on the back step of our house. In time, we mastered some simple duets, but when my father launched into his rendition of 'The Man who Sold the World' or 'Stairway to Heaven', I stopped to listen, hands cupping my face and elbows on knees. I thought that whistling was the extent of his musical talents, but it was magical to me.

Jumpers represented Christmases gone by. Nana always bought a jumper for my dad for Christmas from Marks & Spencer, resplendent with snowflakes and reindeer. Most of them were rarely worn other than on the big day itself, safe in the knowledge that we were unlikely to leave the house. He would rip off the wrapping paper enthusiastically, pretend to be surprised and delighted, and strip off whatever he was wearing in front of us all to put on the new jumper. Sometimes he would deliberately put the new jumper on inside out and back to front and ask, 'What do you think? Isn't it terrific?' Sometimes he would pretend that his head was too big to fit through the hole and battle away until I went to help him. It was always my help that solved the problem. Sometimes his hands would emerge through the head hole in a digging motion followed by the top of his head. We knew this as his mole impression. Sometimes he would kneel on the floor, leaving the arms of the jumper dangling with his hands just visible from underneath the bottom edge, tensed into claws. He would alternately blink against the light and widen his eyes, hooting like a half-demented owl. Sometimes he would rotate the jumper through 90 degrees, put his head through so that his eyes were visible and his ears were pushed forward by the unforgiving neck and wave the empty sleeve about in front of his face, trumpeting like an elephant.

'Oh, that's a lovely fit, Tom,' my mother would remark

after the commotion was over, or, 'That's a good colour on you, Tom.' Anything to avoid actually saying, 'I will never, ever be seen in public with you wearing that,' or, 'Over my dead body will you leave this house wearing that thing.' My mother was always very particular about appearances. She felt that people would judge you by what you wore.

'I've kept the receipt in case you want to change it,' Nana would say, beaming, lapping up all of the compliments about her choice. In those days, I would believe them too.

'Change it, Brenda?' he would reply, horrified at the suggestion. 'Why on earth would I want to change it?'

It became more and more difficult for my father to pretend that he liked the Christmas jumpers that hung unloved in his wardrobe. Eventually, my mother started to insist on taking Nana Christmas shopping and was able drag her away from the novelty jumpers. For the next two years my father was delighted to receive a cream Aran wool jumper and a chunky fisherman's jumper that he could genuinely enthuse about.

'What did you say to the old boot?' I caught him asking my mother as they were canoodling in the kitchen. He always loved that word. Canoodling. Canoodling in the kitchen. There's a word that's just waiting to be caught misbehaving.

'I asked her if she would prefer to buy you something you could wear the whole year round rather than just in December.'

'Genius! And that's why I married you.'

But Nana cast a disapproving eye over my father in his cream Aran. 'Are you sure that you don't want to change it for something a bit more colourful? I've kept the receipt.'

For my part, I missed the ritual and the play acting. It is an unfortunate sign that you are growing up when you stop appreciating the beauty of cartoon ties and Christmas jumpers.

I caved when I unfolded his overalls. Once white but never laundered, every stain represented a morning that we had spent together washing and polishing, peering into bonnets as my father showed me how to check the oil level and change the spark plugs, mending chains on bicycles and removing the innards of tyres to look for punctures, as all the while I pretended that I could recognize a subtle difference in the engine noise after my father had spent hours doing a spot of fine tuning. Listening to him talk about cars was like learning a foreign language. I understood most of the individual words but much of their meaning was lost on me. I didn't let on because I didn't want him to think that his enthusiastic explanations fell on deaf ears. The fact that parts of it eluded me made it all the more magical and mysterious. I spent most of my childhood trying to make up for the fact that I was just a stupid girl, even if it meant disappointing my mother. It seemed obvious to me that my father longed to have a son to play with and to teach.

The world that I inhabited with my father was out in the back yard, the tool shed or the oil-stained drive at the front of the house. There was nothing that made me happier than to be told that I was too dirty to come into the house for lunch and being asked to undress at the back door, while my clothes were put straight into the washing machine. It was a matter of pride when my mother, in an attempt to save my 'good' clothes, went to Halfords and bought me a set of boy's overalls.

While other fathers read their children bedtime stories, my father lulled me to sleep with the Haynes manual for whichever car he was working on at the time, pointing at diagrams and elaborating on the workings of carburettors. If he ever heard my mother coming up the stairs, he would proclaim loudly, 'And they all lived happily ever after,' or, 'And that's what happens if you go into the woods wearing a red cape,' while sitting on the manual he had been reading from. (I would always have a second book to hand in case she ever asked any awkward questions.) If she appeared in the doorway, he would then pretend to be surprised when he noticed her and say, 'I didn't see you there, love. You must stop creeping about like that.' I loved the secrets that we shared. It was almost as if my father and I were the children of the house, while my mother and Nana were the adults. He was as relieved as I was when he got away with something.

'That was a close escape.' He would wink. 'They're always checking up on me.'

'Me too,' I sympathized.

'Well, you are only seven.'

'How old are you, Daddy?'

'Let me see. It was my birthday last April so that makes it seven thirty. Isn't it time you were asleep, Andrea Fellows?'

'Have you forgotten your age again, Daddy?'

'Yes. But it will have changed again by tomorrow, so there's no point worrying too much.'

Behind his suit jackets, I found what I had been looking for. Something to link my middle-aged, balding father to the man I had seen in Uncle Pete's photograph album. A black leather jacket with *The Spearheads* painted on it in white amid a design of an eagle, feathers and arrows. Infused with the smell of beer and smoke, this was the jacket that Uncle Pete had described.

I picked it up and felt the weight of it. Having seen the photograph album, it wasn't difficult to imagine my mother's eyes following my father down the road on the day that they met and Uncle Pete running after him in a vain attempt to impress the girl of his dreams, who would remain just that. I thought of the photos of my father singing, eyes closed with concentration, and of my mother focused on the stage, unaware of the camera, lost in the crowd. And I wished with all my heart that I had known those people.

Chapter Ten

It wasn't that I was uninterested in my mother's world. It was just that oil-stained overalls seemed far more accessible to me than the treasures of her dressing table. I was not a pretty child. When strangers met us and peered at me in my pushchair, the shapes of their mouths changed from the pre-prepared 'Ahh' reserved for all babies and toddlers, to the uncertain surprise of an 'Oh', and they would enquire of my mother sympathetically, 'Takes after her father, does she?' Being a tomboy was an obvious choice.

My mother could look glamorous with a rolled-up towel piled high on her head after washing her hair. And despite my father's constant assurances that she would look good in a bin liner, she had a keen sense of what suited her. She may have looked a million dollars, but when I was young she made her own clothes, shopping carefully for offcuts and ends of rolls after she had calculated exactly how much material she needed. Money was tight, and my mother was frugal but resourceful.

I can remember the sound of heavy-handled pinking shears cutting through the fabric that she had marked out so carefully using a flat triangle of dressmakers' chalk; can picture her leaning over the table with a row of pins in her mouth, each with a different coloured head, spikes projected outwards. With my jaw still on the mend, I could do a reasonable impression of her warnings not to make her talk to save her from swallowing them. She demonstrated how to thread the sewing machine, concentration furrowing her forehead as the material passed under the needle. I loved the sheer magic of watching a dress take shape. I still do. Nothing bought in a shop ever fitted her the way that her hand-made clothes did. She made sure of that, adding extra tucks where the pattern didn't result in the fit that she was looking for.

I wasn't expecting to find anything old and filled with memories in my mother's side of the wardrobe. Once she grew tired of her clothes they were demoted to dressing-up material or recycled into something new for me. An unworn dress and jacket bought for a wedding that hadn't yet taken place brought a lump to my throat. She would have hated the waste of it. I wondered if I should put them on one side for Aunty Faye as the sisters were the same dress size, although they would both say 'same size, different shape' when asked if they had ever thought of sharing clothes. The real issue was not one of body shape but of taste.

I worked my way ruthlessly through her wardrobe, not daring to stop and look at individual items. After I had finished I sat on the padded stool at her dressing table facing the silver-framed photograph of the three of us, me in the middle, gap-toothed and grinning, flanked by Mum and Dad. It had been her favourite family portrait. I must have been about seven, which would have made her thirty-one, him thirty-two. We had visited Russell's Photography Studio and Mr Russell had taken twenty separate poses before he got a single shot where one of us wasn't squinting or pulling a face.

'He can't be very good,' I had whispered far too loudly within Mr Russell's earshot, 'Uncle Pete always gets it right first time.'

Uncle Pete roared when my father told him that, and picked me up to kiss me on the cheek. 'And I'd have been cheap at half the price. Who's my clever girl? Let's see if I've got anything in my magic pockets for you.'

I looked at myself in the central mirror, while the side mirrors reflected unfamiliar angles of my face, somehow making it clearer which features I have inherited from each parent. Although as a younger child I was told I was 100 per cent Fellows, I grew to look more like my mother's side of the family. I've heard it said that nature has organized things so that babies resemble their fathers for the first two years of their lives. This is meant to prevent the fathers from disowning them and leaving. Nana frequently reminded me when I was a little girl that everyone is beautiful at some point in their lives, and that it was not my time yet. She liked to tell me the story of the Ugly Duckling as if this would offer some comfort, but the message it reinforced was that people will love you if you're beautiful, and that those who are not blessed in the looks department were going to have a pretty rough time of it. The only place where I was number one was at home, where I always knew that I was loved.

'You look just like your Aunty Faye when she was your age,' my mother would tell me as she brushed my bushy hair until she was halfway happy with it. 'It's funny how looks run in families that way. If you ever have a cousin, she's going to be just like you.'

'Do you think I look like Daddy?'

'Well, of course, you look like your daddy too!' She swooped to kiss me. 'You're a cross between my absolute two favourite people, so that makes you my number-one girl.' Sometimes she would hug me to her so tightly that all of the breath was forced out of me and I would gasp for air. When she let go, she would have tears in her eyes.

'Why are you crying, Mummy?'

'Oh, I'm not sad, darling.' She would dab her eyes. 'These are happy tears. Do you know how much we love you, baby?'

My teens were tough for me, not because I suffered from greasy hair and acne like some of the girls at school, but because exactly the opposite happened. I was so used to my own image of myself that I didn't even notice it. It wasn't just the new underwear, clothes and make-up that my mother encouraged me to experiment with. At some point between the ages of twelve and fourteen, I became attractive. I wasn't as pleased as I should have been. It had delighted my father that I began life as a tomboy. He never really got over the fact that I got breasts. C cups. We had to stop hugging because they got in the way. I was embarrassed by his embarrassment, almost apologetic. I tried to strap them in place with sports bras, but occasionally, when I was alone in the house, I would take off my top in front of the mirror on my mother's dressing table – the only way of looking at myself from different angles – to get a better idea of what they looked like. My mother had clearly always enjoyed her shape. I hated mine. It took me years to feel comfortable in my adult body.

To the right of the dressing table, a glass jar of cotton wool balls sat next to a bottle of Johnson's Baby Lotion – she said she loved the smell of babies – and her Oil of Olay. A spray can of Impulse. A bottle of expensive bath oil that seemed to be for display purposes only. Pond's Cold Cream. Silvikrin Hairspray. Lavender-scented talcum powder. Astral hand cream. She was faithful to her little rituals. These were the products that she had used as a teenager and that she bought for me until I took more of an interest and replaced them with other brands. I lined them up, rotating the labels until they faced the front. Turning my mother's hairbrush over in my hand, I looked at the stray hairs still tangled in it, honey-blonde against the red cushion. She had taken her make-up bag with her that wretched weekend and I hadn't yet found the courage to unpack the bag of belongings that had been returned to me sealed in clear plastic, but spare nail polishes and lipsticks in various shades of reds lay in a small wicker basket. I used to love watching her put on her face. It didn't work if I sat on her lap as she had to lean so far forward to apply the mascara and draw a perfect line on her upper lid that she was almost touching the mirror. I would be pushed outwards. It was all right if she was just doing a quick touch-up with powder. Lipstick, blot, then a second coat, blow kisses in the mirror. I never understood why you would put lipstick on and then blot it off again. It seemed a complete waste of effort.

My mother was always more of a mystery to me than my father. Occasionally, her eyes would glaze over with a distant look and she would literally switch off her senses. Even if you were standing right next to her, she wouldn't be able to hear a word you said. My father called it her 'selective hearing', but it was almost as if she was in a trance. If you waved something in front of her face, she would snap out of it instantly, sometimes a little cross. When I was small and couldn't reach up high enough, my daddy would pretend he had hypnotized her and that only he could bring her back by snapping his fingers and saying, 'Bananas, bananas, bananas.' That way, if she was annoyed, it would be with him and not me.

Having straightened everything out, I found a cardboard box and swept everything into it with one movement of my right arm. Half-used cosmetics. No good to anyone, but I couldn't bear to simply throw them out.

I decided to take the same approach with her

underwear drawer. It didn't seem decent to do anything else. I removed the drawer and turned round, still seated, to upend the entire contents on to the bed. Bending down to gather up the debris scattered around my feet, I noticed half a dozen photographs among the cotton and silk. Looking at the heap on the bed, I realized that the drawer had been lined with paper and that the photos must have been hidden underneath. There were still more on top of the mound on the bed, face downwards.

I perched on the edge to gather them up like a deck of cards, then turned the first one over slowly as if I was examining a hand. It was a typical photo of a newborn baby. The colour had faded, but there was no confusing the child in the photo with me. People may tell you that all babies look alike, but in this case it was not correct. I was born with a shock of hair that promptly fell out and left me bald until I was nearly two but this child had a neat little tuft of damp, dark hair. There was a peacefulness about the look on its face that made me wonder if I was looking at a photo of my stillborn brother. What other photos would be so private that they would be hidden away from inquisitive eyes? I almost felt ashamed to be prying.

The next photo was similar, but the baby's hands were clenched close to its face. Large hands with fingers facing the camera, a healthy hint of pink in the nails. I turned the next photo over. This showed my mother sitting up in bed, hair loose, pale-faced but beaming, a white bundle in her arms. Next, a close up of her face from the side against the child's, a tangle of hair escaping from behind her ear, the beginnings of crows' feet just visible. The baby is open-mouthed, face straining with effort at the discovery of the power of his lungs. This was no stillborn child. This was one healthy baby. There were several more shots of my mother, counting fingers and toes, cooing, kissing the child's forehead. Then came the shot that I was not expecting. Perhaps the most natural thing in the world – a couple sitting on a hospital bed, holding the tiny child up in the centre of the shot: my mother and a far younger, slimmer version of Uncle Pete.

I shuffled through the rest of the photos looking for the shots with my father in them, the pictures of me seeing my younger brother for the first time, the Fellows family photographs. There were none.

They gave my grandchild away.

She wouldn't talk about it.

I was interrupted by the doorbell. As I reluctantly walked down the stairs, photographs still in hand, I heard Lydia yell, 'Yoo-hoo,' through the letter box. After it clattered shut, the outline of her head appeared in the frosted window.

'Hello there!' she said as if surprised to find me at home. 'Thought I'd drop by and see if anything needs doing. Haven't seen you these last few days, love.'

'Here I am.'

'You busy? Shall we have a cuppa? I've brought some milk and biccies.'

I could tell that she wasn't going to take no for an answer. To tell the truth, I liked Lydia's motiveless fussing. We had no particular history and there was no reason for her to drop round other than neighbourly concern, but she had picked an awkward moment.

As we stood in the hall, I watched her eyes register the changes that I had made to the framed family tree. I could see that she was trying not to frown.

'Oh, I see you've . . .' She nodded, ending the sentence with an explanatory cough.

One evening, I had taken the family tree out of its frame and inserted the date of my parents' death. It had seemed a respectful thing to do at the time. Seeing Lydia's reaction, I wondered if I had been right.

'You don't think—' I began.

'No, no,' she butted in, 'it's just seeing it there in black and white. Bit of a shock, that's all. Wasn't expecting it.'

I stood in the hall looking at my handiwork while she unloaded a carton of milk and some chocolate digestives on to the kitchen work surface and filled the kettle. I tried to visualize the next update and couldn't think for the life of me how to make the entry for my mother's son – my half-brother, if what I was beginning to suspect was true.

She changed the subject. 'It's lovely out. You should have a once-round the park if you get the chance.'

'Can't. I've started tidying my parents' room.'

She looked at me with a mixture of surprise and distaste. 'Isn't it a bit early for that, love? Surely it can wait until the dust has settled.'

'Actually, no.' I took a seat at the kitchen table and looked downwards. 'The house has got to go on the market to pay for Nana's care and, because of what's happened, everyone wants it looking as impersonal as possible.'

'Who's this everyone?' She puffed herself up with outrage. 'This is your home, love! Where will you go?' She sat down on the chair next to mine. My mother's chair.

I shrugged. What happened to me seemed unimportant in the scheme of things.

Her hand folded over mine. 'Are you even working at the moment?'

'No, but they keep on paying me.' I tried the lighthearted approach.

'And this has all been decided, has it? I could murder your lot, you know,' she added as an aside, clawing at fistfuls of air with her hands. 'You've agreed, have you?'

'There was no choice.' I found myself trying to pacify this normally happy-go-lucky soul, but my bravado failed and the tears came.

'Well, it's a proper shame, that's what it is. Ah, come on now.' She circled me with an arm. 'It's more than one soul should have to bear all at the same time. Don't get me wrong, love.' She squeezed. 'I'm so proud of the way you're coping. But it's not what your parents would have wanted for you. I can't do much for you, but I'll have a bed made up for you at ours any time you want it. We've a spare room going to waste and we always like a bit of company. Now let me get you that cup of tea, love.'

To change to subject I asked her how she had met her husband, Bill.

'He was down "sooth" visiting for a weekend. He

81

came back to see me the two weekends after that, and on the third he proposed. I didn't think twice about upping and leaving for Sunderland.'

'That sounds like love at first sight.'

'It was love at first listen, more like. I loved the way he spoke. He called me his bonny lass, his pet. No one had talked to me like that before. How was I to know that was how they all spoke up there?' She nudged me and cackled. 'But I had no regrets. Bill was my rock, you see.

'You know that Kevin's not actually mine?' she twittered. 'My Bill and I got along famously, don't get me wrong, but for some reason we never really hit it off in the bedroom department. I mean, we gave it our best shot, as Bill would say, but nothing happened. So we put in for a child and ended up with Kevin. Two years old, he was. Funny little lad, all these dark curls and a cross little face, like he thought he'd been hard done by. Talking of love at first sight! You grow up thinking that the big love of your life is going to be a man, so it comes as a complete surprise that it turns out to be a child. That you are capable of so much love for one person. I don't give a twaddle that he's not my own, I really don't. I couldn't love him any more than I do.

'I often wonder what he remembers of those first couple of years before he came to us. He'd been fostered but it hadn't worked out. Put with a man with a violent temper on him. They were worried that it might leave him scarred. But I said, "Give him to me and I'll sort him out," and Bill said, "Aye, she will an' all," and they let us take him. He hid behind the armchair in the corner when we got him home. It was as much as I could do to coax him out with a slice of cake. It was about two months before I got a smile out of him and another six months before he let himself go and had a good old belly laugh. I hadn't really noticed that Kevin hadn't laughed until I heard that noise for the first time.' She nudged me. 'Filthy, it was. And the first time he took my hand in his, instead of me having to grab hold of him to cross the road . . .' She sighed and smiled. 'That little hand wrapped around my big, old, clumsy sausage fingers. It was one tiny step at a time with him. He's never been much of a talker – my Bill wasn't either. But when Bill said something, it made you stop and listen. Like it really meant something. I kidded myself into thinking he'd always be there. After he was gone, nothing was right any more. Kevin and me was out of sorts. Sunderland wasn't home without him, so we came back here and lived with my sister for a couple of years while we got our bearings again. That was before we moved in down the road.'

She had been tapping my hand that was covering the photographs. 'That's quite enough about us. What've you got there, then?'

I had to talk to someone and there weren't too many people who dropped in – unannounced or otherwise. She had caught me at a moment of weakness.

'I'm not sure,' I said, taking my hand away to reveal the photos.

'Well, let's have a butcher's.' Lydia took the pile and looked at them one by one, starting with the pictures of the baby on his own. 'Oh, look at the wee bairn.' Her

face widened into a smile. 'Who's this little fella? You?'
I shook my head and shrugged. 'Oh, what a poppet.
Good set of lungs on him, by the look of it and all.' I let
her continue but the comments soon subsided. 'Did
your mother have a child before she was married
to your father?' she asked.

'She was pregnant again when I was quite small.
Uncle Pete gave me a photo recently and it was obvious.
He said the child was stillborn.'

'Uncle Pete? Now, he's your godfather?'

I pointed to the man in the photos. 'Oh,' she
mouthed silently.

'I don't understand why I can't remember.'

'You wouldn't at that age, love. I bet you'll find that
you can only really remember the odd few things
until you are least five. I know I can't.'

'I have a vague memory,' I started, warming my hands
on the sides of the mug of tea. 'I thought it was a dream,
but now I'm beginning to think it actually happened. I
can't remember everything in detail, it was more the
feeling that something was wrong. I was woken up by
my mother in the middle of the night and bundled into
the car, wrapped in a blanket. I was half asleep, so I
don't think I asked where we were going, but I did ask
if Daddy was coming with us. She said, "Not this time."
After that I only pretended to be asleep. We drove what
seemed to be a long way, before my mother pulled over.
I heard her say, "I can't do it, I can't do it," a few times
before she hit the palms of her hands against the steering wheel and then started crying. I think she said, "I

have to do it," at that point. I asked her what was wrong and she said it was nothing and that she would figure everything out. Then she locked me in the car while she went to use a phone box saying that she'd only be a minute.

'She was long enough for me to start to panic that she wasn't coming back for me. I thought that she meant to leave me. I was cold and tired and soon I was crying out for her and banging on the windows. When she came back she told me that we were going home, and that we would have to be very quiet because Daddy was sleeping and we didn't want to wake him up. After she put me to bed, I heard my dad asking where she had been. It wasn't like he was cross. I think he just woke up when she got back into bed. My mother told him that I hadn't been able to sleep so she had taken me out in the car for a drive because that always worked. I knew that my mother had lied to my father and I didn't know why. I can remember feeling sick to my stomach.'

'And you think that this might be the reason?'

'I don't know.' I shook my head. 'I just wonder if everything was quite as perfect as I thought it was.'

'Oh, your parents loved each other.' Lydia dismissed my doubts. 'That much was obvious to everyone.'

'I know.' I thought of them giggling in the car like teenagers on that last day. 'I'm just not sure what happened along the way.'

'Life!' Lydia said. 'It's what happens to all of us. Throws up all sorts of nasty surprises just when you least expect them, I'm afraid.'

Chapter Eleven

My parents hadn't been religious, but the question of whether to have a Christian funeral divided relatives into two distinct camps. Grandma Fellows felt that my father had been raised as a Christian and did not accept that his decisions to marry in a register office and not to have his daughter christened meant that he had rejected his religion. Aunty Faye felt exactly the opposite. Nana, given her presumed state of mind, was not consulted but both sides insisted that she would have given them her full support. They also found my failure to come down for or against either option deeply frustrating. Frankly, I thought that they were all wasting their breath. Nothing could alter what had happened. If there was a God, a concept that I was not very receptive to, and he worked on the basis that how we behave in this life affects our chances in the next, what difference did it make how those of us left behind said our goodbyes? Besides, if I had anything at all to say to God at that time, it certainly wouldn't have been a prayer in the traditional sense of the word.

A black limo collected our party from Aunty Faye's flat, as she felt it best that Nana did not return to the 'family home'. Nana looked immaculate in a black suit, with a pashmina around her shoulders and a pillbox hat. She was so beautifully turned out that it was difficult to remember that she was not quite with it.

'Now, Mum, do you remember where we're going today?' Aunty Faye asked, adjusting the collar of Nana's jacket.

'Tom and Laura's. We're going to Tom and Laura's.'

Aunty Faye looked at me, widening her eyes and raising her eyebrows.

'We used to live together, you know,' Nana confided in me as we walked to the car, showing no sign of recognition. I tucked my hand under her elbow. 'This is my other daughter, Faye. I never had any sons, but I had a grandson once.' It seemed that I had been completely wiped out. Maybe she was aware that there was a delete button to be pressed in the recesses of her mind, but she had hit the wrong one.

As we approached the line of limos, I halted as the twin coffins came into view. An abundance of floral tributes could not disguise them. Suddenly it was all too real. I couldn't pretend this was happening to someone else. In those coffins were the bodies of my parents. And after today even their bodies would be gone. I felt as if I was rolling down that bank at the side of the motorway. I instinctively moved my hand from Nana's arm to my throat, afraid to close my eyes in case I saw the image of my mother that most haunted me. I jumped at the unfamiliar touch of Aunty Faye's hand on my shoulder. 'Deep breath,' she said, her own eyes red and raw. I could only nod.

'There're always people parked in the residents' parking bays.' Nana was chattering. 'My daughter can never park anywhere near her own flat. Taxi!' she called out to the funeral director, who took off his top hat and opened the door of the second limo, sleek and black. 'That was a stroke of luck. I'm not well, you know,' she explained to him. 'I shouldn't be out in the cold air too long. Tell him, Faye.'

We sat on either side of her and each took one of her tiny, cold hands. It was those hands I tried to focus on. The protruding veins, the loose skin, the lines. The inappropriate nail varnish.

'Number 44, Westbrook Road,' she directed.

But as we drove in silence, through my own tears, I saw that she too was weeping, and she didn't question why we pulled into the grounds of the cemetery. There was a part of her that knew what the day was about, even if every fibre of her body was fighting it. A small party waited for us outside the crematorium. Before I could do anything to warn him off, Uncle Pete stepped forward to help Aunty Faye from the car. I held my breath, waiting for the storm, but she allowed him to take her elbow and put his arm around her back, steering her towards the door. I saw him whisper closely in her ear and she leaned in towards him. They looked comfortable with each other, intimate almost. I was glad that some good seemed to have come of the day, even if it only meant a temporary truce. He returned to escort my grandmother, who held on to the crook of the arm that he offered, bent down to her height.

'I thought I told you to bring her straight home,' I heard Nana say crossly as I followed closely behind.

'She's home now, Brenda.' Uncle Pete patted one of her hands. 'They've beaten us to it.' Turning to kiss the top of my head, he asked softly how I was, but his eyes followed Aunty Faye as she greeted the semi-circle of guests who had gathered a short distance from the entrance waiting for instructions.

I attempted a smile. 'I've had better days.'

'Excuse me a minute.' He squeezed my shoulder absently.

'My beautiful girl. He was the one to take her out. He should have brought her home,' Nana was saying. 'If you say you're going to do something, you should do it.'

We followed the pall-bearers, Uncle Pete among them, into the tiny chapel and were seated a few feet away from the coffins. If I had wanted to, I could have reached out and touched the bare wood, felt the grain, lifted the lids. As the words of the service washed over me, I became obsessed with this one thought, and yet my arms were leaden. It was as if I was affected by sleep paralysis, brain signals reaching my limbs, but my body having forgotten how to process them. I couldn't have moved even to save my own life.

I was not prepared for the moment when the curtain was drawn, blocking our view of the coffins. For the mechanical whirring sound. For the whoosh. For my grandmother's strangely distorted wailing as she cried for her daughter, 'Laura! My beautiful girl! Laura! Laura!'

'Wait,' I said blindly as I felt someone take my elbow.

'It's over now.'

'I can't.'

'Say goodbye now.'

I wanted the excuse of my grandmother's dementia. Memories tangled up in time. Shuffled, then laid out on the card table. Incapable of looking after herself. Not responsible for what she was saying. I wanted the excuse of being a small child. Selfish. Self-absorbed. Not expected to understand or to behave.

'Come on, now,' I heard a soft voice say and felt something brush against my shoulder. I wiped my eyes to find Kevin, Lydia's adopted son, standing beside me. 'Time ter go.'

Part Two

Peter's Story

Chapter Twelve

It makes me so angry, the idea that we can reinvent ourselves by having a haircut or changing our clothes. The truth is that we reinvent ourselves with the stories that we tell and retell, justifying our actions to ourselves and to others. Actions are so often without thought, but because we want to give them meaning we analyse and analyse, arriving at a conclusion of what we *must* have been thinking at the time. We are not animals, after all. Anything less is unacceptable. I see it time and time again in my game. A suggestion of, 'I put it to you that you were acting in revenge,' draws only a blank look from the accused. The jury may pick up on the suggestion, but not the poor sod on trial. No prosecutor ever says, 'I put it to you that you weren't thinking,' because it is his job to prove that a crime has been committed. To commit theft, there must be the intent to deprive permanently. To commit murder there must be malice aforethought, not just some idiot who is vaguely wondering what would happen if he were to pull this little trigger. Without thought, we would be left with a civil wrong or manslaughter at best. Most criminal lawyers would be out of a job and the general public would be up in arms because they want to feel that justice has been done so that they can sleep soundly at night. That's how the system works. How society functions.

And then we have the man with good intentions he can never live up to. He fits his story around his original intentions and in the end they become more important than the facts. Sometimes we repeat a story so often that we even manage to convince ourselves that our revisions are real. Take the example of a feud between brothers. Add twenty years of grudge-bearing and you may find that the people involved can't even remember what high-minded principle it was that started their argument. They have no idea how to make amends because they simply can't remember what it is they would have to forgive to be the bigger person. Far easier to carry on with the feuding than admit to any human frailty.

The other thing that I have become increasingly aware of is that there is not just a single version of events called the truth. Life is not nearly as simple as that. Each of us brings to the table our own beliefs, backgrounds and experiences and we all have the potential to interpret a single event differently. One person's experience is a truth of sorts, but it is never the whole story. There is a separate truth for each one of us. The brain is such an incredible organ that if we repeat things often enough, we come to believe them. It can be the use of the phrase, 'I'm not a good sleeper,' that creates the insomniac., the repetition of prayers that creates faith. After almost thirty years of working in the legal profession, I have lost confidence in a system that looks for a single set of facts by relying on the evidence of others based on something as elastic as memory, and labels it as truth. The plain fact is that I wouldn't want to be judged by twelve of my peers, let alone by a higher being. Let's hope that if there is a God, he takes a greater interest in what is in our hearts than our actions, otherwise I fear we're all for the high jump.

The story that I told Andrea as she recovered in hospital was a truth of sorts. One over-simplified version of a potted history of what was a very complicated relationship. It was certainly the truth that I thought she needed to hear. There are things that are better left unsaid. I honestly believe that it is unfair to unburden yourself on another soul when you have no idea how they will deal with that information – if they are capable of processing it at all. I grew up in a decade where free love was supposedly acceptable (although I saw little of it) but talking about feelings was completely foreign. Besides, it would have been quite inappropriate for me, as her godfather, to tell her any more.

I have spent years looking into her eyes and at times it has felt as if I am looking into a mirror, seeing a reflection of my own emotions. With her, I have experienced a little of the love that I hoped I would feel one day for a child of my own. I spoilt her because I never had the opportunity to spoil my own child. Occasionally I have wondered: 'What if?' The great question that haunts all of us. I suspect that I may have a longer list of what ifs than most, but human beings are so much more complex than the labels we like to saddle them with. Even Andrea, whom I like to think of as one of the most honest and decent people I could hope to meet. I know that I only see the side of her she chooses to show me. I expect that she too has moments when she battles with her demons.

I hope with all my heart that if she discovers our story, she will realize that there was love at its centre and that it was strong enough to survive whatever the individuals put each other through, whether in the heat of the moment, intentionally, or in jealousy. Love has many faces. It is not always as pure as St Paul would have us believe and I have found it to be both a blessing and a curse, but I wouldn't have missed out on it for all the world. You cannot appreciate the moments of joy unless you accept the pain that comes hand in hand with them.

In telling you my story, I will try to do away with any embellishments I have added with time. I will try to strip it back to the bare facts – if I can remember what they were. It's such a long time ago that I can barely recognize the person that I was.

Chapter Thirteen

Looking back, it seems that missing persons have always had a huge influence on my life.

An only child, I was born in 1952 and christened Jonathan Augustus Churcher after my father's identical twin brother. I grew up with the vague explanation that Uncle Jonathan had been 'lost' in the war. I remembered the terror of getting lost in a department store after breaking free from my mother's tight grasp on my wrist. The humiliation of wearing reins meant nothing to me after that.

'Who's looking for Uncle Jonathan?' I asked my mother once.

'Shhhhh!' She glared at me, a finger raised to her lips.

On another occasion when he had been mentioned, I suggested as sympathetically as I could, 'I expect they'll find him soon.'

'Jonnie.' My mother shepherded me out of the sitting room door with both hands. 'Go and play in your room.'

As soon as I had a clearer understanding, the idea of

being named after a much-loved brother who had died a hero's death struck me as quite a responsibility. My father had returned from the war physically unscathed but haunted by what he had seen – and probably by what he found himself capable of. In those days his condition was referred to in hushed tones as shell-shock. Sufferers either put on a brave face and got on with life as best they could or hid themselves away. Now we have given it a far grander title: Post Traumatic Stress Disorder and, having such a grand title to describe it, people can be far more open about it without fear of showing weakness.

My father changed from a good-humoured, even-tempered young man to one who looked considerably older than his years and was alternately withdrawn and uncommunicative or demanding and volatile.

'Quiet! Quiet!' he would yell, covering his ears, even though there was nothing louder than the ticking of the clock on the mantelpiece that could have caused his distress. 'Can't you stop that confounded noise?'

My mother would come running, assuming that I had done something to disturb his peace.

'Jonnie, why don't you come and help me in the kitchen and leave your father to his paper?' she would suggest, steering me by the shoulder.

I almost preferred his explosions to the silences that took him as he shut himself away from the world in the parlour for days on end without so much as a book for company. Then, nothing and no one could reach him.

'Take your father this nice cup of tea,' my mother would encourage me, standing behind me at the door.

'And while you're at it, why don't you tell him what we did at the park?'

'We fed the ducks,' I explained slowly, so that he would understand.

'Yes, we did, didn't we?' My mother patted my head.

'Take him away, darling.' He stared into the empty fireplace. 'I don't want him to see me like this.'

His sadness permeated the very fabric of our house. I imagined it circulating perpetually, like the cigarette smog that stained the ceilings and my father's hands indiscriminately. His moods dictated our family life. I learned to monitor them and modify my behaviour, in the same way that you would check the weather forecast before deciding what to wear in the morning. Make hay while the sun shines. Tornado warning: batten down the hatches. Showers expected: remember your umbrella.

It was obvious that he came to regret breaking with the family tradition of calling the first-born son Frederick. I think that it was one of the ways that he chose to punish himself. There were times when my father could barely bring himself to use my name. He developed a stutter as he tried to say 'J-Jonnie.' It must have been quite pronounced because when I learned to say my own name it was with a definite double 'j'. None of this escaped my mother, who feared that he was distancing himself from me. Even she was wary of using my full name, as parents tend to when they want to put the fear of God into you, concerned about the effect this would have on my father. I learned to fear her whispers far more than the times when she raised her voice. It was only in a sharp whisper that she ever called me Jonathan Augustus Churcher: such a big name for a small child, and a sure sign of what was coming my way.

She played around with various shortened versions when I was small, but each prompted a different but distinct memory and a similar reaction: the slight but noticeable pained expression, and a distinct change in the atmospheric pressure.

Brought up in a house where nobody explained anything, especially to a child, I spent my early years studying my uncle's grinning photograph, trying to imagine how he would have aged so that I could form a search party of my own. I could detect the distress on my father's face when his brother was mentioned in conversation and he was unprepared for the intrusion. I had long since given up hope that anyone else would make an effort to find poor, lost Uncle Jonathan and I felt that, as his namesake, it was my duty.

Once, as a seven-year-old on a rare trip to a crowded beach, I was convinced that I saw him up ahead and started running to follow a man who changed direction frequently and easily outstrode me. I ended up completely disorientated, trying in vain to find the way back to my starting point. The problem with beaches is that everything constantly shifts. I didn't appreciate that the tide was going out. By the time I wanted to return to my parents, the beach had grown and its population had expanded. Following the waterline, I was actually moving further and further away from them.

Just as despair was about to set in, I saw a small hut with the words 'Lost and Found' on it. I picked my way over the tangle of limbs to a kindly soul sitting at the door in a deckchair and announced, 'I'm looking for my Uncle Jonathan.'

'Is that who you came with today, lovey?' she asked.

'No, I'm with my parents, but it's my Uncle Jonathan who's lost. Isn't this where all the lost people come?' I danced from side to side to try to look past her into the hut, where a number of children were sitting on wooden slatted benches anchored firmly in the sand. There wasn't another adult in sight.

'That's right, darling. And where are your mummy and daddy?'

'Over there.' I pointed vaguely with a circular motion.

'I think you'd better stay here with us. This is where they'll come if they can't find you.'

I joined the other children, certain that the reason that we had come to the seaside was to look for Uncle Jonathan, and proud to have been clever enough to locate the Lost and Found first. Surely it would only be a matter of time before he turned up? But my initial optimism subsided as the day wore on and my thoughts turned to how disappointed my father would be and the effect that this would have on him. It later turned out that this misery was nothing compared with the thrashing I'd receive after explaining the reason for my disappearance.

It was not just the punishment that upset me, although it was about the worst I had received in all of my seven years. I simply didn't understand what I had done to deserve it. I truly hated my father for failing to appreciate that I had been trying to do something nice for him. And I hated my mother too for not standing up for me and making him understand.

As I lay face-down on my pillow in bed that night, I heard the door opening and feared that I was in for it again. I clenched my eyes shut and pretended to be asleep, but instead of a harsh hand, I felt my hair being stroked.

'Jonnie,' my mother whispered softly (a good sign), 'you must understand how worried we were about you. You must never wander off and get lost like that again. Anything could have happened to you.'

'Is that what happened to Uncle Jonathan?' I asked in all innocence, imagining him lost among armies of men, trying to find his way through to the person in charge.

'Jonathan Augustus!' Her tone changed to one of anger. 'You got lost today. Uncle Jonathan was left behind in the war.' And then I think the penny must have dropped, because her voice lost its harshness. In avoiding the words that might have caused further anguish for my father, she hadn't thought to make things clear enough for me to understand. 'You do know that Uncle Jonathan was killed in the war, don't you? He's dead, Jonnie. And I don't think your father will ever get over it.'

Dead? But he was a war hero who had saved the lives of countless others. How could he be dead? Heroes didn't die, did they? Certainly not in the comic books I read.

Then something strange happened. I became aware that my mother was openly sobbing and she lay down on the bed beside me. I had never seen her with her guard down before and I watched with fascination as the hate melted away into something closer to pity. Displays of feelings like this were rare in our house. The only person who was allowed to be upset or annoyed was my father.

After a while had passed, I announced, 'I think I will be called Peter from now on,' picking the first name that came to mind. I had no idea where the thought came from until the words came out of my mouth. Once out, I wasn't sure I should have said them.

My mother sat up on the bed, wiped her eyes with her hands and straightened her clothes, before saying, 'Do you know, I think that's a very good idea. Peter. Yes, I think we can live with that.' She clung to the name, as pleased as if she had thought of the idea herself. 'Peter Churcher. That's not too bad at all.'

I have no idea what discussions took place behind closed doors that night, but I was never called Jonathan or Jonnie or John at home again. Not by my parents or any family members, or by my teachers in school. Overnight, I became plain Peter Churcher, and it was about as liberating an experience as a seven-year-old is capable of.

I don't want you to think of my father as an unkind man or a bad father. I appreciated his moments of kindness all the more, because I knew that they didn't come naturally to him. It used to frustrate him that I spent so much time admiring his brother's photograph. The grin on Uncle Jonathan's face almost seemed out of place in our gloomy sitting room. Occasionally, my father would rise from his olive armchair, walk slowly to the fireplace and turn the photograph to face the wall, saying nothing. It was my mother who would pipe up, 'That's enough for today, Peter.'

One day I went into the sitting room to find that the photograph was gone. Before I could help myself, I blurted out, 'Where's Uncle Jonathan?' I recoiled instantly with the shock of the sound of my own voice, waiting for my father's reaction. The clickity-click of my mother's knitting needles stopped, suspended in the air, and I could see that she was holding her breath.

My father took the cigarette from his mouth and exhaled slowly, then said, 'He's exactly where he belongs, son. I've found him a new home.'

I had surprised myself so much by my outburst that I didn't feel able to ask where that home might be, although I strongly suspected that it was somewhere I would no longer be able to look at him. It was with sadness and heavy feet that I trudged up the stairs to my room, to find it lit with the yellow glow of my bedside lamp. There, under the lamp's halo, was the photograph, tilted at an angle so that I would be able to see it when lying down in bed. My father, who very rarely entered my bedroom, was standing in the doorway behind me. I hadn't heard him follow me in his carpet slippers.

'You approve, I hope,' he said seriously. 'I know you'll take good care of him.'

'Oh, yes!' I nodded, picking up the picture by the frame. I wanted to thank him, but he disappeared just as silently and the moment passed. I was careful to put the photograph back in the exact same position he had placed it. It struck me later that he must have lain down on my bed to work out where it needed to go and I imagined that I could still see his imprint on the covers. Lying down inside my father's outline and staring at his brother's photograph was the closest that we came to a physical embrace before the days of manly handshakes and backslaps.

As Jonathan Augustus Churcher, I could only have disappointed my father. As Peter Churcher, I was capable of a far closer relationship with him than we would have otherwise enjoyed. Despite this, the uncle that I never met remained the most interesting character in our family history for me. I find it sad that I know so little about him, as my father volunteered only snippets of information. Once I no longer had need of it, the name Jonathan became almost taboo in our house. For the most part, the image that I have of my uncle is the product of my imagination. But how clear that image is, even now! I do know that he hoped to follow a career in the legal profession. And that there was only ever one woman for Jonathan: his childhood sweetheart, Betty, whom he'd met at school and loved from the moment he clapped eyes on her.

I met Betty once when she was well into her

sixties. She turned up at a family gathering.

'On a whim,' she said, after introducing herself, and directed her gaze at the back of my father's head. 'I wondered if enough time had passed. I don't think he knows me. Look at me! I hardly know myself.'

Oh, he knows you all right, I thought to myself. Just look how skilfully he's avoiding you.

She had never married, never had children and didn't seem to have aged at the same rate as those who had.

'Tell me about my uncle,' I asked her. 'What was he like?'

She replied simply, 'He was my Jonnie,' as if I had asked the most extraordinary question. Now, of course, I know exactly how she felt. She was not interested in Jonnie the man of action, Jonnie the war hero.

I recognized a kindred spirit. A person for whom the most important person in her life had been absent for most of it, who had lived with the thoughts of what might have been.

'When I was a child,' I told her, 'no one was prepared to tell me what had happened, so they just said he was lost.' I went on to tell her about my childhood misunderstanding and my change of name.

'You shouldn't have stopped looking for him.' She smiled. 'I never have. Occasionally I see him, too. It was him on the beach that day. I'm absolutely sure of it.'

Chapter Fourteen

Laura Albury. I wish I could tell you exactly when I first met her, but I can certainly remember how it happened. If I had known at the time how important that meeting was, I would have written down the date. Instead, I just wrote her name repeatedly in the margins of exercise books.

At St Winifred's School, it was the rule that anyone who had arrived late had to go and report to the secretary's office immediately. Ironically, they would have to queue there until the secretary had time to deal with them, making them even later for the start of lessons and resulting in an unreasonably severe ticking off in front of classmates. This may well have been a deliberate ploy, to make us understand what it is like to be kept waiting by someone who seems to have no respect for the value of your time. If it was, it was lost on us.

Laura and I had both run from the school gates to the double doors of the main school entrance, arriving at much the same time. I was nervous at the thought of being late, a blot on my otherwise immaculate record. We collided as we both stretched our arms out to push the doors inwards. A flash of white-blonde hair and Laura dazzled me with one of her trademark smiles.

'You first.' I gestured, an automatic response given the circumstances, despite my growing need to use the toilet adding to the urgency of the situation. I was left holding the door, blinking rapidly, as if her image had been burned into my retina and I could see that mesmerizing smile with every single blink.

It was several seconds later that I joined her in the queue.

'I thought you'd done a bunk,' she turned round to say, still smiling.

'And miss all this?' I mumbled, feeling myself redden. I was not the sort of boy that girls talked to, especially very pretty blonde girls. I wasn't equipped with the small talk or the repertoire of witty replies that seemed to be called for.

'Quiet back there!' the secretary called from behind her toughened glass screen, glaring. Laura's head dipped forwards, showing off her neck and the fine, downy hairs that had strayed from the band that was holding them in place. Her shoulders shook slightly, a tell-tale sign that she was hiding her face so that the secretary couldn't see that she was laughing. I could see down the back of her loose-fitting collar to the dark hollow between her wing-bones. I focused on this to take my mind off my bladder. Minutes passed and we shuffled forward.

'Sorry I'm late, miss,' she recited perfectly pleasantly, but without a hint of apology in her voice. 'Laura Albury, Year 2, Form B, Miss Simpson.' I could hear her smiling as she spoke and admired her easy-going manner.

'Laura Albury,' the secretary repeated, looking down the register. 'This is the second time you've been late this month. I don't want to see you in this queue again.'

'No, miss,' she agreed wholeheartedly.

'Laura Albury, Laura Albury, Laura Albury,' I was practising when she turned around and, away from the glare of the school secretary, stuck her tongue out at me, before moving away to the right. I was not the sort of boy that girls stuck their tongues out at. That was when I wet myself.

Chapter Fifteen

Laura was not vain for vanity's sake, but her mother had drummed into her from the word go that she wasn't a particularly bright child and that what she had going for her were her looks and her manners. She was groomed to make the most of both.

'Say thank you, Laura. Your looks will open doors for you, mark my words. But think of all the doors that will open if you're beautiful *and* charming.'

'Thank you, Mummy.'

'You're my little treasure.' And she was rewarded with a kiss on her forehead.

Sadly, her sister Faye lacked the looks, the manners and the desire to please, but she was more intelligent, witty and sharper.

'Faye came top of her year again, Mummy,' Laura announced.

'Well, she's always been my clever girl.' Her mother was not dismissive of Faye's achievements but expectations were high. The fact was that she didn't need to try as hard as others and her teachers were frustrated by the apparent ease with which she breezed through school. They expected her to demonstrate a bit more effort. It was not uncommon for her to be given top grades but still be told to try harder. No one expected anything of Laura academically, but she was never short of praise when she did well.

Both sisters envied each other. Who doesn't want to be loved by everyone they meet? Who wouldn't prefer to be more than just a pretty face? These labels, like my birth-name, affected the girls. Laura didn't stretch herself at school, believing that the future for her would be secondary modern followed by a secretarial course, a white wedding and babies. Faye shied away from the limelight and seemed to almost deliberately make herself ugly.

Mrs Albury counted on Laura's looks attracting the right kind of man from the right kind of background who could provide a good future for her. In her naivety, she didn't seem to realize that those looks would attract all kinds of men. There is no doubt that Laura was used to being admired from an early age – and that she lapped up the attention, particularly attention of the male variety. It was how she looked for approval.

'Laura,' her mother said as she made her stand on a kitchen chair so that she could let down the hem of her skirt, 'I want you to wear this dress when your Uncle Colin and Aunty Barbara come over on Saturday evening. You can stay up a bit later than usual so that you can say hello. I think you'll look lovely with your hair in bunches and that pink ribbon we bought you.

What do you think, Faye?' She turned to face the empty space where her younger daughter had been standing in the doorway. 'Faye! You're next. I need to look at the length of your dress too! Where's she got to?'

Laura would often be rewarded with an invitation to sit on a lap, which her mother didn't object to, or a small gift of pocket money or chocolate, which her mother actively encouraged her to accept.

'Oh, isn't that kind, Laura! What do you say?' Mrs Albury would prompt her to accept the coins.

'Thank you very much.'

'Good girl!' She would then instruct, 'Now, why don't you go and put that in your piggy bank now so that you don't lose it. Then you can come back and kiss everyone goodnight.'

Adults, both men and women, were tactile with Laura and she reciprocated. She was lucky. No one took advantage of her trusting disposition. But what a dangerous lesson to teach a child!

Outwardly, you would not have known that she had a confidence problem. Inwardly, she worried that she would never amount to much and became a grabber of opportunities, without really judging what was right for her. As she grew older, she worried that her luck would run out when her looks ran out. She believed that she only had until the age of thirty to get her life in order, and then it would all be over. Again, this idea was planted by her mother, who blamed her daughters for the loss of her own hourglass figure, conveniently forgetting that there were a number of years between the time when the girls were born and her own thirtieth birthday. When her parents had finished shamelessly showing Laura off, it was her sister she confided in and shared her small rewards with. Faye was not encouraged to dress up and meet her parents' visitors. Faye was denied similar opportunities to shine but I suspect that she would have hated being asked to perform. From the safety of their bedroom or sitting at the top of the stairs peering through the banisters, she listened to the raucous laughter and raised voices, punctuated by snippets of Elvis and Lonnie Donegan.

I remember how my own parents once asked me to recite some poetry that I had learned for school to one of their friends. I found it so embarrassing that I deliberately fluffed a couple of lines to avoid being asked again. It worked a treat. The last thing that parents want to show their friends is that the son they have been boasting about cannot remember words in the right order.

'I wouldn't have had anything decent to wear even if I had wanted to join in,' Faye complained as the sisters retold the stories of life in the Albury household.

Laura's recollection differed. 'Oh, come on, Faye!' She brushed this aside. 'I helped make my clothes out of things that Mum was ready to throw out. It's not like I had anything new and you missed out.'

'They were new to you. I always had to make do with your hand-me-downs.'

I suspect that there was truth in both sides of the story, but there is no doubt that the two sisters were treated very differently.

Laura was one of those rare people who was happy with her lot in life. And if she woke up occasionally feeling slightly out of sorts, she would put on her best dress and take a walk into town. It wouldn't be long before she would attract some admiring glances, and she fed off them like a flower turning towards the light. When I was with her I was alternately proud and embarrassed by the attention she attracted. Depending on my mood I would find myself grinning compulsively or glaring at the whistling wolves. Once, I felt the need to ask, 'Do you really like all this attention? Wouldn't you be happier to blend into the background?'

She replied, a little hurt, even a little shocked that I hadn't realized, 'But this is all I have and by the time I'm thirty it will be gone.'

'Oh, come on!' I almost took this as a joke.

'You don't have to worry about that sort of thing. It's not the same for men.'

No matter how much I protested, she wouldn't be pacified. It made me furious when I discovered that not only was she serious, but it was her mother who had taught her to think that way. What could she have become given the right encouragement? Laura was so much more than just a pretty face. It's a crying shame that she didn't know it.

Chapter Sixteen

As a boy, I expected that I would have to adore Laura from afar, but this idea was quickly quashed. I had no idea what qualities Laura recognized in me at that first meeting or if she simply treated everyone the same. I would seek her out among the sea of faces in the school assembly hall where we gathered daily for morning prayer. It was known more commonly as 'morning mumblings', because we would set ourselves the challenge of getting through an entire prayer without saying a single recognizable word. Knowing what was to come, an invitation from the headmaster to stand and say the Lord's Prayer was enough to cause an epidemic of giggles. Laura always found some way of acknowledging me without drawing attention to herself. It became clear that she had perfected her winking and discreet tongue-sticking-out routine. When I attempted it, I just looked as if I had something in my eye.

If I spotted her in the school playground, I would have been far too nervous to approach a group of girls, but she greeted me with a wave.

'Who are you waving at?' one of her friends asked, sensing a whiff of scandal.

'That's my friend Pete,' she replied simply, killing it dead. There was never any of that sniggering you got from some groups of girls when one of them has waved to a boy as a joke to show him up.

When we passed each other in a corridor, it was our custom to address each other by our full names, even though I was usually plain Pete.

'Hello, Peter Churcher.'

'Hello, Laura Albury.'

You could never have accused Laura of being plain.

Walking home, she would turn round and wait once she knew I was there. One day she called after me and asked me to wait for her, and I knew that the balance had shifted. If nothing else, it seemed that we were going to be proper friends.

'I thought you'd never stop.' She was panting heavily, and put her hand on my shoulder to catch her breath. 'Didn't you hear me? I've been calling after you for ages.'

I wasn't used to being touched and I was literally frozen to the spot.

'Thank you!' She interpreted my body language as a sign of someone being considerate. 'I'm never going to make the netball team at this rate.' The vibrations of her laughter ran down her arm and passed through me like an electric shock, and I woke from my stupor.

'Race you to the end of the road.'

'No! I can't run any more! You'd beat me.'

'Do you think I'd ask you otherwise?'

'You're a rotter, Pete Churcher, that's what you are. A rotter.'

'What is a rotter? Is it like a Rottweiler?'

'Depends what a Rottweiler is.'

'A dog the size of a pony with even bigger teeth.'

'You're making that up. Never heard of it. It's like that time you told me that they're going to send a man to the moon. No, you're a rotter, as in rotten, mean, nasty. Look it up in that dictionary of yours.' Coming from the mouth of Laura, any adjective sounded like a compliment to my ears.

There is no doubt that knowing the prettiest girl in the school does wonders for your reputation, both with the boys and the girls. Because of her, I was finally someone.

'Was that Laura Albury I saw you walking to school with?'

'Yes.'

'How do you know her?'

'You're Pete, aren't you? I'm one of Laura's friends, Cathy.'

'Hello, Cathy.'

'She says you're probably the nicest boy she knows.'

If life at home was dreary, I was happy at school. Our family life was largely unaffected by what went on in the outside world. My father's life ran to a routine timetable, punctuated by small rituals. A daily paper with his breakfast of porridge and tea. A pipe in his favourite armchair on return from work. Dinner on the table at six sharp. The rented television set was switched

117

on once a day to warm up five minutes before the start of the *Nine O'Clock News* on BBC1. (We were always a BBC household – my father never converted to ITV.)

'Where's my shirt for tomorrow?' my father would demand as soon as the *News* was over.

'All ready for you, starched and ironed just the way you like it.' My mother would run to fetch it for him as willingly as a trainee trying to impress a new boss at work, but she was rarely rewarded with praise or even a mere thank you.

He would inspect it and only when he had assured himself that it was satisfactory would he carry it upstairs and arrange it on a wooden hanger, adjusting the collar and shoulders as carefully as if he was actually dressing himself for work. He was a man of the if-a-job's-worth-doing-it's-worth-doing-properly school of thought. My mother lived in fear of accidentally forgetting something that she should have done, and her fear was so great that it actually stopped her from doing anything other than wait on him hand and foot. The four walls of the house marked the confines of her world. The more tragedies she heard about on the *Nine O'Clock News* – the Great Train Robbery, the assassination of President Kennedy – the more nervous she became and the happier she was to keep it that way.

School was my one distraction. And then the eleven-plus changed everything. I almost considered deliberately failing in the hope that I would be kept back a year, but I dreaded the thought of letting my parents down. Having put their single egg in one basket, expectations were high and I was constantly reminded of the sacrifices they had made for me. Besides, I had a certain acceptance of the inevitable. Even if it wasn't this year, I couldn't stall for ever.

When I left St Winifred's for grammar school in 1963, it was in the knowledge that there would be no more waves, no more walks, no more exchange of confidences and, quite possibly, no more Laura Albury. She still had a year to go and I doubted that there would be any shortage of boys queuing up to carry her bags for her. I was right. Whenever I saw her again, she was never alone. Always friendly to a fault, but never alone.

'Hello, Peter Churcher,' she would say with that same bright smile, but that had been our way of talking when it was just the two of us.

'Hello, Laura.' I couldn't bring myself to join in.

Even if I could have found the courage to ask her out, we were too young to be dating, but too old to be childhood friends. If I hadn't deliberately engineered our meetings, there was no way that I would have seen her at all.

Imagine how I felt when I saw a card in the newsagent's looking for a boy for the early-morning paper round that included her road. It was the perfect excuse to cycle past her house every day. If I left her road until last, there was a good chance that I would see Laura as she walked the family's Labrador, Barney, before school. The girls took it in turns, so I was soon on nodding terms with Faye, her shyness eliminating the need for much in the way of conversation. If there was an ambassador for the Albury family, it was Laura.

Not wanting to look too obvious, I sometimes pretended that I hadn't seen her.

'Pete!' she called after me as I sailed past. I looked back to see her broad smile and her wave. I took my time turning round and cycled back as casually as possible.

'You just rode right past Barney and me.' She smiled. 'We might think you're deliberately ignoring us.'

'I didn't see you. You were hidden behind the cars.'

'I could see you just fine.'

'I must have been higher up on my bike.'

'Rotter!' She laughed. 'Have you got time to go my way to school?'

I pretended to look at my watch to check if she would be disappointed. 'I should be just about all right.'

'I know how you hate being late. I'll just let Barney back in.'

After school, I occasionally changed my route home to cycle by St Winifred's and see if I could spot her. Pretending to have been on an errand, I would stop and we would walk home just as we used to. I don't know why I found it impossible to say, 'I thought I'd come and walk you home, just like the old days.' It was the same when I bumped into her at the weekends. Instead of saying 'Would you like an ice cream?' the words that would actually tumble out of my mouth were, 'I was about to get an ice cream. Shall I get you one while I'm at it?'

She'd start to search for her purse, saying, 'Hang

on, I know I've got enough money here somewhere.'

'I've just got my paper-round money,' I would say, feeling extravagant. 'You get them next time.'

Although the end result might have been the same, Laura complained years later that I had never once told her how I felt about her. It's possible that by making our meetings appear to be accidental, I just didn't make her feel special enough.

Chapter Seventeen

When I discuss relationships with other people, they tell me you never love the second or third time around as passionately as you do the first. How, after being hurt, you learn to put up defences, your own invisible force field. Not consciously perhaps. Not even obviously. But they are there, nonetheless. How would I know? I have only ever been in love once. Although you may not think that I was lucky in love, I know that I was fortunate enough to fall in love with the right girl and that my love lasted for the best part of forty years. How many people can claim that?

I am currently working on a divorce case for an undeniably beautiful client – let's call her Michelle. When she walked into my book-lined office in a well-cut suit and high heels, hair smoothed back tightly from her face and a shade of pink lipstick just on the right side of good taste, I thought she lit up the room. Then I began to notice her hard edges. Gradually, I am beginning to think she looks more and more like a stick-insect in drag.

'Where do we start?' she asked, straight down to business.

When I suggested that she told me everything she thought was relevant, I got rather more than I bargained for. She told me how in her teens she had been very insecure and that this expressed itself as jealousy. She imagined that her boyfriend – let's call him Brendan – had a bit of a roving eye. She thought that when he was with her, his eyes should have been on her only. In her mind, he had already betrayed her. She did what she thought every girl had to do to keep her man happy, and a bit more besides. As she gave little pieces of herself away, his confidence grew. She became the needy one, looking for reassurance that he loved her at every opportunity, but his replies were never enough. One day, looking for a stronger reaction, she went as far as accusing him of having the hots for another girl, a friend of his family. A month later she sees them kissing. He denies it. She won't let it rest. Two weeks down the line she discovers them in bed together. Brendan says, 'You drove me away. Before you mentioned her, I didn't even know who she was.' Michelle is adamant. She had always known that one day he would cheat on her.

She goes out with another fellow to make Brendan jealous. Let's call him Rob. Outwardly, she lavishes Rob with affection. He adores her but knows there is nothing behind her kisses. He wonders if he is supposed to buy her love. This time she trades little pieces of herself for an engagement ring. She parades it in front of her friends. Rob comes to realize that she cares more for the diamond than she does for him. One night after drowning his sorrows, he finds himself entangled in the arms of an uncomplicated girl who cares nothing for jewellery. He feels something close to happiness. Michelle feels completely justified when she tells everyone that men are all the same.

She interrupted her flow to ask me, 'Are you getting all this?'

It was only then that I realized I had stopped taking notes and was sitting back in my chair staring at her. I may even have had my mouth open.

'Oh, yes,' I replied, 'I'm definitely getting the picture. Do go on.'

Michelle decides to take revenge on the cheating men of this world by playing them at their own game. She finds a man in a bar with a wedding ring on his finger and asks him to buy her a drink. Several drinks later and she agrees to go 'home' with him and he finds a hotel. She wakes in the morning to find a twenty-pound note on the bedside table. She decides not to share this little story with her friends.

She has had enough. Never again will she be taken advantage of. The next time, she assures herself, she won't give any more of herself away until she walks down the aisle. Unfortunately Michelle is too willing to swap a bit of respectability for love. Once the wedding and the honeymoon are over, she finds that she is expected to give little pieces of herself away every night. And not only in the bedroom, but when she has to play the role of a dutiful wife with her in-laws and his work colleagues. In those moments, she feels lonelier than she ever has before. But she can't admit it, so she retreats to a small place inside herself. Occasionally she looks in the mirror and she can't even recognize the face in front of her. She needs to escape so that she can remember who it is that she used to be.

Unfortunately, her chosen escape route did not take her far enough away from the prying eyes of a well-meaning neighbour. Now her husband is divorcing her. The bastard. She's going to take him to the cleaner's.

For a while, I had been sitting and nodding, waiting for Michelle to give me something – anything – to work with.

'For a man, you're a very good listener,' she told me and I take it from this that she has run out of steam.

'It's my job,' I said, smiling, meaning that I listen by the hour and that her story has cost her the best part of £250. A counsellor might have been cheaper.

'I mean business.' She uncrossed her legs and leaned forward slowly. 'I want him to pay.'

'Just so I'm completely clear, what do you want him to pay for?' I asked, thinking of her insecurities and the other men in her life.

'I want the house, all of the furniture and the car,' she said without hesitating.

'Well, at least we have our starting point. Now, we need to focus on your husband a little more. What sort of a man is he?'

Family law is a depressing line of business. I meet the

Michelles of this world more than you might imagine, ceaselessly looking for the next escape route.

But is it any easier if you have loved just the one person? Where can I go looking now that I need to remember who I am? I start by visiting my old haunts. A young family is living in my parents' house. I can't see them, but the front door is ajar. Somewhere inside a mother is swearing at a child, and the child is shouting back. No one has explained the house rules to them: self-control, self-discipline, self-preservation. Never show your emotions, never answer back. Is it better to grow up in a house where people say exactly what they think? Once things have been aired there is no taking them back, no matter how much you try to forget.

I walk past the double glazing and the paved-over front gardens to the place where I expected to find St Winifred's. In its place is a large block of newly built flats with little personality. An advertising board describes them as 'luxurious accommodation sitting within the footprint of a prestigious school'. A second block sits where I used to play marbles in the play-ground and a third and fourth where the football pitch and playing fields were. I feel as if something else has been stolen from me. Is it possible to mourn the loss of a building as you would a person? Or is it simply that St Winifred's was the shell that I stored so many of my memories in? How is it that my old school was torn apart and I didn't feel a physical wrench?

Taking Betty's advice, I decide to go looking for my

Uncle Jonathan again and drive to the beach where I once thought I saw him: the relative I feel closest to and yet never actually met. Sitting on a low wall, I take off my shoes and socks, tuck the socks inside the shoes, tie the laces together and hang them around my neck. I breathe in the air, smelling salt and seaweed and wet dog. It is a bright day with a good breeze taking the edge off the warmth of the sun, and clouds of the large, white, solid-looking type, fit to take the weight of any god of the Old Testament variety. A day to cheer the spirits. The dog-walkers and bucket-and-spade brigade are out in force, if not the sun-seekers. Mucky kids in sun hats and undies run shrieking from the shock of the icy water. Everyone seems to be with someone, doing something, smiling. Excluded from the world of happy families, I bypass them, walking for what seems like miles, until I have left the roads and crowds with their litter and pandemonium behind.

Walking purposefully but without any particular destination, I watch as the sun sets and the waters turn from blue to grey to golden to obsidian black, and then I walk some more. At a place where the sands meet the cliffs, I toy with an abandoned Diet Coke bottle. With no one to see me, I whisper, 'I miss you,' into it, screw the lid on tightly, and set it afloat on the water. Then I cry the sea-salty tears of someone who is not certain what they have to go back to. An overweight, balding, middle-aged man, weeping over the loss of a love that was never his, the loss of a friend he was willing to betray, the loss of a favourite uncle he never actually met, the loss of a father he never told how he felt, the loss of a name he might have grown to live up to, and the loss of a son who might one day have looked up to him. You couldn't do it by daylight.

Chapter Eighteen

There were any number of times when I could have asked Laura out or told her that I loved her before Tom Fellows arrived on the scene, but there always seemed to be something stopping me. We were too young. I was shy. I didn't think that I was good-looking enough. I valued our friendship too much. There would be plenty of time. It wasn't fair on her when I was going to be leaving for university. Besides, she must have known how I felt, surely?

I didn't feel particularly threatened by her other boyfriends once I realized that they would come and go with surprising regularity. A week, two weeks, three at the most. I made an effort to appear to get to know those that lasted slightly longer. I tried my hardest not to appear to be too jealous of them and I secretly enjoyed their jealousy about my relationship with Laura.

'This is Peter Churcher,' she would explain perfectly naturally, and I would offer my hand. This ritual of Laura's became the test of who was going to make the grade as a boyfriend. Some would look cautiously from one of our faces to the other, waiting for her to expand on the introduction. I listed the possibilities in my head.

'Who has loved me for as long as he has known me.'

'Whom I will compare you to.'

'My best friend.'

'Who will accompany us on some of our dates and will make you feel like a lemon.'

'Whom I tell all of my secrets to.'

'Whose shoulder I will cry on when we break up.'

She never provided an explanation. That was part of her test. The handshake was my own test. I have always read handshakes in the way that some people analyse handwriting.

'Call me Pete,' I would say, looking them in the eye.

I almost felt sorry for one or two of the poor confused souls who fell at the first hurdle and actually asked her to explain. To them, she said very graciously, 'I'm sorry. I don't think this is going to work out.'

The first time she did it, I said, 'That wasn't very fair on him.'

'Oh, Pete,' she replied, 'if he's like that now, what would he have been like a week from now when he asks me out and I have to say no because we're already going to the pictures? Anyway, if I said you were a friend, do you think he'd have been happy with that?'

I should have said it then. 'Laura, what if we were more than friends?' Or, 'Seeing as you're short of a date, how about it?'

If they could prove that they didn't look like the jealous type, she would sometimes reward them with, 'You're going to get to know each other quite well.'

Later, when we were alone, she would dig me in the ribs, her head on one side, and ask, 'Well?'

'Well what?' I pretended that I didn't know what she was talking about.

'What do you think of him?'

'Reasonably firm grip. Good eye contact. He's house-trained. Worth a second chance.'

'That's what I thought.' She hugged herself.

'Not sure if he'll pass the Mrs Albury test.' I couldn't resist leaving her with some doubt. Sunday lunch at the Alburys was the ultimate test. Mrs Albury could tell a lot from the way that a man held his knife and fork and what he did with his elbows while he was at the table.

'You don't think so?'

I shrugged. It was always best not to say too much. Not when Mrs Albury wouldn't be able to resist giving her daughter the benefit of her years of experience.

Of course, I was happiest when there was no one else on the scene. People often assumed that Laura and I were together and it must have put many a prospective admirer off. What is the difference between a male friend and a boyfriend anyway? When Laura complained about a boyfriend, it was always me that she compared them to.

'We never find the need to argue, do we? So why do they feel they have to?' she would say, or 'When you buy me an ice cream, you're not thinking about what you're going to get in return.'

Laura liked to look good for herself and lapped up any attention, but she didn't enjoy the feeling of being on display or of being ogled. She liked to be tactile, but she didn't like to be groped or feel that someone had an arm around her as a sign of possession. She liked to receive gifts, but only when there was no expectation of what would be given in return. She liked to be walked home, but only when she was not going to feel pressurized.

'When do you and I talk about words like "compromise"?' She would occasionally get angry. 'When is it necessary for us to sit down and "talk about it"? When do we ever discuss who's going to pay for what?'

Why didn't I ever say, 'We're obviously the perfect couple. Why don't we just go out with each other?'

The thing was we did go out with each other. All of the time. I didn't understand how to move things on to the next level, short of jumping on her or declaring undying love. For every time that I told myself I had nothing to lose, there was a part of me that knew that I had everything to lose. I didn't want to turn into one of those boys she complained about. And she must have known how I felt about her. Surely, the whole point was that we never discussed it?

Ironically, Laura would tell everyone how I broke her heart the day I told her I was going away to university.

'I'll be home every few weeks to see you.'

'It won't be the same. Why can't you just go to college here?'

In a way, I was delighted that my announcement had had such an effect on her. Who doesn't want to hear that they will be missed?

Why didn't I tell her then? I love you. I've always loved you. I'm always going to love you. This is four short years and then I can earn enough money to make us both happy.

'I'll be able to get a better job if I go to one of the top five universities. It's a really good opportunity for me.'

In fact, I have only ever worked for the one practice and they wouldn't have given a hoot which tin-pot college my degree came from. The senior partner knew my uncle Jonathan during the war and that was the only reference I ever needed.

Chapter Nineteen

I recognized Tom Fellows as the threat that he was the second I introduced him to Laura Albury. By that time, our friendship had survived a four-year separation, working together and the odd admission uttered under the influence of alcohol, which she had graciously chosen to ignore. The change in her was so immediate that I felt I had no choice but to walk away. I even thought about leaving town and putting down roots elsewhere. I had not counted on being charmed by Tom Fellows or the fact that, in time, his friendship would become as important to me as Laura's.

In my early twenties I was the embodiment of everything that was sensible and respectable. I had turned into the professional suit-wearer that my parents had hoped I would become.

'Get a few years under your belt, son,' my father advised me, man to man. 'Thirty is the right age for a man to marry. Plenty of time to shop around.'

I was still young enough for thirty to sound old. I enjoyed work to a degree, I even enjoyed playing the part, but was this really all there was to life: university, job, marriage, children?

You have no idea how attractive Tom's lifestyle was to me. There was no rigid timescale to anything he did. Against the background of our nine-to-five working lives, his pressures were relatively few. He was the front man and driving force behind the Spearheads, a rock band who had achieved local success and were aiming for the big time.

'Enjoy the ride, boys,' he would say. 'It's only a matter of time.'

His belief that they were going to break through was so strong that he had us all convinced. He made only a small amount of money from gigging. Whatever else Tom needed, he made by what he casually referred to as 'making himself useful'. There is no doubt that Tom had an almost extraordinary talent for understanding how things work. Cars came second only to music in his life. He invested the little money that he managed to save in clapped-out shells that looked fit for the scrap heap, but he stripped them down, lovingly welded them back together, sprayed and polished them, and sold them on. I watched him perform these miracles in the double garage at the bottom of his mother's garden. He breathed life into them in the same way that he breathed life into a song. Even as a mechanic, he was an artist. Although he paid his way at home with the vehicle-restoration work, he could never really charge enough to represent the hours that he put in, so he also took on extra work. He gained himself a reputation as someone who could be trusted to do a good job, whether it was car repairs, gardening or small building jobs. When you weren't sure whom to call, you called Tom. If he had been aware of his own worth or if he had become qualified in any of the areas that he already excelled in, he could have made a grand living. As it was, he felt he had to be the cheap option for people who couldn't afford – or couldn't afford to be ripped off by – the so-called professionals. Unemployment was at an all time high in the 1970s.

'Settle up with me when you can afford it,' he would say, not wanting to cause offence.

The businessman in me was appalled. 'You've just done a day's work for nothing!'

'I went to school with his Jimmy.' He scrubbed at his hands until he felt they were clean enough to handle a guitar. 'They didn't have much then, and that was when he was in work, but he would always make sure that he took me to the game if we were playing at home. My dad didn't bother sticking around long enough to do that.'

'What about the materials?'

He shrugged and pointed to a wooden tea chest. 'Spares. When someone can afford a new part, I re-condition the old ones. You never know when they might come in handy.'

'How do you make ends meet?'

'My mum has never let me starve. Pete, you give a little, you take a little.' He put one hand on my shoulder and looked at me as if I was the one who didn't understand how the world worked. 'You know that shipment of tyres I've got stacked out the front?'

'Yes?'

'Do you think I did that all myself? Who do you think helped me unload them?'

'I did wonder.'

'And no one's complained. Do you see anyone else getting away with that?'

In other words, despite the bad-boy image, he was as hard-working and genuine a soul as you could hope to meet. There wouldn't be a single complaint from neighbours if he made a racket on a Saturday morning revving up a car in the road. He was far more likely to receive offers of help. The only person he failed to charm instantly was Laura's mother, but she was a hard nut to crack.

I would never have been able to hate Tom Fellows, or to convince myself that he wasn't good enough for Laura. The story of how he came to be stifled by an office job is a tragedy. It is also the story that I need to find a way to tell Andrea, because it is really her story.

Tom passed the good-boyfriend test with flying colours. For once, there was no need for Laura to introduce me or to explain who I was. He not only recognized the importance of our history, he knew that it was vital to the success of his relationship with Laura. The need to rehearse with the Spearheads in the evenings and his irregular hours meant that dates were going to be few and far between. We were always welcome to watch the practice sessions or gigs, but for every really exciting rehearsal where you felt that you were watching the creation of something important, there were ten when someone couldn't get a chord sequence quite right and they had to go over it again and again. Tom was a hard taskmaster. He demanded commitment and something close to perfection. If Laura had thought that going out with someone in a band was going to be glamorous, she was sorely mistaken.

'I'm bored!' Laura shouted to me, trying to make herself heard above the din.

I shook my head, putting a hand behind each ear. 'Can't hear you!'

The chords stopped suddenly, leaving the sound of Laura yelling 'Bored' hanging in the air. The band all turned and stared, and we hung our heads like naughty school children.

'Sorry, guys,' I tried to explain. 'We're going to go now.' We stood and shuffled backwards towards the door. 'Maybe see you in the pub for last orders?'

Laura waved and I closed the door behind her. Outside, we fell against the wall of the garage laughing as the music started to vibrate again.

Laura was aware that her mother was going to judge Tom on his appearance. While he was keen to meet her family, she was happy to delay this until it was absolutely necessary. The only thing on the plus side for her was that Tom could rarely pick her up or take her home. That was always my job.

Over the next eighteen months there was a shift in the

balance of our relationship. I found myself wanting to spend time with Tom as much as with Laura. It started with an invitation to come and see his latest acquisition in his workshop. He had come across a 1956 MGA at an auction, an absolute bargain.

'She's a beauty.' He smiled knowingly. 'I can't wait to hear what you think of her.'

Why he should have wanted my opinion I will never know. What I saw was a rusting shell propped up on bricks where its wheels should have been.

'Well?' he asked, running a hand over the rear wheel arch, taking in the whole of the curve. 'What do you think?'

'Wow.' I raised my eyebrows, trying to share his enthusiasm. Not knowing what else there was to say.

'She was a steal,' he went on. 'You know what people lack, Pete? Vision! Imagination! That's why treasures like this end up on the scrap heap.'

I nodded. As far as I was concerned, I was one of those people.

'They see something to be cast aside, ignoring the quality of the build. You know what this was? The first of the modern sporting MGs. The first one without running boards. When this came out, it looked so far ahead of its time that everyone wanted a piece of the action. Take a look under the bonnet,' he encouraged. 'Help yourself.'

I toyed with the catch clumsily, and rattled around until I felt movement, then I propped it open. 'What's the size of this thing?' I asked, pretending that I knew what I was looking at.

'Sixteen hundred, push-rod engine. I'm going to make her purr again.'

Although the three of us still spent time together, I started to spend most of my weekends hanging out in Tom's workshop tinkering with cars rather than in the cafés in town with Laura listening to the jukebox.

Tom's mother insisted on calling her garage 'the shed', but it was so much more than that. By day it was where Tom worked on his cars and gadgets, by night it was a rehearsal studio. Tom was surprisingly – even obsessively – tidy, and every possible corner and recess was shelved or stacked high, leaving room for his work-benches, the Spearheads' van and whatever vehicle Tom was working on, the band's equipment and a tatty but comfortable sofa that Tom had rescued. To the untrained eye, it might have appeared cluttered and chaotic, but there was a designated place for everything and heaven help you if you were the person responsible for putting something back in the wrong place.

As the houses were terraced, access for vehicles was via an unmade road that was little more than a mud track running behind the gardens. We rarely bothered knocking at the front door, but went straight to the garage, which was generally where Tom could be found at all hours. Mrs Fellows was friendly enough, and any friend of her son's was always welcome, but it seemed a terrible imposition. The double doors at the back were heavily padlocked, but the favoured few were given spare keys to the side door. Tom's workshop offered more privacy and freedom than I could have found anywhere else at that point in my life. I could forget about the starchiness of the office and the oppressiveness of home where laughter sounded out of place. Tom shared with me the music that had influenced him, the same tracks that he had taught himself to strum along with in his bedroom as a teenager. Unlike him, I hadn't been brought up on a diet of music. I enjoyed it as background noise, but it was hardly my reason for being.

My father hadn't been a music lover; in fact the opposite was true. Most of the music that I had been exposed to was classical or church music, although as a rule my parents were far more likely to listen to news and discussion programmes. My father would have considered listening to music a frivolous pastime that did not fully occupy either the mind or the hands, leaving one exposed to all manner of evil. When he was out, my mother would sometimes allow me to listen to Flanders and Swann by way of light relief. For those of you who are not familiar with their work, I can only describe them as a musical comedy duo, who performed at a grand piano wearing black tie. They followed the great and very British tradition of word play. I understood little of the meaning of the lyrics, but as a child I enjoyed the sound of the language, especially the songs with animal noises, 'I'm a Gnu' and 'The Hippopotamus Song' being particular favourites. By the age of twelve, I had learned most of *At the Drop of a Hat* by heart. However, the Stones they were not. It wasn't possible to impress school friends by knowing all of the words to 'The Reluctant Cannibal'.

Tom decided that he was responsible for my musical education and he wanted me to understand what I was listening to. It was a lesson in history.

'Forget Elvis,' he said. 'We start with the blues. That's where rock and roll began.'

His prescription for musical ignorance was a cocktail of Robert Johnson, Sonny Boy Williamson, Blind Willie Johnson and Howlin' Wolf. Raw recordings, all of them, with hints of long dusty journeys, smoke-filled bars, the comfort of steamy nights to alleviate the general sense of hopelessness, and something else so new to me that I didn't have the vocabulary to put into words.

'What do you think?' Tom asked.

I was more comfortable making a joke of it so I sang my reply, something of a musical cliché, 'Diddly-diddly-diddly-di, Da-da-da!'

He was disappointed in me. 'Well, I suppose that's something. At least you know that Status Quo didn't invent the twelve-bar blues riff. Now we're going to throw you in at the deep end.'

I wasn't prepared for the confusion of 'Tomorrow Never Knows' by the Beatles or the challenging rhythms of *Led Zeppelin III*. Sitting opposite Tom as he strummed along with his eyes closed, I tried to mimic the movement of his body as he kept time with the music. He was mesmerizing, but I found the music difficult and foreign at first. When the breakthrough finally came, it was as if I had suddenly grasped the most complicated mathematical equation you can imagine. A whole new world opened up for me.

That world included guitar gods: Jimi Hendrix, Eric Clapton, David Gilmour, Jimmy Page and Brian May. Great showmen: David Bowie, Marc Bolan, Alice Cooper, Gary Glitter (what a shock that was), Roy Wood and the late, great Freddie Mercury. And great, great songs: 'All The Young Dudes' by Mott the Hoople, 'Walk on the Wild Side' by Lou Reed, 'See Emily Play' by Pink Floyd, 'Satisfaction' by the Rolling Stones, 'Virginia Plain' by Roxy Music. And that was just for starters. I was a convert, and like most converts I became a fanatic.

It was in Tom's workshop that I learned a few chords on the guitar and heard some of Tom's fledgling songs take form. It was there that Tom told me about his plans for the band over shared cans of beer. I learned how to use my new camera, making a study of Tom Fellows and working out the best lighting, the best angle to shoot him from. Many people blessed with natural talent cannot understand why mere mortals cannot do as they do and Tom didn't make the best teacher, but his enthusiasm was enough to carry you. If I described the lighting effect I was looking for, he would be able to create it by setting up the room and making light reflectors using whatever he could lay his hands on.

'Mum.' He would burst in through the back door to the kitchen. 'I'm going to need some tin foil and that old white umbrella of yours.'

'Cupboard under the stairs,' she would say, without batting an eyelid. 'Have you eaten?' she would call after him as he walked back laden down with half of the contents of the cupboard.

Although at least 75 per cent of the credit for the results of my early attempts at photography is Tom's, for the first time I discovered something that I was good at *and* enjoyed. I was soon designated the band's official photographer.

It was a while before I realized that Laura was jealous of my friendship with Tom.

'Do you want to go to the café this afternoon?' she asked.

'Sorry, I can't,' I said – and I was genuinely sorry. It was not so very long ago that I would have found it difficult to refuse Laura anything. 'I've promised to help Tom with the car.'

'Fine,' she said, 'I'll ask Faye.'

'Why don't you come along?'

'Sounds like it involves engines,' she sulked. 'I don't do engines. Not unless they're already inside a car and they actually work.'

'Don't you want to be there when he gets her working?'

'By "her", I presume you mean the car, and the last time I saw "her", she didn't even have wheels. I'm guessing that it won't happen this afternoon.'

I thought she was angry with me for taking up his precious time, which he could have spent with her. Only finally did it register that the real issue was not that Tom chose to spend time with engines, it was that I chose to spend time with someone other than her. At first she had been delighted that we got on so well, but the scales had tipped. She was not someone who was used to being on her own.

One night after watching Tom play, a couple of drinks worse for wear, Laura and I did the Monkees walk home, arms around each other's backs, legs swinging out in wide circles in time with each other, high on pride and freedom. It had been one of those nights when everything had been just right. I had reminded myself to enjoy every moment because it felt like the most exciting night of my life. I had watched Tom on stage, drawing the crowd in, aware of his magnetism, his eyes a little wild. I had stood at the front, picking faces out of the crowd through my viewfinder, people who played to the camera and people who felt that it was an intrusion. My focus would constantly return to Laura, who was sometimes laughing, sometimes coy, sometimes shy, occasionally a little lost-looking.

I knew she hated the fact that Tom couldn't spend time with her when she most wanted to be with him, that out of necessity his priority was to pack up and take his gear home. That when she wanted Tom Fellows what she got was Peter Churcher. Good old reliable Peter Churcher.

When an unexpected rainstorm took us by surprise, Laura clung to me momentarily before we decided to make a run for a bus shelter. We arrived laughing and colliding, much like our first meeting. Laura's perfect hair was matted and her perfect make-up had run. She was panting as she pushed herself against me.

'Kiss me, Pete,' she breathed, closing her eyes. I could have pushed her away, but I saw her furrowed forehead and her look of intense concentration. I looked at her as she opened her eyes again and repeated, 'Kiss me, Pete.' This wasn't a case of mistaken identity. She moved my camera out of the way and placed my arms firmly around her back. 'I need to be kissed.'

You don't want to think too much at a time like that. Thinking could have ruined one of the most exciting moments of my life. There is rarely only one person in any given situation who is taken advantage of. I enjoyed my moment, trying not to worry what it meant.

Laura didn't shock me, but she certainly confused the hell out of herself. The next time I saw her she wasn't apologetic but she wasn't as tactile as usual. Even more telling was the fact that she brought her sister Faye with her. They were as close as any two sisters could be on home territory, but their differences meant that they generally kept to their own sets of friends. I took this as a sign that Laura didn't quite trust herself with me. For the first time, I thought that she might choose me, a reliable boyfriend with a sensible career, over an unreliable genius who, we were both coming to realize, was pinning all of his hopes on pipe dreams, when he might have earned a very good living from his sidelines. Thank God for my sensible career!

For Laura, this was the choice she was constantly faced with over the next few years of her life. In essence, it was exactly the same choice that Tom had: give up your passion and accept option number two. I think her recognition of this parallel made her more sympathetic to his cause. But whilst Tom's passion for music was one of the things that made him so attractive, it made life as his girlfriend very difficult. For Laura, who had longer-term plans, it was impossible for her to imagine how they might make a life together, let alone plan for the family she wanted. While Tom was planning his strategy for world domination, Laura was ready to settle down.

The small snippets of news that Tom shared about possible plans for the band only posed more concerns for Laura.

'I'm looking into Europe,' Tom enthused over a drink in a pub. In those days pubs had real atmosphere which consisted of 90 per cent cigarette smoke and 10 per cent testosterone. 'They really get the rock scene over there and they go wild for live music.'

'More than in London?' I asked, glancing quickly at Laura who had looked away, pretending to take an interest in the bar menu.

'It's actually cheaper to go abroad, believe it or not,' he explained. 'I had a call from a tour booker who saw us in town and he thinks we can pull it off.'

'Will the van make it as far as Dover?' I asked, concerned for Laura.

'The van?' He banged the table with his fist. 'We're talking about a tour bus. It gets us there, we eat on it and we sleep on it. It's like a hotel, but you never have to unpack.'

'It's a bloody caravan, isn't it?' Steve, the drummer, intervened, returning from the bar and setting four pints on the table, covering it in slops. He pulled his long hair away from his face, bent down and hoovered the spillage up with his mouth, before sitting down heavily.

'Waste not, want not, that's what I say. I bloody well hate caravans.'

'Laura's looking forward to it, aren't you?' Tom pulled her close. 'On the road, waking up in a different city every day.'

'I've never been abroad.' She looked at me nervously. 'Have you?'

It wasn't that Laura was excluded from Tom's plans. He thought that she would be prepared to drop everything and come along for the ride. Laura couldn't reconcile this with the white wedding, the semi-detached house and the 2.5 children.

When she talked about doing something to force the issue, it was clear what she meant.

'Don't do anything daft.' I tried to make a joke of it. 'If you tame that man, he may not end up being the person you fell in love with.'

'Trust you to defend him,' she sulked.

'There's nothing to defend.' I held my hands up by my shoulders, palms towards her. 'He's always been honest with you about his plans. On the other hand, you . . .' I left the sentence hanging.

'It's not as if I can ask him to choose me over the band. It wouldn't be fair. Besides' – she looked sideways at me – 'I'm not sure what his answer would be.'

'Don't you think you need to know that before you think about getting pregnant?'

The issue of Mr and Mrs Albury's reaction to Laura's choice of boyfriend still loomed. If Faye had brought Tom Fellows home, I don't think her mother would have given her a hard time (I believe that she was happy if Faye made it home at all), but Mrs Albury had different plans for Laura, whose face was supposed to be not only her own fortune but her mother's pension.

Faye, on the other hand, had grown from a sullen-looking teenager to a somewhat more interesting proposition. She had none of her sister's natural beauty but she looked effortlessly cool in a way that men admired and girls envied. Her look was very contrived: heavy make-up, leather and zips, but you would have noticed her even if she had just been wearing jeans. She looked every inch the rock star's girlfriend. Although Faye had chosen to 'dabble' at art school, her mother was confident that she would either work out that it wouldn't make her enough money or find out how to make money from it. Faye was her clever girl. Always had been. Faye would never have to rely on a man for her living.

What does a boy with a camera do with a free afternoon and the two most fascinating girls in town? If he has any sense he stocks up on film and takes just about the best few rolls of film of his amateur career. Laura loving the camera, Faye hating it, but with equal passion. I had already scouted out possible locations for shoots for Tom's album cover; all I had to do was persuade the girls to pout, glare and to flutter their eyelashes. I played around with the idea of the contrasts between the two of them and between them and the backgrounds. I shot Laura against a background of industrial units and electricity pylons, while I had Faye make daisy chains in the park and pretend to be pushing a toddler in a pushchair, a cigarette hanging out of the corner of her mouth, while the child's mother was distracted. I shot the sisters back to back, side by side, lying next to each other head to toe, and on the swings at the children's playground. I developed those prints in Tom's workshop, which also doubled as my darkroom. He claimed ownership of the better ones immediately for his album cover. Some decorated the walls for a while afterwards, while Faye handed in others as part of the art project that she should have been working on, presenting herself as the true 'artist', making a statement about the role of the model in photography. Her attitude was not one of embarrassment or apology that I was not credited in any way.

'Can you really believe they went for it?' she asked me, amazed that anyone could be so stupid as to be taken in by her poor excuse for an art project. She had come top of her class. 'Bunch of idiots, if you ask me.' That was when she lost all respect for her tutors and decided that art was not for her. The shame of it was that I think she was shrewd enough to work out how to make a lot of money out of it.

Chiefly, what those photographs represented to me was a misplaced feeling of enormous optimism. It is probably just as well that I have no idea what happened to them.

Chapter Twenty

I lost my virginity at the age of twenty-four. I can't claim to have been a late starter as my sex life certainly didn't kick off even then. I had been working in Tom's workshop one evening developing photographs while he and Laura were out together. Bathed in a red glow, having swapped the single light bulb, I was concentrating and didn't hear the door open, but I jumped out of my skin when I heard the chaos that followed. My eyes were accustomed to the half-light but clearly the intruder's weren't.

'Faye.' I was relieved, and offered her my hand to help her to her feet. I should have sensed trouble.

'Well, that wasn't exactly the entrance I planned.' She clutched her coat tightly around her, although the evening wasn't particularly cold. I presumed that her pride, if nothing else, was a little bruised.

'I'm afraid the others are out,' I explained, gesturing around the clutter. 'You've had a wasted journey. It's just me here at the moment.'

'That's what I was counting on.' She smiled coyly,

turning to bolt the side door to the workshop then letting her coat drop to the floor, revealing little more than a black basque, French knickers, laddered fishnets and stiletto-heeled ankle boots. I had the uncanny feeling of being in a dream where the wrong people turn up in the wrong places, but at the same time I was fascinated. I had no idea what I had done to deserve such a display. I wondered if Faye was putting on a theatrical performance and if this was 'art'. If so, it seemed that I was about to become her latest project. Part of me was rooted to the spot. Another part of me wanted to laugh out loud. I was tempted to try and defuse the situation by joking, 'Good God, woman, put some clothes on. You'll catch your death in here.'

She used one hand to push me against the side of the minibus, while she held herself at arm's length.

'Have you ever seen anyone wearing one of these, Peter Churcher?' She ran the index finger of her spare hand along the top seam of the basque, drawing my eyes downwards.

I swallowed, trying to focus on her face. 'I think my mother wore a corset occasionally.'

'And did your mother wear stockings, Peter Churcher?'

I cleared my throat. 'Tights. American tan. And if they were as laddered as yours she would have mended them with nail varnish.'

'She sounds like a resourceful woman.' Her mouth was close to mine. 'Do you like resourceful women, Peter Churcher?' But she did not wait to hear if I liked resourceful women, or any other kind for that matter. Sometimes, you need someone who knows what they want and is prepared to make their intentions all too clear. The fact that she took control seemed to remove any choice that I had and, at the time, the need for any guilt. If I had thought for one moment that she was a shy and retiring virgin, or that she had any strong feelings for me, I would have pushed her away. As it was, I thought of very little apart from her guiding hands.

Afterwards, we sat in the front seat of the minibus while she leaned backwards with eyes half closed and smoked a cigarette, looking pleased with herself. I was happy that our facing-forwards positions meant that I didn't have to look her in the eye.

'Well?' she said at length, enquiringly, still flirting.

'Thank you very much.' I was not sure what it was appropriate to say under the circumstances, unaccustomed as I was, but I had been brought up to mind my p's and q's.

'Do you know what I think?' She moved her hand into my lap. I doubted that I was expected to reply. 'I think that sister of mine has mucked you around for long enough, hmmm? What do you say we make a regular thing of this?'

I must have looked at her in confusion – possibly in horror – as I said, 'But you must know that I'm in love with Laura. I've always been in love with Laura.' I could tell from the speed with which her manner changed that this was completely the wrong thing to say.

'Well, fuck you!' Faye stubbed out her cigarette and let

the end drop to the floor as she struggled to find the door handle. 'You know, that's the type of thing you just might have mentioned beforehand. Do you think I do this sort of thing all the time? Huh? Well, do you?' She stepped out of the cab and slammed the door, turning to face me through the open window. My lack of reply must have spoken volumes. 'You do! You complete and utter arsehole! You think I'm some sort of slut!' Her banshee face disappeared as she moved away to find her coat. When she returned, fully covered, I was staring at my knees miserably. 'Just for the record, Peter Churcher, Laura thinks of you as the brother she never had. Do you know what that means? Let me spell it out for you. It's not that she doesn't care for you, it's just that she will never, ever, sleep with you. Get your head around that!'

But there was only one thing occupying my mind at that moment: how to get to Laura before Faye did.

Chapter Twenty-one

'That's great news,' was Laura's rather surprising reaction when I told her apologetically that I had slept with her sister. I had known that if I waited, sooner or later she and Tom would turn up at the workshop. It was not only Faye who took advantage of the privacy it offered when we were all living under our parents' roofs. Whether they were as puritanical as mine, as protective as Laura's or as liberal-minded as Tom's, it saved any embarrassing questions.

'How is it good news?' I was completely thrown by her, expecting disapproval at the very least.

'Well, if you got together with anyone else we probably wouldn't see each other so much any more, but this way—'

'You don't get it.' I was pacing the floor. 'I told her there can't be anything more to it.'

'You did what?' Laura's mouth dropped and her face turned red. This was more along the lines of the reaction I had expected from her. I looked to Tom for moral support, not wanting to explain out loud to Laura what was obvious to him. 'What the hell were you thinking of? You know how badly she's been hurt in the past and she adores you.'

That was all news to me. The look on my face was enough for Tom. I could see him trying to contain a smile in the palm of his hand, but it was seeping out of the edges.

'I'm sorry,' he blurted when she looked at him accusingly. 'But look at the facts. This is Pete we're talking about. Sorry, Pete,' he appealed to me as an aside.

'No offence taken.' I knew that he was standing up for me, although I had no idea exactly how he might defend me when the situation seemed indefensible.

'There is no way that Pete would have deliberately got himself into this mess. It's obvious what happened.'

'And what is that, exactly?' Laura crossed her arms, facing him squarely.

'Faye seduced him,' Tom explained quietly, mirroring her stance.

'Oh, come on!' Laura looked at me and waited for me to deny it. I hung my head.

'Well, even if she did,' she changed her tack, 'that's no excuse. You could have turned her down gently.'

'It's not as simple as that.' Tom shook his head. 'It's very difficult not to cause offence. If a bloke tries it on and a woman pushes him away, it's like, "Fair enough, you can't blame me for trying." When the shoe is on the other foot, the woman wants a full explanation about what's wrong with her – and God help you if you try to answer that one – and she won't even take the fact

156

that you're involved with someone else as an excuse.'

'I wouldn't know.' Laura was dismissive. I could have said exactly the same thing. Unlike Tom, I had no experience of seducing women and, equally, I had no experience of trying to turn women down, gently or otherwise. There had never been the need.

'Stands to reason,' he countered.

'And what exactly is that supposed to mean?'

'Well, who in their right mind would turn you down, Laura?'

She allowed herself a small smile before composing herself. 'So, you're saying you think that you would cause less offence by sleeping with a girl who makes the first move and then letting her down, than by saying no in the first place?'

Tom and I looked at each other. It was a question that was impossible to answer without looking bad. Tom was the one who nodded. He was the one with sufficient charm to make it sound like the man was the innocent victim in this scenario.

'You're pathetic. Both of you!' She walked to the other side of the workshop and leaned on a bench before turning back. 'Are you going to tell me exactly what happened, Pete, or not?'

'Not,' I said, feeling the need to stand up for myself.

'I thought you had nothing to hide?' Laura accused.

'If it's not too late, I'd rather try to do the gentlemanly thing.'

'So now you start to worry about being a gentleman! You' – she pointed at me – 'I want you to know that you

157

have ruined my evening. And you' – she pointed at Tom – 'can forget it for tonight. You'd better take me home to see what kind of a mess Faye's in. I said that I'd kill the next bloke who mucked her about. I just wasn't expecting it to be you.'

'Hang on a minute . . .' Tom frowned. 'Pete was on his own here this evening. You were the only other person who knew that, and you told me that you and Faye got ready to go out together. You didn't look nearly surprised enough when Pete told you what had happened . . . you *knew* what she was planning. Why didn't you put her off?' Laura turned red and wouldn't look him in the face. 'You encouraged her, didn't you?'

I looked from Tom to Laura.

'Well!' she exploded, her arms waving out of control. 'We can't just carry on like this, can we?'

'Like what?' It was Tom's turn to look accusing.

'*I* can't carry on like this,' she back-pedalled. 'It's just too confusing. I had to take one of you out of the equation.'

'What equation is that, Laura?' Tom asked, gently but firmly.

'It's like . . .' She made one false start before she blurted out: '. . . having a boyfriend in two parts. I have this one wonderful boyfriend who takes me shopping and to the movies and listens to me moan about my day and laughs at my jokes and walks me home at night. And we always have a great time and we never fight. And he has never, ever, let me down. And I have this other boyfriend who I fancy like crazy and we

158

have fantastic sex together but he can't find it in himself to put me first.' She looked at me tearfully. 'I'm sorry, Pete. And I have asked myself time and again' – she was talking more loudly now – 'who I should really be with. And it's making me very unhappy constantly looking at them both and wondering what kind of a life I could have with each of them. And it's not fair, and it's nobody's fault, but I can't do this any more.'

Tom went to her and held her, one hand against the back of her blonde head. 'I can't promise what you want me to promise, Laura. I won't give up the band. I've worked for this and dreamed about it for so long. And there's something else.' He looked at me then held Laura at arm's length, looking her in the eye. 'I don't mind you hearing this, Pete. I haven't asked you to marry me, Laura, because there's a very good chance I can't have children and I know how much you want them. And you should have the chance to have them. A late case of the mumps. It hasn't mattered to me before because I have never met anyone else that I would like to have children with. So, it's up to you. Another unfair choice for you to make. Or maybe it will help you make your mind up.

'I'm going to say goodnight now and ask you yet again, Pete, to see Laura home, because I'd like to be on my own.' He sat down at the drum kit and started thrashing out rhythms so painful and lonely that it made it easy for us to leave.

'Well, that's the end of plan A and plan B,' Laura said to me as we walked home slowly and awkwardly. She was trying to make light of the situation but I could sense how fragile she was, how apologetic and how utterly miserable. On the one hand, marriage had been mentioned, but the issue of children must have floored her.

'Tell me there's not a C?' I said in all seriousness. 'I don't want to be involved in that one, if you don't mind.'

'Any other bright ideas?'

'We could always elope.' It was as close as I had ever come to asking her out.

She laughed in spite of herself, not necessarily the reaction I was looking for. 'So, you're not too angry with me then?'

'Are we quits?'

'I can't speak for Faye, I'm afraid.'

'I think that she can probably stand up for herself. My name is going to be mud in your house. It's going to be very difficult for you.'

'Not unless she admits to my parents what happened and I don't think there's much chance of that. But you may have just lost your Mr-Nice-Guy image.'

'It hasn't got me very far in life so far.'

'I'm sorry, Pete. I'm sorry you had to hear that. I'm sorry I said half of it and I'm sorry I set you up. And I'm going to be even sorrier when I get home. I honestly thought that if you saw Faye on her own, you would see what a beautiful person she is . . . oh, I don't know what I was thinking now.'

'Tell Faye I'm sorry too, will you?'

'Oh, no! That's down to you, I'm afraid.'

But there has only ever been one thing I was really sorry about and that evening didn't even come close to it.

'Friends?' Laura asked with those big eyes brimming over.

'Friends,' I lied.

Chapter Twenty-two

We all treated each other with kid gloves for a while after that. Silences that would have been comfortable beforehand were filled with unspoken words. I seriously considered leaving to give Tom and Laura the space to think, but at the same time I sensed that I was needed to diffuse the situation. In the end, it was Tom who needed to know where he stood and he forced the issue by asking Laura to marry him.

'I knew straight away from how I felt that it's the right thing to do,' she told me.

I wanted to ask, 'What about your plans for a family?' Not wanting to sound the least bit jealous, I kissed her on the cheek in the most brotherly way I could and said, 'I'm really happy for you. You couldn't have found yourself a better man.'

She remained on such a high that the practicalities were unimportant. She even managed to brush aside her parents' open disapproval of the long-haired lout that she brought home and introduced as her husband-to-be. Having never met him before, Tom – on Laura's recommendation – skipped the all-important tradition of asking Mr Albury for his daughter's hand. There is no doubt what his answer would have been. What Laura refused to listen to, I sat through on two separate occasions after being lured into their living room under false pretences.

'Mark my words, he will never be able to provide for her and make her happy,' Mrs Albury confided in me. 'That girl needs security. You've worked with her, Peter. You know that she's never going to go far under her own steam. We wouldn't be so worried if it was Faye we're talking about. She's always had a good head on her shoulders.'

On the second occasion, after sitting through half an hour of nonsense without being allowed to get a word in edgeways, I did the only thing that I could do and walked out. With that, I managed all on my own to do what Faye hadn't. My name in the Albury household was officially mud. It was a relief of sorts. I no longer had to live up to yet another set of expectations about who I was and how I should behave.

'The best man won,' I congratulated Tom, shaking his hand.

'I wouldn't say that.' He smiled sheepishly. 'In fact, I was hoping you would agree to do the honours.' I was flattered to have been asked. Despite the fact that Laura had openly admitted that I was the competition, Tom wanted me to be part of the day. There was no avoiding the fact that it is traditionally the groom's closest friend who is asked to perform the duties of the best man. How could I have refused?

But things didn't settle down. Laura's father suffered a massive heart attack and died. He was only forty-seven and had apparently been in excellent health otherwise. They were all devastated but Mrs Albury was cruel in her grief.

'There's no doubt in my mind who is to blame for this!' she told anyone who was willing to listen. It was the first time that Laura had ever known her mother's anger, having always been her blonde-haired, blue-eyed girl. Instead, Mrs Albury clung to Faye, who had never been the sole recipient of her mother's affection before and didn't know how to react. The dynamics of a family can change overnight. By the day of the funeral, they were at each others' throats.

Although the wedding took place as planned, and Mrs Albury was on her best behaviour for the day, it was never going to be a completely happy occasion. I found myself in the peculiar situation of giving Laura away and acting as best man, while Faye was the bridesmaid. It was strange to see her in a dress that had been chosen for her by Laura and fitted perfectly, with her spiky hair flattened down and curled under at the ends. She could barely disguise a sneer as we faced each other across the aisle in the register office. It certainly took the edge off any other feelings I was struggling with. After she unexpectedly caught the bouquet, she threw it to me, saying, 'See if they work for you, Peter Churcher.'

I felt sorry for Mrs Fellows, who wondered what kind of a family her angel of a son was getting himself involved with. 'The Alburys,' she asked me. 'Do you know them well?'

'Well enough.'

'I mean, I know that they've suffered a bereavement – and I don't want to sound too harsh – but do they always speak to each other through gritted teeth?'

Gritted teeth? I thought to myself. It's the forked tongues you need to watch out for!

I drank too much for courage and made an overly sentimental speech about love conquering all. After the reception, the happy couple left for the coast for a couple of days and I left alone, taking a detour via Tom's workshop and thrashing those drums for all I was worth. I slept in the back of the van, which was as usual filled with some rather suspect bedding. I felt something had ended and I needed to remember who I was before it had all begun so that I could start again. The problem was that Laura had always been there and I could recall so little before her except the gloominess of my parents' house, the desire to escape the confines of its dark brown walls and my father's all-consuming grief.

Eventually I was disturbed by Tom's mother, who rarely ventured as far as the garden, let alone the 'shed', but had been overwhelmed by a desire to mow the lawn in her son's absence. She showed no surprise at finding me there and brought me tea and scrambled eggs on buttered toast, and for that kindness I will be eternally grateful to her.

Tom and Laura moved into a small, rented flat above

a fish-and-chip shop when they returned from their honeymoon. Laura threw herself into making the place look homely and made the most of Tom's carpentry skills and his legendary ability to mend things. Mrs Albury visited and, having proclaimed their new home to be 'nothing more than she had expected', left without having so much as a cup of tea. Laura, who had thought that things would be better once they were married, was beyond comforting. Tom visited his new mother-in-law to try and talk things through, thinking that she would soften once she got to know him, but only managed to make things worse.

'Put it this way,' he told me over a drink, 'the conversation ended with Mrs Albury saying, "Laura's made her bed and she'll have to lie in it," and me saying, "Well, if that's how you feel, then perhaps you'd better stay away."'

'Sounds as if it could have gone better.'

'I'm in the doghouse now. I was on the sofa last night and my back's killing me. This married bliss isn't all it's cracked up to be, you know. Mrs Albury always seems to have liked you. What's your secret?'

'I use a suit and tie as a disguise.'

'I tried that for the wedding and it didn't work. I'm afraid she's going to have to get used to me the way I am.'

The next news was that Faye had left town, no doubt driven away by her mother, and that Laura had been sent to bring her home. Laura found Faye and stayed for two weeks but returned alone. She wouldn't tell her mother where to find her.

'She's staying with some college friends for the summer,' she said simply. 'She just needs some space.'

'Space?' Mrs Albury argued. 'Where could she possibly find more space than at home now that there's just me rattling around on my own?'

She blamed Laura for driving the family apart, completely ignoring the fact that she lost her job for taking unauthorized leave. Although the decision had had nothing to do with me, and I couldn't have influenced it in any way, I felt both responsible and angry.

'Laura was the best secretary we had,' I tried to speak up for her. It was no good.

'She could be the best secretary in this whole damn town and it wouldn't matter,' the senior partner replied. 'Nobody is beyond the rules of the firm.'

'It's probably for the best.' Laura was infuriatingly logical when I reported back to her. 'I probably would have had to give up work when the band go on tour in a couple of months anyway.'

'I didn't know there was anything definite.' I was surprised at this latest news. There were always plans – always had been – but they very rarely came to anything.

She had her back to me when she said, 'Oh yes, it's full steam ahead. All of the university towns.'

'That's fantastic news.' I tried to sound enthusiastic, wondering if this was a show of bravado on her part.

When I congratulated Tom, he seemed less certain than Laura that they would pull it off, but I took this as modesty. He had been this close too many times to let himself celebrate before the actual event.

I was spurred on to take some action in my own life. With everyone else putting down new roots, I decided that it was time for me to move out of my family home. My salary had been steadily increasing and I had been saving without any particular plans. I put down a deposit on a house that was one of a new development being built. Unlike Tom, the thought of restoring something old terrified me. I was happy to wait three months for it to be finished to give my parents a little time to get used to the idea. I was almost twenty-five and, apart from my spell at university and law school, I had always lived under their roof. My father was not a well man and looked ten years older than his age, but he had given up on life long ago. My mother could have been a very attractive, lively woman, but she was like a bee who had flown through a window by accident and spent her days desperately crashing against the glass, trying to find her way back out.

Laura and Tom left in the band's van for an 'advance recce' and promised that they would be back in a few weeks, or that news would be sent about where the others were to meet them. As the band's official photographer, I harboured hopes that I would be invited to join them on tour, although this would have been completely impractical given my job. I heard nothing for weeks.

'Any news, Steve?' I asked when I bumped into him in the pub.

'How should I know?' He shrugged. 'I'm just the drummer.'

A rushed call from a telephone box later confirmed that the plans for the tour had stalled but that Tom had some work in a recording studio doing some engineering work,

'He's doing really well, making lots of new contacts,' Laura told me. 'I don't suppose you've seen anything of my mother lately?'

'Not since the wedding.'

'I know it's asking a lot, but could you find the time to nip over and see how she's doing?'

I didn't like to say so, but I had no particular desire to incur the wrath of Mrs Albury.

'Where are you staying?' I went for a quick change of subject.

'Oh, you know, just some cheap place.' She was vague. 'We can't afford much.'

'Do you think you'll make it home before the tenth?' I asked. 'I'm moving in and I was thinking of having a housewarming.'

'Oh, hang on.' I heard tapping. 'My money's running out. I think the—' The pips went and she was cut off.

Eventually, news was in such short supply that I visited Mrs Albury. She was curt with me before she shut the door in my face. 'I thought you of all people would have known. I seem to be the last person to be told anything. Laura's pregnant and can't travel, so they won't be home until after the baby's born. So now we know why he married her. It's just as well my husband's no longer with us, bless his soul, otherwise he'd have a few choice words to say to that lad, I can tell you. He thought it was bare-faced cheek not to ask for her hand, but it's no wonder given that he'd already taken liberties. But just you wait! Over my dead body will I have a grandchild of mine brought up in a damp flat over a fish-and-chip shop. Mark my words, there are going to be a few changes around here when that girl gets home.'

Part Three

Faye's Story

Chapter Twenty-three

'That's another fine mess you've got me into, Stanley,' my mother keeps repeating endlessly. 'That's another fine mess you've got me into, Stanley.' I haven't got a clue whom she's talking to today, or who she thinks she is for that matter, but, God Almighty, I know how she feels. I just don't know her any more. I have absolutely no idea who she is. 'Let's talk,' she says. 'Why can't we talk about it?' Talk, I ask you! You can't solve all the problems in the world with words.

I never wanted to be a mother. You might think that's selfish, but I think it's realistic. It's such an enormous responsibility and one that I never felt ready for. But suddenly I have a child on my hands. She just happens to be my mother. I know some people don't think I have the capacity to love a child – or anyone else for that matter. Peter Churcher once said to me, 'You don't know what it's like to love someone.' 'That's a terrible thing to say,' I said. But I know how I come across. If only they knew that I've had to shut those feelings off. It's hard for me to admit, but there's a very real part of me that feels as if I don't deserve a child. I seem to push away anyone who tries to get close to me. Maybe it goes deeper and I just don't think I deserve to be loved at all. It's always been easier to say that I don't want children than to think about it. I tell them that I value my independence. And I do. On a good day, I'm very content with my lot. I've got to a place where I'm comfortable with my own company. Except that I now seem to be a full-time carer. And there isn't any financial help, you know. Suddenly, you find that you can't work because your mother needs you and Social Services wash their hands. Just like that! If I hadn't volunteered, they would have had to do something, but now it seems that it's all down to me. Well, it's not on.

'Hang on in there,' her knee-patting social worker says. Don't you just hate the knee-patting do-gooders? When I want someone invading my personal space, I'll let them know, thank you very much. I'm just trying to stay busy and keep out of Mum's way, to be honest, as harsh as that sounds. She's in her own world and I'll keep to mine. In the meanwhile I'm going stir crazy. I'm a prisoner in my own home. I haven't done a yoga class for weeks and even a sighting of a Starbucks would feel like a mirage. Laura would know what to do. But if she was here now, I wouldn't be in this mess. So, in a round-about way, if there's anyone to blame, it's her. Figure that one out if you can. God, there's so much I want to say to her. I can't believe we ran out of time so soon. I didn't see that one coming. I suppose the whole point is that you never do.

I adored my sister as a child. I wanted to be just like Laura. I wanted white-blonde hair curled into ringlets. I wanted perfect white teeth and an infectious giggle. I wanted puffed sleeves and skirts that fell into neat pleats. I wanted white ankle socks with frills around the tops. But most of all, I craved my parents' attention. What I got was the mousy, frizzy hair, teeth that needed braces, the ill-fitting hand-me-downs and the 'Darling, can't you see your father's tired?' I wasn't cross with them. I thought that it was obvious that they would love her more. Who wouldn't?

'You're our beautiful girl,' they would tell her, while to me it was always, 'Why can't you be more like Laura? Laura's such a good girl.' She was just more lovable than I was. I always knew I would have to try a lot harder.

I thought that I could make them notice me in other ways so I worked really hard at school – to begin with. For some reason, on their bizarre system of brownie points, good grades didn't really count for anything if you were thought of as being 'naturally clever'. If you consistently got As but had an off-day and dropped to a B a full enquiry was launched. If, like Laura, you occasionally scraped a C, a cake was baked in your honour. I was in a no-win situation.

Laura wasn't blind to what was going on. She tried to sing my praises to our parents, but they would usually turn my successes into a compliment about her. 'You're so good to support your sister. She wouldn't have been able to get that grade if you hadn't spent last night testing her.' I got to rely on Laura for attention and she

175

was just about as kind an older sister as I could have hoped for. That was enough for the first few years before I learned the phrase 'it's not fair'. Then it got a whole load more complicated.

Even early on, Laura got me out of scrapes. She knew that my parents would never be as hard on her as they would with me, so she owned up to everything that went wrong, especially if she knew I'd done it. Only Laura could admit to breaking one of my mother's precious ornaments and be rewarded with a pat on the head and an 'Honesty is the best policy', even if it was said through gritted teeth. Throughout my teens, I tested her loyalty. I came home drunk. I left a momentous cigarette burn in the living-room carpet. I stayed out all night. Her lies got less and less believable, especially for someone who looked like butter wouldn't melt. I actually thought they fell for them. But that old battleaxe in the other room now claims that she knew all along.

'Why didn't you say anything if you knew?' I asked when she let it slip. There's no way that she would have let me get away with it.

'Sisters are precious things,' she said to me. 'You shouldn't disturb that without good reason.' Maybe it was her way of redressing the balance. Laura was her favourite and there was nothing that she could do about it. You can't help the people you love the most, children included, I suppose.

Sometimes, I'm afraid of what I'd say if I really started to talk to my mother. I'm not sure I could resist asking the question, 'Would you have preferred it to have been me?' Horrible, isn't it? Hugely unfair. But she pushes me and pushes me, and it's the one question I would like to see how she reacts to. Would she avoid answering and accuse me of being cruel? Would she deny it and tell me how much she loves me? Do we feel the need to ask the hardest questions because that's what we really want to hear? And how can I still feel jealous of my sister now that she's gone?

It seemed inevitable that Laura thought she could get me out of any scrape, but I said to her, 'No, that's going too far. I can sort this one out on my own.'

'But you don't understand,' she said to me. 'I need this baby. We can't have any of our own.' She was on the point of begging. Turns out that Tom was not quite the stud that we thought he was after all. I had been planning to have the baby adopted. The difference was that I had never intended to see the baby at all, let alone watch her grow up. I meant to make things as easy as possible for myself. I told her I would think about it. 'OK,' she said. Just 'OK', but she stuck around for a couple of weeks. Made herself useful. 'Promise you won't tell them,' I said to her. I insisted that Mum and Peter could not know that I was pregnant. That was the deal. When she came back with Tom, I said to her, 'You can never tell the child or anyone else who its mother and father are. Especially Peter. As far as everyone is concerned, this is your baby.'

'What if it looks like him?' she said to me. None of us was worried that the child would take after me. We all knew cousins who looked more alike than brothers and sisters and we all knew children who didn't look like their parents at all, no matter how much other people insisted they did.

I told them, 'People are pretty blind to things that are right in front of their noses.'

'Whatever you want,' they said.

I was right. For the first ten years of her life, nearly everyone who met her told her how much she looked like Tom, and she couldn't have been happier about it. What they really meant, of course, was that there wasn't an ounce of Laura in her.

I think she knows. I think that my mother has guessed the truth and will think that she can mend everything with her words. Get it all out in the open, with no thought of the effect that it will have. 'Let's have a nice chat,' she'll say, 'with everyone round the table.' I can see it all now. She just can't see that it's far too late for the truth. We have all become what we have become.

We set up house for the duration in a flat that I was house-sitting for old college friends in south London while they were travelling. Last Tube stop on the Northern Line. Funny place, but one where I wasn't recognized every time I stepped outside and could be a no one – or I could just be myself, depending which way you look at it. Laura had sold everyone a story about a possible tour for the band that fell through, but the truth was that Tom took full advantage of his time here and made some good contacts. Before long, he had found himself a job in a recording studio. He started the day as a delivery boy, took an interest in the address on a parcel, asked if he could stick around for a while, made a few useful suggestions, and found himself helping out. By the end of the day, he had job number two. You had to give him his due, he worked his socks off. 'Got to save some money for the baby,' he said to me. We had this joke: 'This one's free, but I'm going to have to charge you for the next one.'

It was Laura who nursed me through the morning sickness, made sure I was eating properly, came to the hospital appointments, cried when she heard the baby's heartbeat, read all the baby books. Talk about obsessive, I swear the girl almost thought *she* was pregnant. I drew the line when she wanted to sing the baby to sleep every night. 'Give me some space, for God's sake!' I had to say to her at times. But I knew full well that I would have had a horrible pregnancy in a flat on my own. Even though I was miserable about being pregnant, it was good to have people around me who were positive about it. I had a reason to go through with it. I don't think that, once I got my head around it, I ever had a doubt about letting Laura and Tom take the baby. No one else was going to love her more, that much was obvious.

I don't know why they were surprised that I couldn't go home with them. They must have thought about what it would mean for me. To give a child up for adoption and get the occasional photograph is one thing. To see her every time you pop round for a coffee is another. Laura cried when I spelled it out for her. 'But you'll come home after a while?' she asked.

'I've got no plans at all,' I said to them. 'I might try to get a job here.'

I needed them to leave as soon as the baby could travel. I knew that I wouldn't change my mind, but it was too confusing for all of us. Throughout the pregnancy and birth, I hadn't felt the least bit maternal. When they looked at me and asked me what I wanted to call her, I told them it was customary for the parents to name the child. For one horrible moment I thought that they might try to sneak Faye in there as a middle name. I was relieved when she was named after Tom's grandmother, Andrea. She was the one who made the legendary shortbread.

Laura had deliberately put on a little weight over the last couple of months. With a padded bra and a loose fitting dress she looked the part of the young mother. Instant family. Just add water. I refused to hold the baby while they packed. I couldn't bring myself to wave them off in the van and stayed inside reading a book. I watched with mixed feelings from behind the net curtains as it moved slowly off down the road. Unable to decide whether to dance round the living room or weep, I turned the stereo up loud and let myself cry, then I washed my face in cold water and removed every remaining trace of baby from the flat. I had to be hard with myself. It was the only way to get through it.

It was clear to me that I could never go back home. My plan was to earn some money for a while and then travel. Later, when Andrea was old enough to know that she had an aunt, I thought that it was wrong that I never saw her. I didn't allow myself to feel any emotional attachment, but the poor girl looked just like me at the same age. It brought back memories of myself as a child and in my early teens, feelings of insecurity that I thought I had got over. I only ever allowed myself to be an occasional visitor to my old life, bringing presents from wherever I had been, sending postcards, but I could never bring myself to be physical with her. I envied how easily Peter threw her up in the air and swung her round by the arms, sending her into spasms of giggles. He could only afford to be that close because he didn't know. It was obvious that Laura and Tom had kept their side of the bargain. I never imagined that it would be so hard for me to keep mine.

Part Four

Andrea's Story

Chapter Twenty-four

It was the first time that I had left the house other than for the funeral and I had accepted an invitation from Lydia to join her and Kevin for tea.

'Nothing stuffy,' she said, 'just a fish-and-chip supper in front of the telly. You won't even have to talk if you don't want to.'

I had never been inside Lydia's house before and it amused me that it was so familiar and yet so different. It was a little like being Alice in Wonderland. Nothing seemed to fit.

'That just about sums us up, doesn't it, Kevin?' Lydia joked, the cough only a short way behind. 'I always knew we lived in topsy-turvy land.'

The house was littered with Kevin's 'inventions', half-built projects and gadgets for everything you could think of and a lot more besides. Dad would have loved it. In fact, it was right up his street.

'I never even knew I needed my reacher-upper until he made it for me.' Lydia showed me a claw-like contraption for reaching things in the tall kitchen cupboards. 'But I was forever standing on chairs to get things. Then one day I came home and he said, "I've made this for you, Ma," and I thought, Well, he's noticed that all on his own without me asking. He's not as daft as he looks. So now and then I drop hints, "I could do with something to help me get lids off jam jars," or something, and I can almost hear his brain working. A couple of days later, he'll have come up with some gadget or other. Shall we go through?'

We joined Kevin in the front room where he was already in front of the television.

'There you go, love.' Lydia handed him a plate with the fish and chips still in the newspaper on top. 'Nice bit of haddock for you. Want any ketchup with that?'

He unwrapped the parcel as carefully as if he thought that the fish was still alive, sniffed the contents and said, 'Salt and vinegar?'

She beamed at him. 'Just how you like it.'

'Thanks, Ma.'

'What are you watching, love?'

"'S'about kids bein' brought up by men who aren't their fathers.'

'Adopted, like?'

'No.' He swallowed a mouthful of chips. 'Where the woman's done the dirty.'

'Oh, I see.' She nudged me. 'I don't mind a bit of scandal.'

'It's not scandal, Ma, it's science!'

'Silly me! I thought it was sex,' she chortled. 'That all right for you, Andrea? You comfortable?'

'Shush, Ma!' Kevin frowned. 'Ah'm watchin'.'

The presenter, a man with glasses, a high forehead and curly hair, was explaining how women are attracted to different men at different times of the month. They had carried out tests by showing pictures of various men to the same women and had asked which they found the most attractive at different times in their cycle. Those who were normally attracted to the bespectacled, artistic or intelligent-looking men for most of the month suddenly found themselves drawn to the square-jawed Adonises when they were ovulating. He concluded that women could detect which men were the most fertile firstly by looks and secondly by the exchange of saliva.

'Ooh, I know exactly what he means,' Lydia told me in a loud whisper. 'Sometimes I feel like De Niro, other days it's Pacino, but then I'm quite partial to the one who did all them Nescafé adverts and all.'

'Anthony Head?' I asked.

'I'm not that bothered what his name is.' She winked. 'I wouldn't even mind if he forgot all about the coffee.'

'Get over you!' Kevin laughed with her.

I was envious of their obvious affection for each other, feeling so alone in the world. 'Do you ever wonder about your parents?' I asked him.

He looked at Lydia, who nodded at him to go ahead.

'What for?' He dismissed the idea.

'I just thought that you might have wanted to know who they were.'

'That's my ma sitting next to you,' he said, and turned

back to the television. We watched for a few minutes and I assumed that he had finished. Lydia looked approvingly at him. Then he went on: 'What's important is the person who tucks you in at night.'

'That's right, love,' Lydia said. 'But you did ask a lot of questions in your teens, didn't you? And we looked into it for you. And that nice lady said you should think about it and that you could make up your mind if you wanted to know when you were eighteen.'

'And did you?' I asked.

Kevin shrugged. 'Thought about it.'

'But you didn't take it any further?'

'Like I say, that's my ma sat over there.'

'We've got his birth certificate in an envelope upstairs, but we've never opened it, have we?'

Kevin shook his head. 'Nope.'

'And we had your da with us until you were twelve, didn't we?' Lydia prompted. 'We miss him, don't we?'

'Yup,' Kevin said with an intake of breath.

'Every day, we miss him.'

'I don't think I've ever seen my birth certificate,' I said with sudden realization.

'Not found it clearing out all that stuff?' Lydia asked. 'You'll have to get yourself a copy. You might need it for all the legal stuff at some point.'

'Maybe I will.' But my thoughts were on that other child and what his birth certificate might say.

'You finished with those?' Kevin asked, eyeing my chips.

'Help yourself.' I offered him my plate. 'I'm full.'

'Put them on the newspaper for him, there's a love,' said Lydia, dipping a chip into some tomato ketchup. 'That's how you like them, isn't it?'

Later in the kitchen, Lydia insisted that I sat down while she washed up and made a brew. 'What do you think of that, then? Licence for every woman in the country to throw themselves at some weightlifter and say, "I just can't help myself. It's science." I think they were after the weightlifters all along, but settled for the blokes with the money, then as soon as they had a drink or two inside them . . . wallop.'

'I don't know. I'd settle for one bloke, forget the two.'

'Been a while, has it?' she asked, laughing at my shocked face. 'It's all right, I'm not your mother.'

I joined her. 'You?'

'About fifteen years, I'd say. So don't you go feeling sorry for yourself! I'm glad you asked him that question, you know.'

I raised my eyebrows at her. 'Have you talked about it?'

'Not for a long time.' She looked content. 'It was nice to hear Kevin say it to someone else. That I'm his mum and that what went before doesn't matter. You know, every day, there's something that makes me thank my lucky stars that we found each other, but that was quite something.'

'I thought for one minute I'd put my foot in it.'

'Oh, no,' she said happily, 'not one bit, love. You ready for that tea now?'

Chapter Twenty-five

The visit to Lydia sparked an interest in me that I hadn't felt for a long time and I decided that I would piece together my family tree in earnest. The only problem was that with my parents and Grandma Fellows gone, and Nana teetering on the brink of reality, I had no one to ask about our family history other than my aunt. She was unusually short with me when I approached her.

'You can count us all on the fingers of both hands. You're wasting your time.'

'But what about Dad's father? There might be a story there.'

'He left when Tom was very young. Your dad didn't want to know who his own father was. If he's still alive – and I very much doubt it – Tom obviously never wanted him to meet you. So I would leave whatever story there might be well and truly buried if I were you.'

'Did you know your grandparents?'

'A little.'

'Is there anything you can tell me about them?'

'They were old,' she said sarcastically.

I decided to consult the local register office. Not knowing where to start, I found that I had to ask for assistance, already feeling wobbly. The clerk found a volume covering the five-year period from 1975 to 1980.

'I'm sorry,' he told me after helping me to search under the year of my birth. 'There's nothing under your name for that date.'

'Are you sure?' I could already feel that my eyes were brimming with tears and I blinked to try and keep them back.

'Absolutely sure.'

'There must be a mistake. Could you please check again?' I tried to brush a tear away with a quick swipe of the back of my hand while he was looking down the columns to humour me.

'Are you all right, miss?'

'I'm fine. I'm just in a bit of a . . .' I was desperately avoiding his gaze. 'Is there a . . . ?'

'Shall I get you a tissue?' he offered.

I nodded and he disappeared. I checked the next page of columns and the page after that, then turned a number of pages in frustration as much as anything else. It was only when I reached the entries for 1980 that I wondered if there would be an entry for my stillborn brother. As I had no idea of his name, I focused on the column for the mother's name. And there it was in black and white. Laura Fellows gave birth to Derek James Fellows on 25 July 1980. Only one detail was missing: the father's name. Unusual for a married lady.

'Here we are.' I looked up guiltily from the register to find that the clerk was holding a box of tissues. 'I see you've had another look. Found anything?'

I shook my head. 'Where do I go from here?' I asked.

'You need to try the Family Records Centre if your birth wasn't registered here. That's where the records from all of the local offices are held. I'll write the details down for you, but it would mean a trip down to London.'

I could feel tears welling up again and was glad of the tissues on offer. A trip to London was out of the question. A walk into town had been as much as I could handle.

'If you need the ladies,' he confided in me, 'there's a washroom down there on the right. It says "Staff Only" on the door, but that's just to stop people walking in off the street.'

I tried to smile vaguely in his direction before stumbling off in the direction that he had indicated. Once inside the safety of a cubicle, I sat and allowed myself the luxury of a few sobs before I made myself take deep breaths and blew my nose. I would have liked to have found the clerk and apologized, explaining that my parents had recently been killed in a car crash and that although I had thought I was ready to face the world again, it was too soon. Aware of the effort that would be involved in saying those few short words aloud and accepting the pity that would follow, I decided to leave him with the opinion that women are hormonally imbalanced, emotional wrecks.

In need of comfort and unable to face an empty house, I called on Lydia who prescribed a sit-down and a cuppa, her solution to most of the world's problems. 'You'd better come on through.' She busied me into the kitchen, mentioning as she passed the front room, 'Andrea's here, Kevin.' She chattered away as she boiled the kettle and assembled the tea-making equipment with all the seriousness that my father used to employ when cleaning shoes. Then, after placing the pot on the table, topping it with a padded tea cosy and arranging cups and saucers, she sat with her forearms on the table and her hands clasped together.

'Your turn.' She nodded with a smile. 'I'm all ears.'

I told her about my trip to the local register office, my dismay at having failed to trace my own records and my discovery about my brother. I also told her that I would have to put my search on hold as I couldn't face a trip to London.

She looked thoughtful, 'Well, I just might be able to help you out there. Won't be till next month, mind, but I'm due a visit to see a dear old cousin of mine who lives in Surrey. I go every year and we always treat ourselves to a trip up to town to see a show. I've always liked a good musical and, with the best will in the world, we don't get a good musical round here, do we? I'm sure I could persuade her to tag along. You give me those details and I'll sort it.'

'Will they let you if you're not family?'

She smiled. 'You fill in a form giving a reason. I'll

write "family research". I just won't say whose family I'm researching.'

I was so grateful that I almost burst into tears again. She put one of her large arms around me and hugged me to her. 'Ah, you see! There's always a solution. But don't you go thanking me yet. You don't know what news I'll have for you. Families have this knack of throwing up a few surprises.'

'Mind if I have a word with Kevin?' I asked. 'I want to ask what he thinks about something.'

'You go right ahead, love. He's in the front room putting his feet up. I'll finish my tea. I haven't sat down once all morning.'

'Hello, Kevin,' I announced myself and perched on an armchair. He was slouched on the sofa, his shoulders hunched up and his feet on the coffee table in front of him. 'I hope you don't mind, but I thought you might be able to give me some advice.'

'All right,' he said, uncertain, his eyes still focused on the television.

'I've started to look into my family history and I've found out enough to know that there's going to be a couple of surprises in there. It looks like I might have been adopted too. What do you think I should do?'

'What do you want to do?' He answered me with a question, only his mouth moving.

'I don't know. Why do you think you never looked at your birth certificate?'

'Ah already know who Ahm.'

194

'Do you mean that you know who you are, or who your birth parents are?'

'Both.'

'Is it important to you who your birth parents are?'

'Yes an' no.'

'Can you tell me why?'

'Yes, because Ah wanted to know they were good people. No, because Ah already had Lydia an' Bill.'

'Don't you want to know why they gave you up?'

'If they hadn't, Ah wouldn't have lived with Lydia an' Bill.'

'Did you wonder why they couldn't take care of you?'

"Course Ah did.'

'Did it make you angry?'

'Sometimes.'

'Have you ever met them?'

'Yes.'

'Spoken to them?'

'Aye.'

'Did they know who you were?'

'No.'

'Did you want to tell them who you are?'

'Nope.'

'Why not?'

'Ah didn't want to change anything. Ah like living with Lydia. Ah couldn't have axed for better parents.'

'What do you think I should do?'

'D'yer think you know the answer already?'

'No. I just have this feeling.'

'Did you have a happy childhood?'

'Yes.'

'Would you have changed anything if you could?'

'No.'

He shrugged and I gathered that our conversation was over. On the one hand, conversation with Kevin could be frustrating, because he only answered exactly what had been asked and volunteered so little. On the other hand, he made things seem so refreshingly simple that I wondered why I spent so many hours fretting over unimportant details.

'Thanks, Kevin.' I stood and took my leave, and wandered into the kitchen, where Lydia was drying up.

'You done out there?' she asked. 'Staying for lunch?'

'I think I'll be off now, if you don't mind.'

'But we'll be seeing you soon. And I'll let you know how I get on.'

Despite Kevin's assurances, I felt that my life was on hold until I had traced my birth details. Although I had nothing concrete to go on, I couldn't stop my mind from churning. I had always been told that I looked like my father and we had been extremely close. I had never looked remotely like my mother. I toyed with the possibility that I might have been my father's child with another woman. A groupie from the band, possibly. That would also explain why I had never been told that I was adopted. And as both my mother and father obviously adored children, I assumed that they would have only given my brother up for adoption if they could not take care of him themselves. Possibly he'd been disabled. Would there have been such a great stigma about this that they would have pretended he was stillborn? Like Kevin, I had enjoyed a very happy childhood and I wouldn't have changed anything for the world. But what was at first a welcome distraction from the other thoughts that plagued me soon grew into an obsession.

I started to quiz Uncle Pete about the band more and more, especially about the people who hung around with them. As always, he was a reliable source of information and far more willing than my aunt. Even if his memory needed a little jogging, he was usually able to supply photographs. These were particularly useful as he had enjoyed taking shots of people's reaction to the band. He talked about how he had tried to capture the atmosphere at the Spearheads' early gigs. In those days, audiences dressed up just as much as the band and his focus was on the most outrageous, among them Aunty Faye showing a side of her I had never seen before. He told me how bands like Pink Floyd and Genesis, with their original line-ups, and artists like Bowie and Roxy Music had introduced a theatrical side to music. Although the Spearheads weren't influenced by the punk explosion, its impact could be seen in the clothes that the crowd wore, particularly with my aunt's art-school group, who wanted to stand out and to shock.

'Your dad always said that the Spearheads would have done better if punk hadn't happened,' Uncle Pete said. 'Tom thought that their moment was stolen from them. After the Sex Pistols, everyone thought that they would have a go. There was one Sex Pistols gig that was seen by

Peter Hook and Morrissey. Without the Sex Pistols we wouldn't have had Joy Division or the Smiths. Plus, there is nothing that affects record sales like the death of an artist. Nineteen seventy-seven was a bad year for music. First we lost Elvis, then Marc Bolan and most of Lynyrd Skynyrd. That reminds me! All this talk and I almost forgot! I thought you might be interested in this.' He handed me a tatty white sleeve with a cut-away circle in the middle. 'I found it when I was clearing up.'

'Is this what I think it is?' I asked, looking at him.

'It's probably a collector's item.'

I pulled the record from the sleeve and held it by the edges as if it was a priceless antique. ' "The Spearheads",' I read. ' "What Were You Thinkin' Of?" and "Sugar Mama"'.

'The B side is the cover of a Sonny Boy Williamson track.'

'Can we play it?' I asked.

'One small problem, I'm afraid.' He shrugged apologetically. 'I don't own a record player any more. You're going to need to find someone who still listens to vinyl.'

'I can keep it?'

'You should own a copy of the recordings of Tom Fellows. I don't expect you've ever heard him playing before. If there was any justice in this world, he would have been up there with the best of them.'

'Have you got any photos of him rehearsing in the garage?' It was there that I thought people might have been relaxed enough to let down their guards. I spent the afternoon trawling through face after face before

Uncle Pete mentioned to me, 'Of course, I was never at their recordings or any of the gigs when they went on tour. I was always working.'

'They went on tour?' That broadened the search considerably.

'When you were very young. You and your mother stayed with me so I could help out. You probably don't remember. Faye would be able to tell you more about it. The band sometimes stayed with her in London in the early days.'

'Do you know where she lived?'

'Small place. Can't remember the name, but I do remember that it was the last stop on the Tube. I went there once myself, but that was years ago.'

I could almost hear my mother saying, *You're a cross between my absolute two favourite people, so that makes you my number-one girl.*

Was it possible that my father had had an affair with my aunt? I remembered the photographs from the album when my parents were so obviously in love, and my aunt's distress that there were no photos of her. But how could the same person who was attracted to my mother also have been attracted to her sister, even if it was only for one night? 'Chalk and cheese,' my father used to say, shaking his head in disbelief. 'Who'd have thought that two sisters could be so different.' Having said that, the Faye in the photographs was not the Aunty Faye I knew. She wasn't even the Faye I remembered as a child. She was someone you would notice in a crowd as they were watching you. Someone that you wouldn't forget easily. Not obviously beautiful, but interesting. Edgy. Dangerous-looking.

'Did my aunt ever go out with anyone in the band?' I asked.

'Faye?' He frowned, as if it was possible that I might have been talking about someone else.

'She looks like the girlfriend of a rock star. Or maybe even one herself.'

'I loved the contrast between your mother and Faye.' He didn't take the bait, or maybe he ignored it, but instead enthused about a photograph he had found of the two of them. 'They were completely different ends of the spectrum. Looking at Faye in these shots, you'd never believe that she was this shy little girl who wouldn't say boo to a goose.'

'I was born seven months after my parents' wedding,' I mused, trying to pull him back to my direction.

'Between you and me, you were a bit of a surprise. Your parents actually thought that your father couldn't have children. Your mother had no idea she was pregnant when she got married. I don't want you to go thinking that your parents were marched up the aisle. Completely the opposite, in fact. I think your grandparents would have done anything they could to stop it.'

'Really?'

'They thought that Tom was completely unsuitable.'

'What was wrong with him?'

'He was dangerous, had long hair, no job to speak of. I probably shouldn't tell you this, but your parents were blamed when your grandfather had the heart attack that killed him. The wedding almost didn't happen at all.'

'See! That's the problem with living with Nana. They never talked about things like that with her there.'

'I expect that there was quite a lot they didn't talk about. It took your grandmother years to get over it. And quite a while for her to get used to Tom. She was a tyrant in those days.'

'Nana?'

'I've found myself in her bad books once or twice and I can tell you that I wouldn't have wished her on my worst enemy. She was quite a force of nature.'

I was reassured by what Uncle Pete told me. That their best friend had been around when my mother was pregnant pushed the nagging doubts to the back of my mind.

'Now, has that answered all your questions for today? Do you think I can have that tea you promised me hours ago?'

'Yes. That's it – unless you can tell me why I can't trace my birth at the local register office. I don't seem to exist on paper.'

He nodded. 'That would depend on where your birth was registered. You see, you weren't actually born here. I didn't meet you until you were two weeks old.'

I was greatly relieved to hear this. 'Then I've been asking the wrong questions!'

'So that's what this is all about. You don't think that you're Laura's daughter?' Suddenly, Uncle Pete looked a little off colour and put out an arm to steady himself.

'Must have got up too quickly,' he explained, when I asked if he was feeling unwell.

Later, before he left, he put a hand on both of my shoulders and said, 'When you were a little girl, I would look at you sometimes and feel as if I was looking at a mirror image of myself. Have you ever felt like that before?' I could feel his hands shaking.

'Are you sure you're feeling better?' I asked, embarrassed by his sudden intensity. I put my own hands up to steady his and removed them from my shoulders at the same time.

'I'll take that as a no, then.' He looked half relieved, but his gaze was still fixed on my face and his expression was a question mark.

'Sometimes I look in the mirror and I don't even recognize myself any more.'

'I thought that was my age.' He laughed. 'That shouldn't be happening to you for a few years yet.' Then he was suddenly serious. 'It will get easier. Give it time.'

Left alone, I took the record and wandered upstairs to my parents' bedroom, their domain. Even half cleared of their possessions, it was the place where I felt closest to them. I sat at the dressing table in front of the three-sided mirror and turned the side mirrors inwards so that I could see an infinite number of reflections of myself. As a child, I had perfected the art of staring at the main mirror. Sometimes when I did this, a tiny detail in one of the side mirrors would jump out at me. Uncle Pete's question had touched a raw nerve somewhere. Something I couldn't quite put a finger on. I looked for some evidence that I was my mother's daughter. Having spent the afternoon studying photographs, I had a very clear image of what she had looked like at my age. But the faces that looked back at me in profile were not my mother's. They were not my father's. Suddenly, it was very clear to me what Lydia would find on her visit to London. There was no doubt in my mind that I was an Albury – but I was certainly not a Fellows. It was equally clear that Uncle Pete had just arrived at exactly the same conclusion, and his reaction had been one of shock. No wonder my aunt had tried to put me off researching our family history! My father – if I could still call him that – had been right to suggest that a tree was not the most accurate way of illustrating our family, but I now realized that wasn't only due to his absent father. Our story was obviously far too complicated for that.

Part Five

Peter's Story

Chapter Twenty-six

As much as I had been hurt by their lack of contact while they were away, Laura and Tom made it difficult to be angry with them. They turned up at my new house unannounced with the baby, a bottle of wine and stories of their travels and their momentous return.

Tom did a fine impression of Mrs Albury, declaring, 'I will not, under any circumstances, allow a grandchild of mine to grow up in a flat above a fish-and-chip shop.'

'And the thing is,' Laura explained, 'that was her idea of how to offer us a roof over our heads. She thought she was being nice.'

'It just happened to sound like a declaration of war.' Tom snorted. 'She seems to think that I'm completely incapable of supporting a family.'

'So what did you say?' I asked.

Laura smiled, trying to stop herself from laughing. 'It was a classic.'

'I said "I couldn't agree with you more, Mrs Albury." ' Tom shook his head as he remembered his own cheek.

'That's why we're moving to the flat next door above the launderette.'

It was true. They were swapping a flat with one bedroom for a flat with two, but the rent was going to be the same. The landlord had been impressed with Tom's handiwork in the smaller flat, and he had a few odd jobs in mind for the new one. In fact, he was fairly confident that he could pass some work in Tom's direction at some of his other properties.

'You should have seen her face.' Laura laughed until the tears ran down her cheeks, but I noticed how drawn she looked despite the few extra post-baby pounds, which were exaggerated by the dress she was wearing. There was something different about her, but I supposed at the time that giving birth was a life-changing event.

'Still, this place looks nice enough.' Tom looked around him. 'It's a good size. You must have a spare room or two going to waste.'

'I've got a few jobs that need doing if you're offering.'

Everything about the baby's face and hands was scrunched, protesting that she had been quite happy where she was before she had been disturbed. I hadn't seen too many babies up close before, but I stroked her hand and she grasped mine.

'She's got a strong grip,' I said.

Laura looked at me large-eyed as if she was desperate for my approval, but when she turned back to the baby, I saw a side of her that I had not seen before.

'You're going to make a fantastic mother,' I told her.

'I hope so.' She was shy in her new role, not yet confident.

Tom slapped me on the back. 'So, when are you available for babysitting?'

'I'm glad to see you didn't have any problems . . . what with the mumps and all.'

'No,' said Tom. 'Apparently everything is in perfect working order. Just needed to find the right woman.'

'Well, what do the doctors know?'

'Precisely.'

'So, what news of the band?'

'First practice for five months next week.' He rubbed his hands together. 'Minus one drummer, the traitor. You coming? Might even have to go and wet the baby's head afterwards.' Laura looked questioningly at him. '*If* I can get a late pass.' He looked at her winningly with his palms pressed together as if in prayer.

'Oh, go. Go! I've got to get used to being the one without a social life. This' – she nodded to the bundle in her arms – 'is what I wanted, after all.'

'Yes!' Tom mouthed silently, triumphant, behind her, punching the air with a fist.

My eyes passed from one to the other, watching the interaction with the baby. Laura was quieter than usual while Tom carried on more or less as he always had, talking about his engineering work at the recording studio and how he now understood what his album could sound like. But when the baby cried, it was Laura's expression that changed to one of panic, and it was Tom who swooped mid-flow to throw Andrea over his shoulder as naturally as he would a guitar. He sang a few lines of a song that I hadn't heard before that clearly had 'Andrea' in the lyrics, while walking and patting her back in time. The noise stopped almost immediately and Laura visibly relaxed.

'That's Andrea's song.' Laura yawned. 'Excuse me! We had a bad night last night. Change of scenery and meeting the grandmothers must have done it.'

'Still working on the chorus. I'll nail it tonight.'

Glad as I was to have them back, it was clear that I would have to change to fit into Laura and Tom's new world. I was only partly right. Laura had thought that having a baby would be the way to tame Tom, but it wasn't to be that easy. Tom was a natural with Andrea from the start. He understood how babies worked without reading manuals on the subject, while Laura was forever consulting medical dictionaries or rushing to the doctor. Although it was occasionally hand to mouth, he had no problem earning enough money to support them, running the band and getting up in the middle of the night with Andrea. He had more energy than the rest of us put together. Keeping irregular hours had prepared him for life with a baby. We nine-to-fivers were used to our eight hours' sleep, but Tom had always grabbed a few hours whenever he could, wherever he could. In his mind, there was no reason to change because nothing needed fixing. He had the best of every possible world.

'Ideally,' he confided, 'we would have liked a little more time on our own before Andrea came along, but we made the decision to start trying straight away in case it took a while.'

Of course, he had no idea that Laura had been trying long beforehand.

'Having a baby makes things a bit more difficult – but not impossible,' he explained. 'Everything just needs a bit more planning.'

But the things that he wanted were still not necessarily the things that *they* wanted. The big issues were still looming.

Chapter Twenty-seven

Things settled down into a routine and for a while Laura and Tom were happy – and I was happy for them. It gave all of us the chance to be real friends again and, in a way, Laura and I were closer than we had been for years.

'I can't get out much,' Laura claimed. 'Having a baby is a much lonelier business than I thought it would be.'

'Well then, I'll just have to come round to see you more often.'

I made sure I dropped in on her regularly and I was always impressed by what I saw. Although she didn't plan to go back to work, spurred on by Tom's resourcefulness she built up a small stream of income by doing dress alterations at home and the occasional more ambitious dressmaking project. When she needed a break, or if she had a deadline to meet, Tom took Andrea to his mother's or on his rounds, where he found no shortage of volunteers to watch her while he fixed dripping pipes and leaking cisterns. Andrea even came to band practice, where the hangers-on would keep an eye on her while she slept, or dance her on their knees when she woke. She was not necessarily a beautiful child, but one whose face was completely transformed when she smiled, so adults loved to entertain and amuse her. As a photographer, I got to know that face as well as I do my own. The only people in the arrangement who didn't get to see as much of each other as they would have liked were Laura and Tom, but hadn't that always been the case?

The band's new drummer was quite a find and gave the music an added dimension that it had lacked. After a few weeks back in rehearsals, Tom knew that he had a song on his hands that was a single.

'This is the one, boys,' he said with certainty.

Rather than take the band on tour, he called his friends in London and managed to negotiate some free time at the recording studio where he had worked. The Spearheads were away for two nights, sleeping on the floor of Faye's flat. Tom returned with a grin on his face and a tape in his pocket, which he planned to take to record companies in person.

Laura voiced her concerns to me privately. 'I only hope he's not building himself up for a disappointment.'

I shook my head. 'This is the song that's going to make it happen.'

'Do you think so?' she asked, with a smile that made me know that she too believed this was the one. We were all trying to hold back our enthusiasm.

Things moved slowly until a copy of the tape made its way to John Peel, who was known for his support of new bands and played it on Radio 1 a few nights in a row, albeit late at night when few people were listening. The few people who did hear it phoned in and wanted to know where they could get hold of it. Then the phone started ringing. For the first time, Tom had managers and record companies chasing him. Tom was firm that he wanted to stay in control in terms of management.

'I want you to be the band's solicitor,' he told me. There was no asking involved.

'I'm afraid I don't know the first thing about media law,' I explained. 'You need a specialist.'

'What I need is someone I can trust,' he said, 'and if that means you're working outside your area of expertise, so be it.'

'Tom, as a friend . . .' I protested, but he insisted.

'As a friend, I know that you'll do the best job that you can. And that will do just fine. Don't say no. I need you.'

How could I have refused? We shook hands on it.

The contract terms on offer were shoddy, there was no doubt about that. I was against them signing.

'I'll take the responsibility,' Tom said. 'We've got to get the single out there while people are interested. We'll do the best we can with what's available and renegotiate once we've started selling records.'

'You're the boss.' I passed the contract to him and he signed. Even Tom the family man was less focused on money than he should have been.

On 1 December 1977, the Spearheads' first single was

214

released up against some pretty stiff competition for the all-important Christmas number one. The track had been ready in the autumn, but delays, as we soon learned, were commonplace. Tom was confident that his market was completely different and that sales wouldn't be affected. He wasn't aiming for a Christmas number one. That was the reserve of the novelty songs and Christmas carols. The previous year, Johnny Mathis had charmed everyone over the age of sixty with 'When A Child Is Born'. Nineteen ninety-seven would be the year for Wings with 'Mull of Kintyre'. It even beat Bing Crosby's 'White Christmas' to the top. I loved the sound of bagpipes for weeks one and two. By the time it had been at the top of the charts for nine weeks, I was with Tom. What did it have to do with 1977?

David Bowie had sung about heroes, Talking Heads had sung about a psycho killer, Iggy Pop had a lust for life, the original disco diva, Donna Summer, shocked with 'I Feel Love', the Bee Gees were 'Staying Alive' and Freddie Mercury announced, 'We Will Rock You'.

It had been the year of the Queen's Jubilee and the Sex Pistols had reacted with 'God Save the Queen', the year that *Star Wars* was released, the year that Steve Biko died in custody, and we put the 'Great' back in Great Britain with the launch of HMS *Invincible*, one of the largest ships ever built. But you would have been forgiven for thinking that the only thing that mattered was the fate of a giraffe called Victor who tore a leg muscle at Margate Zoo.

The Spearheads' single sold, but not enough to chart. For the first time in all the time that I had known him, Tom was unable to keep up his happy-go-lucky act. This mattered desperately to him and all of his talk about just waiting for the right opportunity must have been echoing in his ears.

Laura tried to comfort him. 'Maybe the timing wasn't right.'

The record company were fairly clear what they thought had gone wrong: the Spearheads' lack of live dates.

'Oh, no,' Laura said disbelievingly, as Tom delivered the news to us in their flat. 'Apart from the fact that I'll be here on my own, if you're not earning, what are we going to live on? How will we pay the rent? You said your plan didn't involve being away from home. I won't be able to work if I'm looking after Andrea full-time. We can't just hand her back when it doesn't suit us, you know.'

'It's not *my* plan, love.' Tom spoke quietly with his head in his hands. 'I thought that we could manage without, but if we don't sell some more records, the contract will be cancelled and we'll end up owing them for studio time. It's money that I don't have and I can't ask the lads.'

'Is this true, Pete?' she demanded.

'I'm afraid it is. The band is obliged to do everything to help market the release, otherwise they'll be in breach of contract.'

'Well, why the hell did you let him sign the damned

thing?' Laura post-baby was more confident: happier to speak her mind than she ever had been before, and less afraid to say what she thought. She had someone to protect other than herself.

'It's not Pete's fault.' Tom paced the floor. 'It's a standard contract term in this business. There's not one record company that would give out a contract that says the band doesn't have to tour.'

'We had a deal!' Laura was trying to contain her anger with limited success. Even though her voice was not raised, her colour was.

'Ten dates. If this doesn't work, I'll give it up for good and I'll get a proper job.'

'Two weeks,' she negotiated.

'A month.'

'A month, and if it doesn't work, a permanent job. And what will we do in the meanwhile?'

'Stay with me,' I offered. 'I'm not going anywhere and I can help out in the evenings. You might even be able to get some work done.'

'Oh, we couldn't,' Laura stammered, looking at Tom, suddenly unsure of herself.

'I was involved in arranging the contract,' I insisted. 'It's the least I can do.'

Tom turned to Laura. 'I'd be much happier if you would. I don't like to think of you here on your own.'

'I could go to my mother's,' she offered.

'Do you want her to think you've gone crawling back? She'll be bad-mouthing me the entire time I'm away.'

'Then your mother's . . .'

'Look.' I picked up my coat to leave, sensing that I was in the way. 'If I've embarrassed you by offering, then I'm sorry.'

'Pete, you're our best friend in all the world.' Laura looked at me appealingly. 'We don't want to take advantage. I always end up leaning on you and it doesn't seem fair.'

'I wouldn't have said anything if I was going to be put out. But just a suggestion. If Faye's not working at the moment, what about asking her to stay with you? She hasn't been home for a while and you must be missing her.'

They both started speaking at once. 'I don't think that's a very good idea.' 'Faye really doesn't like babies.' 'And she's not very well.' 'We'd love to come and stay with you if you'll have us.'

'Obviously another useless idea on my part. Was that a "yes" I heard in there somewhere?'

Laura smiled at last. 'That was a yes!'

'Well, that's settled.' I made as if to leave.

'Where are you going?'

'To lock all my valuables away.'

'Valuables?' she joked. 'You have valuables? You never told me.'

'Thanks, mate. You're an absolute star.' Tom shook my hand at the door. 'There's not many men I would be prepared to trust with my little girl. And there's only one I can trust with my missus.'

Trust. It's a very fragile thing.

Chapter Twenty-eight

I quickly learned that you can't live in the same house as a young child without getting involved. Andrea was fifteen months old and mobile; a handful. For the first couple of weeks, I felt that Laura and I were pussy-footing round each other. We were overly polite and constantly apologized as we got under each other's feet or passed each other in the narrow hall. Laura was excessively tidy and took a great deal of care to put everything back exactly where she had found it. Tom had trained her well.

I noticed how she gathered her dressing gown around her tightly when she was wearing night clothes so that they were completely covered, even though she was wearing far more than she ever did by day. The door to the spare room was always firmly closed, although Laura fretted that she wouldn't be able to hear Andrea in the room on the opposite side of the landing. I knew it was being alone with me that she was uncomfortable with, so I steered conversation towards Tom and the baby.

Despite the awkwardness, I liked the feeling of life in

the house. Although I had wanted my own space, there had been a considerable difference between the idea and the reality. I had imagined a house where a stream of people would pop in for coffees, but I ended up working late and going out more than ever to avoid the loneliness. I hated the way my footsteps echoed in the empty, sterile rooms. Even if we didn't talk as much as we used to, I liked the sound of the clicking and whirring of the sewing machine as Laura worked. I liked the sound of her laughter as we watched *The Two Ronnies* on television. With Tom gone, we listened to very little in the way of music. I liked coming home to the smell of cooking and a shout of, 'The kettle's on. Do you fancy a cuppa?' I even liked the sight of washing on the line and the pram in the hall. These were all the things that made the difference between a house and a home. It reminded me of my parents' relationship. Not quite open, rarely honest, but always the consideration, always the cheerful front.

When I woke in the night to the sound of crying, I would listen for Laura's footsteps and the small comforting sounds she made. If Andrea didn't calm down, I would hear Laura move downstairs and put the kettle on. Only when they settled did I allow myself to go back to sleep. The first time that Laura didn't get up when Andrea cried, I wasn't sure what to do. I listened at Laura's door and thought I could just make out heavy breathing and the very occasional snore. I tried putting a dummy in Andrea's mouth, but I knew that Laura was not keen for her to get too used to it. I talked quietly to the baby and put one hand on her stomach, patting. When that didn't work, I picked her up and slung her over one shoulder as I had seen Tom do, and sang the first childhood song I could remember, 'Row, row, row your boat, gently down the stream. Merrily, merrily, merrily, merrily, life is but a dream.' Laura was delighted that Andrea had slept through the night for the first time since the beginning of their stay, but was insistent that she had not slept well herself.

My secret was discovered a few nights later when Laura got up to go to the bathroom and found me sitting in the box room singing to Andrea. I heard a sharp intake of breath behind me and turned round to find Laura standing in the doorway in the half-light, her dressing gown hanging loosely, exposing a pair of spotted pyjamas.

'Shall I take her?' she asked.

'It's all right. I haven't dropped her once yet.'

'I didn't hear her,' she whispered, more herself, 'but I was woken by a strange noise. Any idea what it was?'

I carried on singing, 'Merrily, merrily, merrily, merrily.'

'That's it! Have you been up long?'

'Half an hour or so.'

'I'll take her now, shall I?' She held out her arms this time.

'We're getting along just fine.'

'I can see that. I'm just worried that you're in court tomorrow and you might need your wits about you.'

'Hush, woman. You'll wake her. It's hardly worth my

while going back to bed now. Why don't you try to get another hour or so?'

'I'm fine. At least let me make you some breakfast.'

'It's a deal.'

'You know,' Laura said, sitting on a spare chair, 'you're very good with her.'

'I've been practising these last few nights.'

'You've been getting up?' She was genuinely surprised.

'I'm a bit of an insomniac,' I lied. Instead, it seemed that I was awake as soon as Andrea was, in tune with every noise she made.

'And there's me thinking she was sleeping better.' Laura laughed, propping her head up with one hand. 'Oh, God! This is exhausting.'

'Why don't you go back to bed?'

She shrugged my comment away. 'Maybe I should have her in with me. Then she might not wake you.'

'I'm enjoying it!' I insisted. 'The whole point of you staying was so that I could help out and you wouldn't be left to do everything yourself.'

'It was, wasn't it?' Her shoulders were limp and her feet pointed unselfconsciously inwards, strangely childlike.

'Bed!' I commanded.

'You're sure?' She yawned, looking at Andrea, concerned.

'When I was fifteen, I was regularly trusted with a neighbour's baby and I even got paid for it, if I remember rightly. Now, if I had been those parents, I wouldn't have trusted me, but that's not the point.' Then, without thinking I asked, 'Are you going to get her christened?'

'We haven't made a decision yet.' Laura yawned. 'I know Tom's mother would like us to. At this rate Andrea will be in school before we make our minds up.'

'If you do, I thought I might qualify for the role of godfather.'

At that moment, Laura raised her hand to her mouth and quashed a small noise. 'Excuse me.' She made her other hand into a stop sign. 'Hiccups. Drink of water.' She pointed to the bathroom and disappeared.

Chapter Twenty-nine

Tom returned buzzing with stories of life on the road and my two favourite girls returned to the flat above the launderette. The only thing that dampened Tom's enthusiasm was the fact that Andrea seemed to have forgotten him. What had turned into five weeks was a long time for a small child. Instead of 'Andrea's Song', the only thing that would settle her was 'Row, row, row your boat'.

'Couldn't you have thought of anything else? Maybe something with more than two lines?' he complained in Laura's direction.

'That was Pete's doing.'

'Pete?'

'I did a little of the night duty,' I admitted. 'It was the first song I could remember from my days as a choir boy.'

'A choir boy? Now I know you're kidding me.'

I pretended to be offended. 'I'll take that as an insult.'

'Well, you're banned from singing to my baby from now on.' He held her away from me protectively. 'I can't have it that every time I go away she takes ages to get used to my voice again.'

'Every time?' Laura raised her eyebrows, although her mood was still jovial, picking up on what she assumed was a throwaway comment.

'Too right,' said Tom, concentrating on Andrea, and I watched Laura turn away to regain her composure.

'So,' she asked when she turned back, deadly serious, 'will you be staying for long?'

For some time, I had noticed that they seemed to be storing up their most serious conversations for when I was with them. Although I couldn't call them arguments, I felt I was mediating some fairly weighty negotiations. Of course, I had no idea how things were when I wasn't there. I pretended to deliberately misunderstand.

'No, I think I'll be off now.' I bent to kiss Andrea's forehead. 'There's my girl. Don't you go growing too much before I see you next time.'

'Oh, you don't have to go yet!' Laura stood, physically placing herself between me and the door.

'Early start tomorrow,' I explained. 'It's going to be strange. I'm going to miss that little one. The house will feel empty.'

'Thanks for taking care of things.' Tom smiled. 'I wouldn't have felt happy going otherwise.' Behind him, I saw Laura bristle. 'Couldn't have done it without you.'

'I hope it was worth it,' I replied.

'Oh, it was worth it all right.' He winked and moved away from the door to shield the baby from the draught.

'See you soon, Laura,' I said. 'Pop round any time.'

'Thanks, Pete.' Safe in the confines of her own home, she was comfortable enough to kiss me on the cheek.

'Talk to him if you're unhappy,' I added quietly.

'I was going to when you so rudely interrupted,' she joked. 'I know! I shouldn't do it when you're there.'

'It's not fair on either of us. I'm beginning to feel as if I'm expected to take sides.'

'I want him to do well. It's not just being left on my own with Andrea. It's just . . . well, you know I've never been any good on my own.' There was a wobble in the corners of her mouth when she smiled. 'I thought things might change when we got married. Or at least I thought that I might feel differently . . .' She put one finger to her lips, hushing me or hushing herself, and closed the door.

I wanted to say, Enjoy him while he's here. Don't spend your time being angry. I wanted to say that she had known who he was when she married him. I wanted to tell her that if she wanted the boring, stay-at-home alternative she should have picked me. It was a good job she closed the door. I might have been tempted to tell her that she never needed to be alone.

It wasn't long before Tom was under pressure to tour again. Record sales had been boosted by the live dates, but the single had narrowly failed to reach the all-important top forty. The feedback was that it was a respectable start, but they had failed to capture the imagination of their audience. The record company wanted more live dates, a follow-up single and only then would they agree to the album. Tom was so keen to secure the album release that he would have agreed to any terms. After hearing Tom strumming it softly to himself, the single that they wanted was 'Andrea's Song'. He was strongly against this. Not only was it not a Spearheads' track; it was personal and had no place on the album.

'I'm losing any control I ever had,' Tom confided in me. 'They've got no interest in what we're about. They just want to see the money roll in. And I haven't seen a penny yet. It's not as if I can even offer a carrot to Laura to keep her happy.'

A second set of dates was scheduled and Tom tried to piece together money for the rent while he was away by working extra hours for his landlord at some of his other properties. The results were so good that there was talk about a further rent reduction in return for a certain number of hours' labour. 'Maybe he'll pay us to live here before long,' Tom joked.

'Which is great,' Laura told me unhappily as we shared a cheap bottle of plonk at the flat, 'unless you need cash to buy some of the luxuries of life like food and nappies. This might have worked when we were going out, but we're married and we have a baby. We never see each other. When he's here, he's either working or rehearsing. Or I'm so tired that if he offers to take Andrea for a while, I just try to catch up on some sleep. I don't want to feel as if I'm nagging all the time, but that's just the way it is at the moment.'

'Have you thought about going to live with your mother for a while?' I asked.

'Now, there's another thing.' She took a sip from her glass. 'She's been so unreasonable and rude about Tom that I'd feel I was betraying him. But there she is, all on her own in that big house. She's still getting over Dad, and Faye hasn't been home to see her. And here we are, cooped up in this flat that we really can't afford. But she's going to say: "I told you so. I knew that you'd have to come crawling back sooner or later with your tail between your legs . . ." '

'That's not bad as impressions go.'

'Years of practice. But the point is, she won't be able to resist it, because that's just the way she is. And I could probably cope, but Tom will see it as yet another insult aimed in his direction.'

'What about Tom's mother?'

'She's wonderful. Would do anything for us. But again, Tom wants to stand on his own two feet and not keep running home as soon as the going gets tough. I think it's called male pride.'

'There's always the garage. She'd never notice you were there.'

'Do you think he's ever going to make any money from the music?' she fired at me suddenly, as serious as I had ever seen her.

'I think that he just needs one lucky break.'

'One lucky break,' she mused. 'Is that the same lucky break that I would need to become a model, or maybe an actress?'

'He's incredibly talented.'

'I've never doubted that for one moment. And I know how committed he is. But it's going to destroy him if it doesn't work out.'

'I know,' I agreed, nodding.

'And in the meanwhile, it's destroying us,' she said bitterly, shocking me with her honesty.

'Don't say that.'

'Why?' She was adamant. 'I'm the one who has to be realistic.'

'Because if it doesn't work out, he's going to need you to help him pick up the pieces. It's hard to give up on your dreams.' I looked her in the eyes. 'You can't let them go without a fight.'

'But you didn't fight, did you?' Inappropriate though it was, it was the first time that she had ever really acknowledged that I had feelings for her. 'Wasn't I worth it?'

'That's the drink talking.' I didn't want to reply.

'Well? Wasn't I?' Laura demanded.

'You know what you mean to me,' I muttered, trying to put my feelings to one side.

'I never knew exactly how you felt.' She put one hand over mine. 'Because you never once said.'

I looked at the table in front of us. 'I saw the way that you looked at him, and I knew I didn't stand a chance. And you told me that you knew you had made the right decision.'

'If that was true' – her eyes brimmed over – 'then tell me why it was so difficult?'

'Don't do this,' I said, getting up, not knowing how to react and deciding that the only rational thing to do was leave. 'It's taken a long time for me to think of you as just a friend. Don't spoil it now.'

Chapter Thirty

I answered the door with Andrea on my hip. Mrs Albury pushed past and closed it, looking at me accusingly. 'So it's true what they're saying,' she fired at me. 'You have set up house with my daughter!'

'Mrs Albury,' I said loudly for Laura's benefit. 'Welcome to my home. Laura's in the kitchen. Would you like a coffee?' And then under my breath through gritted teeth, 'Or perhaps you'd care to inspect the sleeping arrangements?'

'Mum!' Laura appeared in the hallway, 'We're staying with Pete while Tom's away.'

'And he knows about this, does he?'

'Of course.' She laughed off the comment as lightly as possible. 'Tom didn't want me to be on my own.'

'Well, it's highly irregular, if you ask me.' She sat down at the kitchen table and said over her shoulder in my direction, 'I'll have that coffee now, if you don't mind.'

'Mum! I think you could show Pete a little courtesy in his own house.' Laura sat down opposite her. 'He's not a waiter.'

'I'm the grandmother,' Mrs Albury tapped her chest forcibly. 'What about the courtesy that should be shown to me? You think it's easy living round the corner from your daughter and having every Tom, Dick and Harry tell you that she's taken your grandchild and moved in with that solicitor chappie as soon as her husband's out of town for a few days? And it's not the first time, is it? You conveniently forgot to mention that, didn't you?'

'And you wonder why?' Laura raised her voice to match her mother's. 'Look at the way you're reacting. The truth is, I thought you might have thought badly of Tom for leaving me with Andrea.'

'Work is work,' Mrs Albury replied. 'Needs must. But this is wrong. Mark my words, the whole town's talking about it. And they can all see I'm rattling round in a big house on my own.'

'Do you think it's easy asking your mother for help, when she's criticized your choice of husband from the start?'

'I'll take Andrea next door,' I said and wandered through to the living room, ignored. This only resulted in voices being raised further, and Andrea started to grizzle. I set her down on the floor and distracted her with a toy, enjoying her reaction, while keeping one ear on the conversation next door.

'I have not! I only said that I was worried that he would never be able to support you. And it's true. Look me in the eye and tell me you're not worried about money. I would have preferred you to have chosen a man with a profession behind him, I'll admit it. Or at least a permanent job. Am I not allowed to express a little concern for my daughter? But I would never criticize Tom. You've only got to listen to folk around town to know what a good man he is. I hear he did some work for the Stevenses last month when Bob was out of work and he wouldn't take a penny for it. That's the sort of man you married, Laura, so why are you afraid of asking your own mother for help?'

I heard Laura laugh out loud.

'Well, what's that for?' her mother asked. 'I can't see what's so funny.'

'You see!' I could imagine Laura shaking her head, 'That's your idea of an offer of help. The neighbours are talking, Mrs Jones has told you how wonderful Tom is and suddenly you're on his side.'

'There are no sides, Laura.' Mrs Albury was stern. 'Not when there's a child involved.'

'We're very happy here, thank you.'

'Not too happy, I hope. Don't you put your marriage at risk, Laura. I know your history with that man.'

'The man that you're referring to is my best friend!'

'Exactly!'

'And what is that supposed to mean?'

'You think that there's such a big difference between a husband and a best friend? It's a much finer line than you think. You have put yourself in a position where you could cross that line very easily. I'm not saying that you would do it deliberately, but mark my words—'

'That's it!' I heard a chair scrape. 'I've heard enough.'

'I don't mean to hurt you, but I wouldn't be doing my job as your mother if I didn't say these things. Do you think I want to see you upset? And you should think about how it looks, not because you care what the neighbours think, but for Andrea's sake. It's not just you any more. You're a mother, for goodness' sake.'

'Pete,' Laura called unnecessarily loudly, 'my mother has to leave now. Could you bring Andrea through so that she can say goodbye to her.'

Laura had her arms crossed in front of her and was standing by the doorway to the kitchen, while her mother was still seated. She stood as she saw Andrea toddle into the hall holding my hand and smiled, kneeling down to kiss her fine, feathery hair. 'Goodbye, petal. Come and see your nana soon, won't you? You take after your daddy, my love, don't you?' And she stood to look me in the eyes, tight-lipped. 'Goodbye, Peter. Give my regards to your parents. There's a fine example of a marriage.' It might have sounded like a kindness but it was a criticism. As far as I was aware, my parents barely knew the Alburys. I heard Laura's sharp intake of breath behind me. There was nothing to be gained by reacting so instead I herded Mrs Albury towards the front door as quickly as possible.

'I'll pass on your regards,' I said.

'Tell Laura that her mother is a lonely old woman and would like to see more of her only grandchild before she dies.' (She hadn't reached fifty at the time but she had aged visibly since she lost her husband.)

234

I watched her walk down the path and then close the gate.

'Has she gone?' Laura called out from the kitchen, where she was sitting with her head in her hands.

'She's gone.' I shut the front door and, turning, I crouched down to Andrea's level and held out my arms. 'Come to your Uncle Peter,' I said to her.

Laura sighed. 'Bolt the door behind her, would you?'

I knew Laura needed space and so did I, for that matter. 'I'm taking Andrea upstairs for her nap. I'll sit with her for a while and read.' I waited for a reply that did not come. Climbing the stairs slowly with Andrea's hand in mine, I peered over the banisters to see the back of Laura's head bent over the kitchen table.

Later she appeared looking dishevelled, and sat in the spare chair in the nursery of what had once been my bachelor pad. 'I'm going to have to talk it through with Tom, but I think we're going to have to go and live with my mother. Then we won't have to worry about money. We can all stop fighting and Tom won't have to give up on his dreams.'

'I know.'

'I hate all this moving.' She tried to smile. 'I have nowhere I can call home any more. And we've been really happy here. Andrea is so settled into her routine.'

I nodded, not without an element of pride.

'We make a good team, don't we?' she said, bringing one hand up to my shoulder. 'I can't think of any part of my life that would work if I didn't have you as a friend.'

'Can I say something without causing offence?'

'Go on,' she sniffed nervously.

'Your mother is a bit of a tyrant.' I tried to make a joke of it.

She laughed. 'She certainly speaks her mind.' But then she became serious: 'But why, oh why, does she always have to be right about everything? Do all mothers have that knack?'

'Mine never says what she thinks about anything. We get along just fine like that.'

'I'm so tired of fighting. I need things to be simple.'

We were quiet for a while.

'I used to be a rock chick once, you know,' she said to Andrea, picking her up when she started to stir. 'Before I was your mummy. One day, Uncle Pete will show you his photos and you'll ask, "Who was that beautiful lady?" And he'll say, "That was your mother when she was very, very young. And she was, quite simply, magnificent."'

'She still is.'

Part Six

Andrea's Story

Chapter Thirty-one

'We need to talk, love,' Lydia said, bustling past me into the hall. I watched her waddle into the kitchen, which she had made her own in the absence of anyone taking a real interest in it. I had become a microwave cook. It wasn't that I didn't know how, I just found it depressing cooking for one. My staple was jacket potatoes, with a little melted cheese if I was feeling adventurous.

By the time that I had entered the room, she had taken charge and was already filling the kettle. 'I've got news for you and a small confession to make,' she announced with her broad back to me. It was only when she turned around that I realized how flustered she looked. Her hair was curled damply around her face and her skin was red and clammy.

'Let me do that.' I reached for the tea bags. 'You look as if you need to sit down.' When she offered no resistance I added jokingly, 'Now I know I should be worried.'

She responded with a little laugh and brought her hand to her mouth as if to stifle it. There were no signs of merriment in her eyes and she was clearly in distress.

'Lydia, what's wrong?' I asked, deeply concerned. 'The news isn't too terrible I hope?'

She shook her head.

'Kevin's OK?'

She nodded quickly, frowning, her mouth still clamped in place.

'And you're all right?'

Again a nod.

'Well, thank God for that.' After depositing a cup of tea in front of her – a proper cup and saucer, the way she liked it – I took a seat and waited for her to begin. 'You'd better put us both out of our miseries then.'

'I never thought I'd be this nervous,' she managed, before putting her hand back in place.

'You can't leave me in suspense now.' I put my hand on the arm at the end of the offending hand. 'I need to know, no matter what the answers are.'

She took a deep breath and said, 'Well, here goes. This is hard for me so it might come out wrong. I had my own reasons for offering to go to London for you. You see, after my Kevin told me that he will always think of me as his mum, I suddenly realized that I don't know anything about where he comes from. I was that desperate for a little one at the time. I don't even know the name that his parents gave him. It didn't seem important before. And there's something else you should know. My Kevin's always believed that you're his sister.'

I laughed, having expected something far more terrible. 'But why would he?'

'Someone might have let him think that your parents were his birth parents.'

'Who would have done that?'

She sat, stony-faced, before explaining. 'There was a stage in his life when he needed to know. He needed to believe in something. After we lost my Bill, he went through a very difficult patch. Everyone had always let him down and here was someone else who had left him. Except that there was no one he could blame this time. Maybe it was my fault for uprooting him when he already had so much change to get used to. We knew that he had actually been born locally even though he was pushed from pillar to post. To me, it felt like I was bringing him home. Maybe I only thought about what was best for me. I honestly thought that we would be all right if we stuck together. He found it hard to settle. When he tried to make friends, the kids at school claimed they couldn't understand a word he said. Well, he started to play up. I couldn't control him and the police were involved. This is a small place and your parents were so well known. Tom has always been Tom, and everyone loved him. And your mother was . . . well, she was just beautiful. If you wanted an example of a perfect couple, they were it. I didn't mean anything by it, but I let slip that your mother had had a child at about the same time as he was born, which was true. Kevin assumed I meant him.'

I listened in silence. Lydia had become one of the people whose judgement I had come to trust the most, but here she was telling me that she had let her adopted son believe that some of his nearest neighbours were family. She misread the look on my face and thought that I was shocked that our family secret was public knowledge.

'I'm afraid that you can't keep anything to yourself around here. My sister told me. Everyone was so upset that your mother lost her child. I'm sorry, love. I should have told you, especially when you showed me them photos, but I wasn't expecting to see your Uncle Pete in there. That threw me. Not even the local gossips knew about that.'

I shook my head. 'But they lost the baby. Why didn't you explain to Kevin that he couldn't have been their son?'

'I tried to, love, I really did!' She held my hand. 'Maybe I'm not telling this right. I made one throwaway comment. It wasn't like we were having a big discussion about where my Kevin had come from at the time. But he had lost so much. He clung on to the *idea* of it, more than anything else. He needed to believe something, so he latched on to that. It didn't matter that it couldn't have been true.

'Almost straight away, he became a different person. He was the one who told me that the house had come up for rent two doors away. He was the one who wanted to move here. Finally, he thought he knew where he came from and he stopped fretting about who he was.'

By now she had seen my face. My jaw was nagging as it always did when I was tense. I found that my hands were clenched into fists. 'I can almost understand the rest. But why did you agree to move down the road? Didn't you think that you were encouraging him?'

'You're angry and I don't blame you. But be angry with me, not him. Try to understand, love. His own parents didn't want him. He spent his first few years with a man who was cruel, then he lost the first man who ever showed him some love. And on top of that I moved him all this way to a place where he knew no one, and then had the nerve to be surprised when he went a bit wild! Now you understand why I was so happy when he said that I was a good mum. I'm not really sure I have been. This was the only thing he's ever asked me. I made sure I kept a close eye on him, but he never would have said anything to anyone. Definitely not to them. I'm sure that at the back of his mind, he knew that they couldn't have been his real parents.'

I thought of all the times when Kevin had wandered down the road to exchange a few words with my dad's feet as they stuck out from under a car, and of the times that my dad had defended him to my mocking grandmother. Of the occasional nods that we had exchanged in the street, because he would have found anything more embarrassing. Of the way that he had blushed when my mother had rewarded him with a smile. I knew that Lydia was right; he wouldn't have said anything to anyone, least of all to us. He was indulging a private fantasy, nothing more. How could I feel threatened when the objects of that fantasy were gone? It was something else that had died with my parents. Another loss for a boy who had already lost so much.

Thinking that the speech was over, I said, 'It's ironic, really. My dad always wanted a son.'

'Yes, love,' she said dismissively.

'That's not all?' I was aghast. What more could there be?

'Your birth certificate.' She began again softly. My eyes followed the envelope as she retrieved it from her handbag, placed it on the table and pulled a certificate from it. 'Andrea, love, you're not on your own in the world after all. Your parents are alive. And what's more, they're no strangers. In fact, you know them very well.'

I nodded and sighed deeply as I read and confirmed what I already knew. That I am the daughter of Faye Albury, student, and Peter Churcher, solicitor, born in Morden, Surrey.

'You know?' she asked, confused.

'Only just recently. It's been staring me in the face all these years, but it's as they say: sometimes you can't see what's right in front of your nose.'

'Well? What are going to do about it?'

I shrugged. 'I don't know if I'll do anything.'

'But you must!'

'Lydia, the only parents that I have ever known are gone. For whatever reason – and I'm sure that there must have been a good one – my real parents either didn't want me or couldn't look after me. My parents chose not to tell me. And bearing in mind who my real parents are, I can see how awkward that would have been. And very confusing for me too. At least one of them knows exactly who I am and where I am, and hasn't told me even now.' It was more difficult to admit this – and everything that it meant – than I had imagined. Isn't the mother-and-daughter bond supposed to be the closest bond there is? Thinking things and saying them out loud are not the same. Suddenly, it was all too real. I was another lost soul, searching for something to latch on to.

'Oh, you poor lamb.' Lydia cradled me with a heavy arm.

'I've never been that close to Aunty Faye.' I sniffed. 'She always kept her distance. She's very entertaining in small doses and she was a really exciting person to have as an aunt. But she was never exactly what you would call reliable. There's no doubt she would have made a terrible mother.' I tried to smile despite the tears.

'But your Uncle Pete? He's been like a second father to you. He loves the bones of you.'

'I don't think he knows for sure. There are moments when I'm sure he suspects something, but suspecting and being sure enough to risk confronting my aunt?' I sighed. 'They're two completely different things.'

'I think you're right, love.'

'It's not for me to tell him.'

'He might need to hear it more than you think. He's all alone in the world too.'

I shook my head. 'I still need time to get my head around it. For now it's enough that I know.'

'Then it's best I leave you to your thoughts,' Lydia said.

'What did you decide about Kevin's birth certificate in

245

the end?' I called to her as she was putting her coat on in the hall.

She appeared at the kitchen door again. 'Do you know, after all that, I decided to leave it exactly where it is for now. I would feel terrible going behind his back. I'm no good with secrets, me. I wouldn't be able to keep it to myself if there was something I thought he should know.'

'Maybe he'll want to open it now that my parents have gone,' I suggested.

She shrugged. 'Maybe.'

Alone again, I took down the family tree from its place in the hall and stared at it for some time. Then I took it out of its frame and crossed out my own name from the place where it had appeared under my parents' with heavy black lines. Unable to work out how to redraw it, that is how I left it. Our very average, straightforward family had been wiped out. I was not unhappy with the end result. It reflected exactly how I felt. I no longer knew who I was or where I had come from. I was completely lost.

Chapter Thirty-two

It was about that time that Nana started running away from Aunty Faye's and finding her way home to Westbrook Road. The first time she pretended that she had gone shopping and forgotten her way back to the flat, so she gave the cab driver the only address that she could remember. But who goes out shopping with a small suitcase fully packed? The next time she arrived on the doorstep, pinching my cheek and saying, 'Nana's home to take care of you now,' with the ingredients for her famous rhubarb crumble in a carrier bag. I humoured her and let her get on with it, unable to track my aunt down on her mobile and unsure what to do next. Aunty Faye arrived later, flustered and apologetic, insisting that she had only left her mother on her own for a few minutes.

'Stuff and nonsense!' Nana reprimanded her. 'You always were the most awful liar. Had to get your sister to do your dirty work for you so you didn't land yourself in it. Out all night then creeping in at the crack of dawn. "Of course I haven't seen your earrings? What, these? I got them down the market." And who was it who broke my favourite vase? "The next-door neighbour's cat must have got in through the window." Very talented cat. Handy with a dustpan and brush, it was. Managed to sweep all the pieces into a neat pile behind the door. I've heard it all before. Thinks I was born yesterday, this one. Well, let me tell you, I'm not nearly as daft as you think I am.'

I was beginning to suspect she was right.

'Seen your father?' Nana asked me over dinner and I almost choked.

'For goodness' sake, Mum!' Aunty Faye scolded her.

'Dad's . . .' I faltered. It still sounded too harsh to say that my dad was dead. But there was also the added confusion that the person that I had always thought of as my dad was not related to me at all. My real dad was very much alive. In fact, here I was with my mother and my grandmother. It was only my grandmother who didn't need to change seats in the new arrangement. I wondered if this was as good an opportunity as any to talk to my aunt, while the two of them were there.

'Oh, not that one,' Nana interrupted. 'Your other father. The one who always wears a suit. What is it we have to call him? Your *godfather*, isn't it?'

'Uncle Pete,' Aunty Faye patronized, rolling her eyes in my direction as if to say, 'Here we go again,' but I looked at Nana more closely. What did she know?

'Peter Churcher.' She nodded. 'He was our paper boy, you know. Funny thing. He kept on delivering the dailies years after we stopped using the newsagent he worked for. They overcharged your father once and that was that as far as he was concerned. Peter still turned up every day right on time. We didn't pay him a penny. Why do you think that was, Faye?' She waved a fork in my aunt's direction, who returned her look with narrowed eyes. 'Nothing much wrong with my memory, is there, sweetheart? Ah, the stories I could tell given half the chance. Do you know, seeing the two of you sitting there together, you could be mother and daughter.'

'Can't you see how tactless you're being, Mum?' Aunty Faye snapped, standing up to clear the plates away, although no one had finished. On her way back to the table, she touched my shoulder. It felt unfamiliar and cold. 'It's too early to be making comments like that. We're all still very fragile.'

Maybe that was it, I thought. Maybe she was waiting for the right moment to talk to me.

'Too early for you, perhaps,' Nana said. 'Some of us may want to talk about it. Some of us may be *dying* for the chance to talk about it!' She turned to me. 'Can you imagine having to stay in a place where you're not allowed to talk about your own daughter? Where you are treated as if you're mad because one minute you're up and the next you're down. And, yes, I admit it: I can remember what happened thirty years ago far more clearly than I can remember what happened five minutes ago. Sometimes I get a little lost in the past and I'm not sure how to find my way back. And there are times when I'd prefer not to find my way back at all.' I found myself nodding at her. She twisted around to face my aunt, leaning on the back of the chair with one elbow, raising her voice more than was strictly necessary. 'It's called grief, Faye. It's called mourning. I can't just switch it on and off to suit you. Maybe you should try it. You've usually got such a lot to say for yourself.' She nudged me as if she had said something very clever.

'Do you want me to say something, Mum?' Aunty Faye turned back, looking pale and world-weary, straining to keep her voice low and even. 'What would you like me to start with? You see, you have the advantage over me here. I can't pull out a photograph album and say, "Look. That's how I remember my sister. On her first day at school. In the first dress she made for herself. On her wedding day." Because – and I'm not blaming anyone for this, don't get me wrong – because I had to see her afterwards. And that is the image that will stay with me for ever. So while you might want to sit around and have a nice, cosy chat, forgive me if I'm not quite ready for that. I'm still stuck in that nightmare. I'm not even ready for tears yet, let alone talking.' It was a dignified speech and she sat down at the end of it.

I felt that I should say something. 'I'm sorry that you had to go through that.'

'Sorry?' she snapped. 'Don't be sorry. I was glad that they asked me. Who do you think I would have preferred to have done it? You?' she challenged me, not expecting a response. Every time that I began to feel some empathy with her, to make a connection of sorts, she batted it neatly away and we were back to square one. 'You?' She turned to Nana, who looked pale at the thought. 'Peter, perhaps? It would have finished him off. No. It was much better this way. But if you think that I can forget about it just like that, well . . .' She shook her head.

'Good!' Nana proclaimed, bringing her hands down on the table. 'Good! We're talking at last. As a family.'

'No!' Aunty Faye was still speaking softly, but despairingly, knowing that the point she was making had not sunk in. 'Aren't you listening? I'm not ready to talk yet. And I don't think I should have to apologize for the way that I need to deal with this. You get to be up and down. Can I just please be allowed to be quiet?'

'But what about Andrea, all on her own here?' Nana asked. 'Who's going to look after her if we all just hide ourselves away?'

'I'm fine. I have people to talk to,' I insisted. I suddenly felt an overwhelming sense of responsibility for the two of them. Nana, who thought that she could make everything all right with words, and Aunty Faye, who wanted to shut herself away but couldn't. 'Anyway, I'm such awful company that I think I'm better off on my own half the time.'

'Like mother, like daughter.' Nana stroked my face. 'I'm always here for you, dear. Any time you need me.'

'Yes, well, I think it's time we left Andrea in peace now.' Aunty Faye took Nana's elbow, looking around for her handbag.

'Your bag's in the other room,' I remembered and

went to look for it. On my return I heard hushed voices.

'Enjoying yourself, are you?' my aunt asked sharply.

'Oh, I was just getting warmed up,' Nana replied, and then noticed me. 'Ah, there you are, dear. Well, it appears that somebody believes it's way past my bedtime.'

'Love you, Nana. Fantastic rhubarb crumble,' I said as I hugged her.

'There's life in the old girl yet.' She was pleased. 'Next time, I'll make us a roast dinner. I bet you haven't had one of those for a while.'

'And you, Aunty Faye.' I embraced her and felt her stiffen, her arms pinned to her sides. She wasn't even ready to hug me. How could I redraw the family tree with Faye Albury as my mother? She didn't *feel* like my mother. I was aware of her resistance. She was fighting it with every bone in her body. It was not part of who she was and it was clearly not who she wanted to be.

Part Seven

Peter's Story

Chapter Thirty-three

Be careful what you wish for. You fall in love with a
would-be rock star, you get a rock star, if you're lucky.
You try and turn him into a stay-at-home husband, you
end up with one unhappy man. Laura's mistake was
that she underestimated Tom. He was someone who
kept his promises. A man of his word – and a far better
person than I could ever hope to be.

When the band's next single didn't chart, Tom knew
that he had to make some decisions to save his
marriage. Those changes were not necessarily what
Laura expected. If she thought that Tom would be able
to slip neatly into a nine-to-five routine, she was mistaken. He was a person who threw himself into
whatever he did, even if it wasn't what he had wanted to
do in the first place. He didn't see himself as a plumber
or a decorator or even a mechanic. He decided to study
engineering. There was no doubt that he had the
aptitude for it. This meant that he worked during
the daytime, putting his practical skills to good use and
making ends meet. At night, he went back to school.

And in the early hours, he sang Andrea to sleep when she woke, and wrote his essays. He found a satisfaction in it that didn't quite live up to playing the guitar, but offered him some small compensation.

All of this meant two things. Firstly, the Fellowses did not have to be beholden to Mrs Albury, although Laura had been prepared to accept the olive branch that had been begrudgingly offered. And secondly, I was still needed. There were never more than a couple of days that went by before I heard from Laura wanting a chat or needing a small favour. She accepted Tom's absences more gracefully than she had done when he was away with the band. She seemed surer that he was working hard for their future. I doubted that Tom could ever be more driven than he had been fronting the Spearheads, but I was impressed with his humility in accepting that things had come to an end and his commitment to his family. I didn't once hear him moan or say 'if only'. But I missed him. While Laura had time for old friends and her extended family, Tom had emergencies or lectures or study to attend to. Even if he was in when I called round, he barely had time to grab a bite to eat for himself, let alone stop for a chat. I had reached a point in my career where I was relatively comfortable without having to burn the candle at both ends. Tom was burning the midnight oil. I have to say, it impressed his mother-in-law no end. Her good-for-nothing son-in-law was fast becoming someone she was proud to boast about in the queue at the post office when she went to collect her widow's pension. Mrs Fellows, on the other hand, had always been proud of her son, and was not quite so thrilled to see him worked to the bone. Tom had always been lean, but he began to look drawn and his legendary cheekbones became even more pronounced. He tried to laugh away her concerns, but to keep her happy, he often popped round and let her make him a fry-up in his lunch break.

'You're wasting away,' she would mourn. 'Just look at you.'

'Well, now's your chance to change all that.' He would rub his hands together. 'What have you got for me?'

There was nothing she liked more than to watch her son eat a home-cooked meal. Ironically, when I joined them occasionally (it was the best time to catch Tom), I can't recall ever seeing her eat. She was the kind of mother who wasn't happy unless your belly was full, but would go without herself. I enjoyed eating at her kitchen table, the lack of formality and the flow of easy conversation between them. It was nothing like the kind of relationship I had had with my parents and it was everything that I felt a family should be.

She often embarrassed me with questions about whether or not I had a young lady and if marriage was on the cards.

'Pete can't get involved with a woman,' Tom would say to shut her up. 'The only reason I'm still married is because he's my stunt double.'

'You're a true friend,' Mrs Fellows would declare, but she had even less of a clue than Tom did. He was far closer to the truth than he could have thought possible.

Tom had been aware that I was in love with Laura from the very beginning. He had even recognized that it had been a possibility that Laura would prefer the so-called sensible option to a man who couldn't offer her financial security. What he was not very good at, and where I had always excelled, was reading Laura Albury. Laura, as she had always acknowledged, was not very good at being on her own. Rule number one. Neglect her, even with the best of intentions, and she withered. Pamper her and she glowed. Nothing had happened deliberately. Nothing had been planned. At least not the first time. But Laura had found herself feeling neglected and she had turned to me for attention, and the love and respect that I felt for Tom was no match for the depth of feeling that I had for her. Just as Mrs Albury had predicted, we crossed the sacred line between friendship and love, and once crossed there seemed to be no way of returning. I had expected Laura to say that it was a mistake and that it could never happen again, but she didn't and it did.

While Tom was working so hard for the future of his family, we spent lunchtimes and afternoons and evenings in each other's arms. The only rule was that their house was out of bounds. They were not snatched moments. The snatched moments were the times that Laura spent with Tom. But they were stolen moments. Stolen from another lifetime where, if things had been different, there would have been no Tom Fellows and it would have only been the two of us.

In the time that we shared, there was an unspoken

rule that we would not make plans for the future, but Laura talked about the past and the 'what ifs'.

'What do you think would have happened between us if Tom hadn't come along?' She would ask as we lay facing each other.

'The nineteen-year-old you wouldn't have been interested in the twenty-year-old me. She was looking for someone a bit more adventurous.'

'The twenty-five-year-old me would have been interested in the twenty-six-year-old you.'

'But then there would be no Andrea.'

'True. But there might have been a little Pete.'

Laura definitely saw our time together as an escape from her reality. She said that she didn't have to think about being a housewife or a mother or a daughter or a sister when we were together. What she liked the most about our relationship was that she could be herself. We had known each other for so long that there was nothing that we needed to hide – even that faraway look that told me she was thinking about Tom, or the occasional guilty tears. It was all part of the deal. Forgive me for sparing you more detail than that, but my memories are precious and they are private. I think that we have already established that I am hardly a gentleman, but I would like to remain gentlemanly in some things at least.

Tom often joked that there were three of us in his marriage. Sometimes I thought he knew that it was more than just a joke. But nobody wants their nose rubbed in it.

Chapter Thirty-four

'Laura wants another baby,' Tom told me over a beer at the pub closest to their flat. When you have to create extra hours in the day from nothing, not a moment is wasted in walking elsewhere. We were sitting in a dark, smoky corner, away from the regulars who had congregated noisily around the bar.

'Really?' Having narrowly prevented myself from choking, I found it difficult to think of any other response. My mind was racing.

He nodded. 'Doesn't want Andrea to be an only child. Thinks I might spoil her.'

'Never did us any harm,' I joked. 'Not that I remember being spoilt.'

'Too right.'

We sat in silence for a while. Was it possible that Tom had sensed there was something going on and that this was his way of warning me off?

'It's not good timing,' he went on. 'My course is coming to an end, but I'll be on an apprentice's salary, up against all the youngsters who don't have families to support and can work for a pittance. It's going to be a lean couple of years. We're not out of the woods yet, by any means.'

'What does she say about that?'

'She says we'll manage. People do. But there's something else.'

'What's that, then?' I had seen many a guilty man look innocent with ease, but I didn't know if I was capable of hiding my feelings.

Tom looked at his glass, holding it with both hands. 'I'm not sure we can have another child. We've still got the issue of the mumps to get over.'

'But what about Andrea? They were wrong about her.'

'Andrea was our miracle. We've already seen the doctors. Let's just say I had one sprinter who was ahead of the pack. Very little chance of that happening again.'

I had no idea that there had been time for sex and talk of babies and doctors' appointments in their marriage. This was all news to me and I felt that I had been betrayed, even though I knew it was illogical.

'What about adoption?'

'That's just it.' He shook his head. 'I think I could love any child, but Laura says that she wants one of her own. No. This time the doctors say that our only hope is this new treatment called IVF. Have you heard of it?'

'Louise Brown, the miracle baby.' I took a sip. 'I read about it in the papers but I have to say I thought that it was a one-off.'

'No, they want to develop the idea so that they can treat couples. They're actually looking for volunteers, believe it or not. I'm not at all keen. I don't want Laura to be used as a guinea pig. I'm not even sure I agree with the idea of it. But she's willing to try anything.'

I had to be honest. I couldn't understand how a woman who already had one child of her own could be desperate for another.

'So what now?' I asked.

'I want her to be happy, I really do. But as soon as she has one thing she wants, she's on to the next. I can't keep up. I'm working flat out as it is. Plus, I don't want to see her hurt if it doesn't work out. God only knows, I know what it's like to feel that sort of disappointment. We've got one beautiful girl and I'm grateful for that, to be honest. For a bloke who never thought he'd be a father, to have one child is a bonus.'

'Laura's always known her own mind.'

'And she's used to getting what she wants, I know. Did you find life tough as an only child?'

'I found being a child tough in general. But it had more to do with the atmosphere at home. What about you?'

'It's always just been me and my mum. And that was how I liked it. We've always got on like a house on fire. No complaints there.'

'Whereas you might feel differently if you had a battleaxe for a mother.'

'To the lovely Mrs Albury.' Tom raised his glass in a toast. 'Ah, she's not so bad. I do believe I'm finally growing on her. She even stuck up for me the other day when Laura complained that we never eat dinner together. She said that she was lucky to have a man who works so hard for his family. I was so surprised I could have kissed her.'

'I've never asked you about your dad—'

'There's nothing to tell.' He cut me short. 'He didn't want me and I never needed him.'

'Do you know if he's still alive?'

'He's always been dead to me.'

'Fair enough.'

The bell rang for last orders and Tom checked his watch.

'Time, gentlemen!' the barman yelled and Tom downed the dregs of his pint.

'Saved by the bell. Time for the nightshift.' He grabbed his jacket. 'Same time next week?'

I sat and finished my drink, thinking how ludicrous the situation was. Laura and I couldn't carry on like this. Even though she hadn't promised me anything, I had let myself believe that all was not right at home and that there was still a chance she would choose me. Listening to Tom, I wondered if I was what was holding the marriage together or preventing it from working. Perhaps the only fair way to resolve things once and for all would be if I removed myself from the equation. Laura had tried to do this once before. Now it was my turn.

The mechanics of this were far easier than I had imagined. I felt no desire to go anywhere in particular. I had always been good at throwing myself into my work when things were not right in other parts of my life. For some time, my firm had talked about opening an office in the north-east of England and I volunteered to go. They began to make preparations immediately. This gave me time, but not too much time, to prepare mentally.

I was too weak-willed to break things off with Laura before I left. Neither was I able to resist mentioning the conversation that Tom and I had had. She was typically unrepentant.

'I can't keep on putting my life on hold until everything is perfect,' she said.

'But what about us?' I asked. 'Doesn't this mean anything to you?'

'Don't you see it means *everything* to me?' She cupped my face. 'If I didn't have you, I couldn't go out into the world and be the person everyone expects me to be.'

'Have you thought about what you would do if you got pregnant now? Clearly, you're trying. How would you know who the father is?'

'It would be very unlikely to be Tom,' she said bitterly.

'How can you be so sure when you have Andrea?'

'We're sure. Don't ask me how, but we're sure.'

I shook my head, not understanding her certainty. 'That makes it worse. What would you do if you got pregnant and the baby was mine? Would we just carry on like this?'

'I don't know all the answers. I'd love to pretend I do, but I don't.' Laura was tearful. 'Tom's given up his dreams for me and Andrea. You know what that has cost him. I don't think I could leave him now.'

This only cemented my feeling that I was doing the right thing. Laura said that she treasured our relationship but that her marriage took priority – even if there was a child involved. Faye had been wrong when she said that Laura would never sleep with me, but she was also right; I had never stood a chance against Tom Fellows. I was at a time in my life when it was no longer good enough. When I picked up Andrea and swung her around, or carried her on my shoulders, or when she took my hand as we crossed the road – and especially when she called me 'Daddy' by mistake – I felt a yearning to be a father. It was no longer just about the girl for me. I wanted the whole package. There would never be another Laura as far as I was concerned, but maybe with a new start and the bigger picture in mind, a family might be possible.

Then one afternoon, Laura caught me hugging Andrea too close for too long and telling her that I would never be more than a phone call away.

'You're saying goodbye!' She was wide-eyed and shocked. I didn't answer but turned around to face her. 'But why?'

I held her to my chest. 'Don't you see I have to? How long can we put ourselves through this?'

'You say it as if it was torture, whereas I've had some of the happiest times of my life with you this last year or so.'

'I want more than you're prepared to give me, Laura. I always have.' I stroked her hair. 'If we carry on like this we're going to start to argue and it will be just like every other relationship you've tried to escape from.'

'But you can't leave me.'

'Mummy, why are you crying?' Andrea interrupted, her hands tugging Laura's skirt. As Laura let go of me to explain to Andrea that she was very, very sad, I made a cowardly escape, touching Laura's blonde waves for what I honestly believed would be the last time.

Part Eight

Faye's Story

Chapter Thirty-five

I hadn't been home for over three years when Laura came to stay with me, bringing Andrea with her. I was used to Laura coming on her own because of Tom's schedule, but I immediately sensed that this time something was different. Being in such close proximity to Andrea made me nervous. I drank too many gin and tonics to compensate, which made Laura eye me critically. She may as well have come straight out with it and asked me to stop drinking in front of her child. 'Whose child?' I imagined myself asking.

Andrea was boisterous. 'Aunty Faye' this and 'Aunty Faye' that. Jumping on the furniture and wanting to be the centre of attention. Every new discovery was followed by a shriek of delight that produced smiles from Laura and goosebumps on the back of my neck. My flat was hardly child-proof and neither was I.

I was relieved when Laura put her to bed and order was resumed, but it was short-lived. I had no idea of the secrets that Laura had been keeping. They were hard to take in. An eighteen-month affair with Peter Churcher. Peter gone. Things going downhill at home. And now this. Laura pregnant and thinking that it was a sign that she should be with Peter after all.

'A sign!' I remember saying. 'Did you think it was a sign when I was pregnant? The man's so virile that I'm amazed it took you so long.' Then she told me that she had been on the pill for the first year. She had only stopped taking it when she knew she wanted another baby! 'But Tom's sterile. What were you thinking of?' I asked her.

'I know. I tried to get him to try that new IVF but he wasn't keen. It's such a mess.'

I asked her if she had been in contact with Peter.

'No!' She was horrified. 'He so desperately wants children. I can't tell him about the baby unless I'm ready to leave Tom.'

That was a shock, hearing it out loud. Peter desperately wanting children. I felt anger and regret. Nobody had thought to mention that to me when I was pregnant and needed advice. When I told them that I didn't want Peter to know about the baby, no one tried to persuade me otherwise. There was nothing but agreement that I was doing the right thing.

'But why Peter, of all people?' I asked her, genuinely keen to know why she would have played away from home with someone so involved in the situation.

'We love each other.' She seemed surprised that I needed to ask. 'It's always been Pete and me. Even with

Tom, it would never have worked without Pete. There's never been a time when it was just Tom.'

I honestly don't think that she saw her affair with Peter as a betrayal of Tom, because she had known Peter first. She had loved Peter first.

'You mean to say . . . ?' I began to ask, wondering how long it had actually been going on for.

'No.' She seemed to find it amusing that she had managed to shock me. 'It was never all about sex with Pete. In fact, the sex was a bit of a surprise. I thought that we had gone way beyond that stage, to be honest. We'd kissed before, but it hadn't led anywhere. I didn't think it would that time either, but I was wrong. Pete's the only person in the world that I can be myself with. Apart from you. With everyone else it's an act. Do you know what I mean?'

'How on earth would I know what you mean?' I snapped. 'I've never been that close to a man.'

'I'm not just talking about men,' she said, 'I'm talking about having to pretend you're something you're not all the time.'

'Well, you've brought Andrea with you,' I said. 'Let's see how I get on with her for starters.' That was a conversation-killer. But really! Didn't she ever think about what she was saying?

Like me, the easiest option wasn't one that Laura was prepared to consider.

'How can you want a child so much and then decide to get rid of it because it's inconvenient?' she asked.

'Even if it might save your marriage?' I challenged, playing devil's advocate.

'So be it.' She shrugged, but her face betrayed her fears. She knew what was at stake.

On another evening she asked, 'How would you feel if Pete brought up Andrea with me?'

Up until then the thought hadn't crossed my mind. I had been so far removed from the situation that I hadn't had to think about it. I had never been in love with Peter Churcher so it wasn't a case of being jealous. But when I gave her away, it wasn't to Laura, but to Laura and Tom.

'I thought so,' she said, looking at my face.

'I haven't said anything yet,' I protested. I've thought about that conversation so many times since.

'You don't have to.' Laura always told me that Andrea was the best gift I could have ever given her. But you can't place conditions on gifts. You don't give someone a gift and tell them they can never tell anyone about it. Andrea was never a gift. She was never just mine to give. 'That would be too weird for you. I shouldn't even have asked.'

Did she expect me to protest, to tell her that it would be all right with me? I hadn't created the problem but now she wanted me to hand her a solution. I was already living far away from my home in an attempt to escape my past. How much further would I have to go to avoid the deceit that would accumulate? Oh, no! This time she was asking too much. But what alternatives were there?

'If you leave Tom, could you leave Andrea behind?' I asked, afraid of the answer.

'That's not an option,' she replied.

'Then we have a problem,' I said unnecessarily.

But the number of options were running out. And time was an issue. How long would it be before Tom noticed and Laura was forced to make a decision? When Laura left London to return home, she was no nearer to arriving at a conclusion. I had not told her that whatever she did would be all right with me. For the first time, as I waved my so-called niece goodbye, I started to think about what would be best for her as well as for me. I started to think like a mother.

A few weeks later, Laura phoned from a telephone box in the middle of the night and reversed the charges. She tearfully told me how she had tried to leave Tom for Peter, but hadn't been able to.

'I couldn't do it to him. God knows I tried.'

'Where's Andrea?' I was surprised that my immediate thoughts were for her rather than my sister.

'She doesn't know anything about it. She's asleep in the car. It's just a bit of an adventure as far as she's concerned.'

'What are you going to do now?' I asked her.

'I'm going home to face the music,' she said.

'What's that going to involve?'

'I have no idea. It's up to Tom now.'

'Does Peter know?'

But she had already hung up on me and the question was left hanging. No matter how much I mulled things over in my mind, I couldn't think of a solution that would work for everyone. Laura had assured me that she would never tell Peter about Andrea, but if her future lay with him, how would she be able to keep it from him?

Part Nine

Peter's Story

Chapter Thirty-six

I could hear a commotion at the reception desk and excused myself from the meeting I was conducting with the intention of asking whoever was responsible to keep the noise down. I hesitated when I heard Tom's raised voice saying, 'Well, you'd better drag him out of his meeting and tell him that Tom Fellows wants to talk to him about his wife.'

The next thing I knew, I was reeling from a blow to my face and my nose was bleeding. Instinctively, I sat down on a low chair and bent forwards. I knew that Tom was not a fighting man and he was unlikely to hit me again unless I stood up against him.

'You stupid bastard,' he was shouting. 'You've gone and ruined everything.' But instead of raising his fist again, he sat down next to me and held his head in his hands.

'Shall I call the police, sir?' the receptionist whispered as she bent down to hand me a wad of tissues.

'No, no. Make us some coffees and show Mr Fellows to my office while I wash my face.'

'Will you come this way?' she asked him, but Tom followed me into the men's toilets and looked at my reflection in the mirror. Denial wasn't an option.

'I left, Tom,' I explained. 'I left because I knew that I couldn't finish it any other way.'

'Oh yes, you left all right,' he hissed. 'But did you know you left her pregnant?'

The colour of my face was answer enough to tell him the answer. 'How can you be so sure it's mine?' I asked, quickly backing off as he moved towards me again, expecting another blow. Instead he prodded my chest with an index finger.

'You knew that we were planning another child.' His voice was raised but steady. 'What did you think would happen? That I'd agree to IVF and that you could do the job instead? And then what? Tell me, Pete, because I don't understand!'

'I didn't know she was pregnant,' I said. 'Do you think for one minute I would have left if I had known?'

'What would you have done? Stayed and fought for her?' he scoffed.

'It's not as simple as that,' I replied. 'Laura would never choose me over you and I wouldn't want her to change her mind because she's pregnant.'

'If you believe that then what the hell were you doing sleeping with my wife in the first place? I trusted you!'

'I'm truly sorry, Tom. I never meant for it to come to this.'

'Those times she stayed in your house! How long has it been going on for? Three years, is it?'

'Nothing happened then, I swear it.'

'Am I supposed to be grateful for that? How many times have we sat down to eat together? The three of us? How many times have you and I gone for a drink? I don't know how you've been able to look me in the eye all this time!'

'I—'

'Don't!' He raised the palm of his hand to me, opening the door with the other hand. 'Don't even try to give me excuses.'

It slammed behind him and I knew better than to follow him. If he hadn't been such a good driver, I would have worried about him on the journey home. He had travelled 200 miles to vent his anger. I knew that he had come to see me to avoid taking it out on Laura.

I spent days waiting for the next contact, but there was nothing until Faye phoned some two weeks later. I hadn't heard her voice since the wedding and I was surprised to hear it then.

'Tom's left her, Peter,' she said. 'She's too proud to come to you, so you're going to have to make the next move. She needs you.'

'You knew?' I asked her, stunned.

'Of course I didn't know at the time.' The scathing Faye was back. 'Laura's only just told me about it. Why on earth my sister would choose to have an affair with you when she had Tom Fellows at home is, quite frankly, a mystery to me.'

Even then, it was not that simple. There were other people to think about. Andrea might be old enough to understand a little of what was going on. Then there was Mrs Albury who felt that protecting the reputation of her family was her role in life and Mrs Fellows whom I would not have hurt for the world. I went home with the excuse of visiting my own mother, who was by then in an old people's home. In the end, with my father gone, instead of being released into the world again, she was lost. She reverted to calling me 'her Jonnie' with no one there to scowl at her every time she used my name. To me, it sounded as if she was talking to someone else and added to the illusion of unreality.

I rang the doorbell of the flat with trepidation. I had been gone for over four months and I was afraid that Laura might be angry or feeling too guilty about Tom to want to see me. Andrea spotted me first through the window and I watched her jump up and down excitedly. She clearly announced my arrival to her mother, so it was not a complete shock for Laura to find me on her doorstep. Nonetheless, she was surprised and cautious, cradling her bump protectively with one hand.

'Faye phoned me,' I explained. She brushed her blonde head against my shoulder. I'd love to say that she flung herself at me but neither the circumstances nor her bump would have allowed for that.

'So there's no need for me to start from the beginning,' Laura said, closing the door. Then, seemingly changing her mind: 'How much did she tell you?'

'That you're pregnant and Tom has gone. Why didn't you call me?' I asked.

'You left too, remember. And after what I had said to you I don't blame you one bit.' She smiled. 'How do you think I should have put it? "I'm pregnant and Tom's gone, so would you mind coming home and taking up where we left off?" You deserve more than that.'

'So where does that leave us now?' I asked, taking her hand.

'Well, I'm five months pregnant with a three-year-old in tow and no income, and you live two hundred miles away. I can offer you a cup of tea, but I'm afraid I haven't got the energy for anything more.'

'Have you got a better offer?' I hung my coat on the peg in the hall.

'You're not seriously . . . ?'

'Laura, I've been in love with you for as long as I can remember, you're pregnant with our baby, and for once, there's nothing standing in our way.'

Andrea bounded into the hall. 'Uncle Pete, Uncle Pete! Guess what I am!'

'A frog.'

'No.'

'A kangaroo.'

'No!'

'A jumping bean.'

'No, silly. I'm Tigger.' She grabbed my hand. 'Come and play with me. You can be Eeyore. Mummy's Pooh Bear because she's so fat.'

'You can always rely on a three-year-old for the truth! Darling, the grown-ups were just about to have a cup of tea.' Laura tried unsuccessfully to pull her away.

'But he promised that he would come and play with me any time I wanted,' she protested.

'That is true,' I admitted, getting down on to all fours, hopeful that nothing would be more irresistible to a pregnant woman than a man being good with children. I crawled into the living room languidly, muttering about the perils of thistles.

'You've got five minutes!' Laura said in her pretend strict voice. 'Then the adults need to talk.'

'Is Daddy staying with you?' Andrea hissed at me as soon as she thought we were out of earshot, barely missing a bounce.

I sat up on my heels to marvel at her directness. 'No, darling,' I said solemnly.

'Do you know where he is?'

'I'm afraid I don't.'

'That's OK,' she said cheerfully. 'I can look after Mummy. Only she's very sad.'

I winked. 'We'll have to see what we can do about that.'

The sun was shining through the window, throwing shadows on the wall opposite.

'Do a rabbit,' she pointed, referring to her favourite game of shadow puppets. I left my first and second fingers upright and wrapped the other fingers and my thumb inwards, rubbing the fingers against my thumb to make the rabbit's nose twitch. 'He-he-he-he! What's up, Doc?' I mimicked. This produced a giggle.

'And a crocodile,' she commanded. I held the top of my hand stiff and snapped my thumb against it.

'Never smile at a crocodile,' I sang, deliberately low. Then I made the crocodile take off after the rabbit and a chase ensued.

She was unimpressed. 'Do a bird.' I joined my thumbs together and flapped my fingers, moving my hands diagonally up the wall, and cawing like a demented seagull.

'Do an elephant!' she demanded. I was stumped. I had no idea how to do an elephant.

'You do an elephant,' I suggested, after experimenting unsuccessfully.

'No, you do it!'

'No, you do it!'

'Five minutes is up!' came a call from the kitchen.

'Sorry,' I shrugged, and pretended to be making a very quick getaway. 'No elephants today.'

'Read to me later!' Andrea called after me.

'"Please can you read to me later, Uncle Pete?"' her mother corrected, shaking her head.

I joined her at the kitchen table. 'Was that really only five minutes? I'm exhausted!'

'I'm afraid she's not been getting the amount of attention she's used to. I can't keep up with her at the moment and the grandmothers had to give up trying a long time ago.'

'I enjoy being in demand.' I smiled. 'It's not so long ago I struggled to find people who wanted to play with me.'

'That's because you can't do elephants,' she joked. 'If you don't learn, Andrea will get bored of you quickly enough.'

'Can you do elephants?'

'Can *I* do elephants?' She was mock-serious, then: 'No, I can't do elephants. That was always Tom's job. He was the elephant man.' She smiled sadly.

'Boy, are we in trouble.' I took her hand. 'How long has he been gone?'

She addressed the table. 'Five weeks.'

'What have you told Andrea?'

'That he's away working.'

'And the grandmothers?'

'Grandma Fellows obviously knows the truth. It's a small town. If my mother doesn't know already, she will soon.'

'You haven't told her?'

'And have her say "I told you so"? It's one thing thinking it yourself, but to have your mother say it to your face . . .' She exhaled noisily.

'How long do you think it's going to be before Andrea starts asking questions?'

'Pete, Tom could still come back,' Laura said deliberately slowly. 'I don't want to tell Andrea anything before I know what's happening.'

'Has he been in touch?'

'He sent money for the rent. No letter. No address. Just the money. For all I know, he might just need some space.'

'So, it wouldn't help if I asked you to move in with me?' I asked hopefully, but already knowing the answer.

'It helps me to know that you're still here for me. It broke my heart when you moved away. I thought that

284

it was the last I would see of you.' It was an evasive answer, but an honest one.

'So where does this leave us?' I looked at her down-turned eyes. 'Is there any "us"?'

'For me, there always has been, but I know that that's not good enough for you any more.' She turned her eyes to me. 'Give me time. We both owe Tom that much.'

'How much time? In a few months that baby will be born into the world fatherless.'

She nodded with equal concern. 'Give me two months.'

'And what about in the meanwhile? How will you manage?'

'I have help,' Laura said humbly.

'What if that help disappears?' Mrs Albury could be so changeable that I wouldn't have put it past her to with-draw her support if things weren't organized exactly the way she had in mind.

'I'll manage, Pete.' Laura sounded weary. 'I have to manage.'

'Let me come and see you at the weekends,' I implored.

'How would it look if Tom came home and found you here? This is still his home, until he tells me otherwise.'

I pushed my chair back and stood.

'Are you leaving?' she asked, her look one of panic.

'I'm going to read to Andrea. She's waiting for me.'

'There's no happy ending now, is there, Pete?' She raised her eyes to me. 'If Tom comes back, I lose you, and if we get to be together, it means that I have lost Tom. You do know what you'd be letting yourself in for, don't you? I don't know if Tom's told you, but I'm not an easy woman to live with.'

It was then that I knew that I had no intention of losing either Laura or Tom. They were both too important to me. We shared such a complicated history. If it was within my power, I was determined that we would not lose each other, regardless of the sacrifices it would involve.

Chapter Thirty-seven

Over the next few weeks, I was determined to track down Tom, using all of the tools that I had at my disposal through work. I spent my weekends in my home town, visiting all of our old haunts and letting it be known that I was looking for him. Tom had always been so visible in the community that I quickly dismissed the possibility that he was staying locally. His college confirmed that he hadn't handed in any coursework and that they assumed he had left. They explained that many a talented pupil takes this route in the approach to the final exams. Those he worked for regularly were as keen for him to get in touch as I was. His services were very much in demand and sorely missed.

It seemed most likely to me that he had packed his guitar and returned to London in search of work as a session musician or in the recording studio where he had made a name for himself almost four years previously. I turned up on Faye's doorstep unannounced, afraid of being refused if I phoned first.

'What on earth are you doing here, Peter Churcher?'

she asked me. It was a question I didn't quite know the answer to myself.

'Can I come in?' I asked her.

She took one look at the luggage I was carrying. 'You can't stay,' she said, turning and leaving the door open for me. It was not a friendly start, but it was at least a start.

'I was wondering if you had heard from Tom.'

'I don't understand you!' Faye faced me with arms crossed over her chest. 'Laura needs you there with her, probably the best chance you have of catching her in a moment of weakness, and here you are trying to track Tom down. Are you mad?'

'Faye, you know as well as I do that Laura won't be happy if she loses Tom. I'm certainly not going to step straight into his shoes if there's any chance at all that they could still work things out.'

'So now you worry about doing the right thing! That's just typical of you. Don't you think that you're a bit late for that?'

'I wish I could say that I'm acting selflessly, but the last thing I want is for me to move in with Laura and for Tom to turn up afterwards. Think how confused Andrea would be if nothing else.'

Faye's mood seemed to change and she perched on the corner of her sofa, 'How did things get so complicated?' she asked. 'I'm supposed to be the one in our family who gets into scrapes and Laura is the one who bails me out. It's always been that way. Tom is supposed to be the young, good-for-nothing troublemaker. And you're supposed to be the respectable one. If we could all just stick at what we're good at, everything would be fine.'

'Have you heard from him, Faye?' I asked again, softly.

She looked at the floor. 'No.'

'You're not helping anyone by keeping anything from me . . .'

'Will you let me finish! Don't you dare use your solicitor tactics with me! I haven't heard from him. I've heard *of* him. He's been seen around town, busking down the Underground and playing the pub and club circuit.'

'Any idea where I should start?' I took a notebook and a pen out of my jacket pocket.

'All of the smaller venues. The Half Moon at Putney. The Swan at Fulham. The Sun Inn at Clapham. The Borderline. The Hope and Anchor in Islington. That should do for starters. They'll be able to point you in the right direction.'

'Thank you. That's a big help.'

'Have you got any idea where any of those places are?' She frowned at me with the level of doubt that you would direct at a small child.

'I'll look for the stops on the Underground. That's how I found you.'

She left the room and returned with a book in hand. 'Your bible. The *A–Z*. I can do without you phoning in the middle of the night to tell me you're lost. Guard it with your life.'

'I came to ask you something else as well,' I told her before I left. 'Won't you go home, Faye? You've been away too long and Laura needs a sister at a time like this. Andrea needs her aunt. You know how difficult things will be once your mother finds out what's going on.'

'This is my home now.' She was stubborn. 'I have a job here, friends, a life. They are welcome to stay any time they like.'

'This isn't your home. It's a rented flat. You deliberately haven't put down any roots here.' I looked around for examples of how bland and unloved the place felt. It reminded me of my own rented flat in Newcastle, but I had the excuse of only having been there for a few months. 'You haven't even hung any pictures on the walls. It still looks exactly like it did when you were visiting.'

'Well, it's a fine thing that after all this you think you know what's best for my family.' Faye shut the door on me with a slam. I had taken no more than a few steps, when I heard it being opened behind me. 'If you find him,' she said, 'be sure to let me know.'

I waved over my shoulder, the copy of the *A–Z* still in hand, walking in the direction of the Underground station. No matter how hard Faye tried to appear, I could rely on the fact that she loved her sister more than most sisters are entitled to expect.

Tom had covered his tracks carefully. I got the distinct impression that he didn't want to be found. Apparently, none of the people he worked for knew where he lived or how to contact him. They all relied on him staying in contact with them. I told more than one of them that I didn't consider that it was any way to do business, instantly regretting how pompous I sounded.

'And what line of business would you be in exactly, Mr Churcher?' I was asked by a surly, stocky man with a shaved head. I was taller than him, but when he folded his arms across his chest and stood with his legs slightly apart, he seemed to double in size. I had no doubt that he was used to defending his territory.

'I'm a solicitor.' I felt safer behind the mask of my professional role. 'But this is a private matter. A family matter.'

'Your name ain't Fellows.'

'No, it isn't,' I conceded.

'Well, Mr Churcher, this ain't a solicitor's office and you ain't family.'

'I've brought a message from the family. If you can't tell me how to reach him, would it be possible for you to get a message to him?'

'*If* we 'ear from him, I should be 'appy to pass on your message. More than 'appy.'

'That's very kind of you,' I said, jotting down details of where I could be contacted and a brief message. I left similar messages at various locations around the capital. I wanted Tom to know how much I had wanted to get in touch and how hard I had tried to track him down. Over the weeks that followed, I returned to the same venues to see if those messages had been passed on and if there was news. I felt that some of the landlords were lying, and that some knew exactly who I was and were judging me, but only one greeted me by name.

'Back again, Mr Churcher?' He was pulling a pint.

'I was wondering if you'd heard from Tom Fellows since I was here last.'

'A word of advice, Mr Churcher, if you don't mind. I've passed on your message like you asked. You're an intelligent man. It's obvious he 'asn't been in touch or you wouldn't be gracing us with your presence again. What conclusion can you draw from that?' He put the pint on a bar towel in front on me. 'If a man doesn't want to be found, there's no finding 'im. No charge this time.' He nodded at the pint. 'We operate a pub here. A place where people come to escape their worries. I like to think we do that very well. If you're not 'ere for a pint, I'm afraid you have no business being 'ere.' He moved on with a clap of his hands. 'Right then, who's waiting to be served? What can I get for you, sir?'

I didn't darken his doorstep again.

Two months passed and there was no news. It was time to pay Laura another visit; it would not be long before the baby arrived.

'Pete,' she said, opening the door with one hand, her other on her hip. She had grown considerably larger since the last time I saw her and she leaned backwards to balance the weight of the baby. She smiled wearily. 'I hear from Faye that you've been playing the detective.'

'Can I come in?' I asked.

'The coast is clear for once. Andrea's having tea at a friend's.'

She showed me into the front room, which was littered with piles of baby clothes.

'I've been sorting out all of Andrea's old things. Some of them look as if they've hardly been worn.' She picked up a Babygro. 'Can you believe she was ever this small?'

'Seems like only yesterday.' I smiled. 'How are you?'

'Huge – as you can see. Tired. Trying to keep it all together for Andrea's sake.'

'So you haven't heard from Tom?'

I watched her lip quiver. 'Just an envelope with the money for the rent.'

'I'm so sorry, Laura.' I reached out to touch her knee. 'I've tried everywhere I could think of.'

'I didn't ask you to.'

'Are you angry with me?'

'With you? No!' She tried to smile through the first onset of tears. 'You've always looked after me. How could I be angry?'

I had a sudden thought. 'I don't want you to think that because I've been looking for Tom that I'm not interested.'

'I understand. I really do.'

'Is the idea of a future with me so horrible?' I tried to be lighthearted.

'You know that when I say yes to you, I'm giving up on Tom.' She let her head drop.

'I know, I know.' I put an arm around her and let her head rest against my shoulder.

'Do you think he's given up on us?' she asked, her eyelashes heavy with tears.

I chose not to answer but hushed her as I would Andrea when she needed comforting. 'I'm here now.'

She responded by holding on to the hand on her shoulder. Her touch felt child-like rather than like a lover's.

After a while, when she was calmer, she asked, 'Where do we go from here?'

'Well.' I tried to stick to the practicalities. 'We've got to get ready for this baby. If you're willing to have me, you need to decide where you would like to live.'

'I want to stay here.' She was adamant about that. 'I don't want to move to Newcastle.'

'I've already told the firm that I consider I've done my time at the new office, so that's not a problem. I've just got a few things to finish off there. Would you consider moving to my house? There's no shortage of room there.'

'That seems best,' Laura said, looking around her at the cramped living room. I could tell that she was not ready to let go yet. There were too many memories in that one small room, in the flat that had never belonged to them. The shelves that Tom had put up. The stand that he had fixed to the wall for the rented television. The boiler housing that he had built. The folders of his course work for college. Their wedding photo on the wall. Evidence of a four-year marriage. I knew that she was wondering what Tom would do if he came back to the flat and it was empty. I was wondering the same thing myself.

Part Ten

Andrea's Story

Chapter Thirty-eight

I think that even completely normal families avoid talking to each other about the things that really matter. And so it was with us. At the age of twenty-five, some months after the parents who had brought me up had died, in my mind I started the gradual journey from being Andrea Fellows, daughter of Tom and Laura, the product of a stable and loving family, to becoming Andrea Churcher, daughter of Peter Churcher and Faye Albury, whose relationship seemed to see-saw helplessly. Of course, I didn't consider changing my name by deed poll. I hadn't even confronted them. Although there were times when I wanted to demand answers, I waited and waited for one of them to broach the subject with me. Not knowing where the conversation would take us, I wasn't sure that I should be the one to start it. How could I speak to my aunt who had made it so clear that she wasn't ready to talk? How could I talk to Uncle Pete, not knowing if he had spoken to my aunt yet and how much he knew. It was far easier to talk to Lydia.

'I don't think you can assume that there was one party

who was right and one who was wrong,' she said. 'It wasn't like it is today. Twenty-five years ago, you were either marched up the aisle or all choice in the matter was taken out of your hands. From what you've told me, the timing would have been just awful. Your grandfather had just died and your mother and father were more or less blamed. The whole family was falling apart, for goodness' sakes! It sounds to me as if your aunt must have been very strong. Just imagine, you decide that you're not ready for a child of your own, so you let your sister take her. How do you think that feels? Now imagine that you sacrificed a lot of things in your life to cover up the secret and suddenly it's out in the open. You think you've been lied to at the moment, but what if she thinks she's protecting you?'

'I don't need to be protected,' I snapped. 'I need to know who I *am*.'

Lydia was bullish. 'I know it's all come as a shock, but you know who you are just fine, missy. Do you think that Kevin will change overnight if he finds out who his birth parents are? No! Don't give me that. But what about your aunt? She spent years pretending to be someone she's not. And your godfather? Now, if anyone's been lied to . . .' She shook her head.

'So are you saying that I shouldn't ask them?'

'I think it will all come out in the wash in its own time. It's complicated. There won't be an easy answer because there are people and feelings involved. And, of course, if there was going to be a point when your aunt thought you should know, the two people who should

298

have been the ones to tell you would have been your mum and dad. Because, no matter what, Tom and Laura will always be your mum and dad. That isn't going to change. Chin up, love.' She put one chubby hand on either side of my face and planted a kiss on my forehead. 'You're going to be just fine.'

In a strange reversal of roles, my attitude towards my aunt and my godfather was one of parental concern. I began to feel responsible for their feelings.

Uncle Pete (after all these years it is still difficult to call him by any other name) had started acting erratically around me. I caught his sideways glances when he didn't think I was looking. I knew exactly what he was thinking. *It's been staring me in the face all these years. How didn't I notice before? She has my chin and her eyes are spaced exactly the same width apart as mine.* He was particularly tactile with me, touching my arm, putting a hand on my shoulder, hugging me before he left. And he tried to tackle some of the difficult subjects with me that I would have preferred to avoid. Money. Work. Wills. Disposal of the house. My feelings. The future. But more than that, the advice that he gave me changed dramatically. In the past, I went to Uncle Pete when I wanted the advice of an older, more experienced person, but didn't want the advice of a parent. He made me think about all of my options, both legal and illegal on some occasions, and warned me about the ramifications of the various paths, but never in the past had he told me what he thought I should do.

'I'm your godfather,' he explained when I challenged

him. 'I've always taken that role very seriously. I'm responsible for your moral welfare, not legal advice.'

'I don't need you to change. Not on top of everything else.'

'I'm afraid that everything's changed and that probably includes me. There's only one thing that hasn't, and that is that I will always love you as if you were my own daughter.' I had been distracted but now he had my full attention and I watched as he bit his bottom lip and drew blood.

'You're bleeding,' I said, hoping that he would say something more.

He sucked on his bottom lip and seemed surprised to taste blood. 'So I am.'

'Did you ever want children of your own?' We were so close that I decided to try and draw him out, but his face looked so pained that I regretted it the moment the words were out.

He was distracted by shouts from outside.

'What's that racket?' he asked, striding to the bay window in the living room that overlooked the street and pulling back the net curtains. His face was turned away from me, but I could see that he had kept his hand close to his mouth.

'It's the tenants from next door. They're moving out today. Their landlord has told them that he is going to sell and they've decided to move on before they're pushed out.'

'No need. They would have been entitled to stay.' His voice was flat.

'I think they just wanted to be in control of the situation,' I said, thinking of Lydia's comments about my aunt's situation.

He scratched his head. 'Who owns the house? Do you know?'

'Thinking of moving in next door?' I joked.

'That's exactly what I'm thinking.' He turned back towards me, his face a little red, but otherwise recovered.

'You're kidding!' I was genuinely taken aback.

'I've got an embryo of an idea.' He was suddenly boy-like in his enthusiasm. 'I haven't thought it through yet, but hear me out. We're both orphans. I have a house that I'm kicking around in. You have a house – and I mean "you" collectively – that you're kicking around in, while Faye and your grandmother are cooped up in that flat of hers going stir crazy.'

'But Nana needs looking after. She's only with Faye until a place can be found for her in a home.'

'There's nothing wrong with your grandmother! I've known that woman for most of my sorry life and she's no more senile now than she was at forty. Difficult? Yes. Manipulative? Yes. But batty? No more than you or I. If you want to see her go downhill, put her into care. I saw what it did to my mother in a matter of months and I wouldn't wish it on anyone. Does she really strike you as being ill?' he challenged.

'I thought she was behaving strangely, but now I'm not so sure.'

'She has lost two of the people she loved the most in the world and been thrown out of her own home. She's

301

entitled to act a little strangely! God knows, I'd be climbing the walls if I was in her boat. I know it won't be easy, but with three of us, we could give her all the help she needs.'

'You're not suggesting that Aunty Faye moves in as well?'

'That's exactly what I'm thinking of! She'll have to do her bit as well. Of course, I'm not suggesting that we all live on top of each other. Or maybe I am! There would be enough room to turn the two houses into four flats if we wanted to. Or to have a bedroom and a sitting room each at the very least. How do you think she'll react to the idea?'

'She's going to hate it. Aunty Faye comes and goes as she pleases. She doesn't like to be tied down.'

'Given the choice, few of us do. But these are unusual times and we need be a bit creative. I know for a fact that your grandmother meant to live in this house until the day she dies. Your parents wouldn't want you to be turfed out of your home at a time like this. Your grandmother's will gave permission for your parents to live in the house for as long as they needed once she was gone, and they were to hold it in trust for the family. It would have gone to Faye and eventually to you. But, in the meanwhile, the lion's share belongs to her. It's her house and I know Faye thinks she means well, but she's wrong. Your grandmother should be allowed to come home.'

'Uncle Pete . . .' I paused, not quite sure how to ask the question. 'Do you and Aunty Faye actually get on?

At all, I mean.' I thought of Aunty Faye referring to him as 'that dreadful man', of her suggestion that he had deliberately excluded her photos from his album as if he had erased her memory. And that was before we came to the question of the lies.

'Get on?' He looked stumped for a minute. 'We're both stubborn and set in our own ways and we've always fought like cats and dogs. But we have history.' I watched him flinch. 'We couldn't go our own ways even if we wanted to. That's almost as important as getting on. You're all family as far as I'm concerned.'

That was just it. We would be what was left of the Churcher family and the Alburys, all living under one roof. What had once been the roof of my family home.

'How much will all this cost?' I almost hoped that we could rule the idea out on the grounds of expense. This could go one of two ways. It would either be a complete disaster or the perfect solution. But the risk was too great.

'To you? Nothing! I have a house to sell. Don't worry about the money. I just want to know what you think about the idea.'

I nodded doubtfully. 'It could work.'

'Do you give me permission to try and track down the owner of the house next door and talk to Faye?'

Could he have a conversation about houses without talking about families? I wondered. Did this mean that he was ready for that conversation with my aunt?

'Are you sure it's what you want?' I wanted to be cautious, concerned that he would change his mind.

'What I want?' He looked as if he would burst. 'I get to try and do something right for a change. Opportunities like this are not to be missed.'

Part Eleven

Peter's Story

Chapter Thirty-nine

There was far less time between my return to my home town and the birth of the baby than we had expected. Maybe it was the stress of the move from the flat. Andrea was in familiar surroundings and didn't question the reason why she was going to stay with Uncle Pete. It was all an adventure to her. As long as she had her toys, she was happy. She already considered the room that we had used as her nursery to be her bedroom and was no trouble at all. The physical work involved in packing was one thing. The emotional wrench was quite another. What to do with those wedding albums and Tom's things? I put no pressure on Laura either way.

'You don't have to decide now. Let's just pack everything and we can put it all in the loft. You can just unpack what you need.'

Then there was the need to explain the move to her mother. Laura wanted to have that particular conversation with Mrs Albury on her own, so I took Andrea to the park with a bag full of stale crusts to feed the ducks.

Andrea wouldn't eat crusts at that point, so the local ducks did quite well.

Laura returned tearful and angry. I put Andrea in front of the television and made Laura some tea as she sat at the kitchen table.

'What did she say?'

'Exactly what I knew she'd say. That there would be no going back once I'd made this decision. Why couldn't I just move in with her so that she could take care of us both? Did I have to move in with another man so soon? That I should be thinking about Andrea as well as myself. That I should be thinking about Tom before I gave up the flat, because it's his home too. Why does she have to say these things? She must know that I wouldn't make a decision like this without thinking about it!'

'She's your mother. It's what mothers do.'

'Is it? Or is it just what my mother does?'

'She only wants the best for you.'

'Then why can't she just say that? Why does she have to make it so difficult?'

There was a ring at the doorbell and Laura jumped up full of anticipation. My heart sank as I saw that she was hoping even then that Tom had come home. 'Shall I get that?' I asked as Laura wiped at her eyes.

Andrea was in the hall, keen to find out who the visitor was.

'Nana!' She took control as I opened the door to Mrs Albury.

'Have you got a kiss for me?' She bent down to the

level of Andrea's face before straightening up to her full height and looking me in the eye. 'Peter,' she said sternly, handing me her coat, and I saw that she was wearing a housecoat over her dress. 'I've come to help pack. My daughter shouldn't be doing any heavy work in her condition.'

'I'm sure she'll appreciate it.' I turned to hang her coat on the row of pegs in the hall that Tom had made. 'She's in the kitchen.'

'Mum,' I heard Laura say, simply.

'That's my girl,' Mrs Albury said, as softly as if she was talking to Andrea, 'My beautiful girl.'

I left them alone.

Laura went into labour three weeks before her due date. I dropped Andrea off with Mrs Albury and took her to the hospital. It was made quite clear that Laura didn't want me to be there for the birth. I felt a mixture of disappointment and relief.

The doctor was Chinese and seemed to have trouble understanding me. 'First baby?' he kept asking.

'Second baby,' I told him repeatedly.

I sat. I stood. I paced. I drank tea with powdered milk from a vending machine. I read and reread the same article from the *Telegraph*, unable to absorb anything. Eventually I slept, curled up on three armless chairs.

When I saw the doctor emerge every once in a while, I asked, 'How is she doing?'

'First baby often long labour.' He smiled. 'Not to worry. You go home. Sleep. Come back.'

'Second baby,' I told him, pointing to the floor. 'I'll stay.'

309

He shrugged. 'Maybe long-time. I go sleep.'

'Can I see her?

She was lying on her back, knees raised, moaning softly. Her eyes were closed and she had a few beads of sweat on her brow, which the midwife dabbed at with a damp flannel. Her hair was loose and darkened strands clung to her face.

'Are you the husband?' the midwife enquired and Laura asked instantly, 'Tom?'

'Shhh.' I leaned forwards. 'It's me. Pete.'

'Pete. How long has it been now?' She frowned, her eyes open.

'Eighteen hours.'

'What time is it?'

'Four thirty.'

'Morning or afternoon?'

'Afternoon.' I smiled. 'But it feels as if it could be the middle of the night. How are you doing?'

'Tired.'

'Do you want anything?'

She shook her head. 'Why don't you go and give Andrea her tea and tell her I sent you to give her a big hug from me.'

'Is that what you want me to do?' I stroked her forehead.

She nodded, closing her eyes and turning them away. I bent to kiss her. 'I'll be back later.'

Mrs Albury was naturally anxious for news when I knocked at her door.

'Nothing yet,' I told her. 'They say it could be some time.'

'How is she holding up?'

'She's tired. Half asleep.'

She nodded knowingly.

'What's normal for a second baby?' I asked.

'Everyone's different.' She shrugged. 'But the second one is usually easier than the first. It was certainly that way for me.'

'I had no idea it could go on this long.'

She looked at me dismissively. 'Why would you?'

'Laura wanted me to give Andrea her tea.'

She sniffed. 'Doesn't she think I'm up to the job?'

'I think she wanted to give me something to do to stop me making a nuisance of myself.'

'Have you eaten?'

'Not yet.'

'Think you can manage fish fingers, mash and peas for three?'

'I'll give it a go.'

'Andrea!' she shouted up the stairs. 'Your Uncle Peter's here.'

I heard the toilet flush and Andrea appeared at the top of the stairs, still straightening her clothes. I felt myself smiling, as I always did when I saw her.

'With Mummy?'

'Mummy's fine,' I called up to her. 'She asked me to come and get you some tea. You're going to stay here tonight with your nana. Won't that be nice?'

'Wash your hands,' Mrs Albury told her. 'We're having fish fingers.'

'Fish fingers,' Andrea began to chant. 'Fish fingers and

311

baked beans. Fish fingers and baked beans. Fish fingers and baked beans.'

'Do you have any baked beans?' I asked Mrs Albury.

'I think I'd better nip out and get some. Can you hold the fort? You can make a start on those spuds.'

The baby was born after another eighteen hours, just after 11.30 a.m. Laura had not slept for the best part of three days and was exhausted, but her expression was peaceful at last when I was invited to meet my son for the first time. He was pink and so long-bodied that it was difficult to believe he had fitted inside the curve of Laura's belly. I found the way that he curled up his frog-like legs close to his body almost miraculous. He was so small and precious that I felt clumsy holding him in my arms. In his curled position, he was no longer than the length of my two hands. With his legs stretched, he was almost the length of my forearm. He was a new life with ancient and animal-like qualities all at the same time. He was both ugly and perfect. I was fascinated by every movement he made; the way he yawned, the slight twitching of his closed eyes, the way his mouth moved instinctively before he had even suckled for the first time. When the midwife took him out of my arms to place him at his mother's breast, I felt his absence.

Laura smiled. 'You haven't said anything.'

'I'm speechless,' I admitted, sitting down heavily on the side of the bed. 'I've never felt anything like it before. Why didn't you warn me?'

'He's going to be a good father, this one.' The midwife winked at Laura before leaving the room. 'I can tell.

You've got two minutes then I'll be back,' she said to me. 'She needs to rest now.'

'You can't put it in words,' Laura said. 'You wouldn't have understood.'

'I know it's been really difficult recently but I'm so glad we got to share this.' I put one hand to her face and she moved to kiss it. I can honestly say now that it was the happiest moment of my life. I thought that it was the beginning of a journey. There is nothing like the birth of a child to give you hope and make you think of huge potential. I watched the person I loved the most look at our boy with such emotion reflected in her eyes. For a single moment, there were only the three of us in the world and it was all that mattered. If I had known what was to follow, I would have asked for five minutes more when the midwife returned. I would have kept on asking for an extra five minutes, just like Andrea at that age when she wanted to stretch each day to its limits.

'I'd better go and tell your mother that she has a grandson,' I said reluctantly.

'And Andrea that she has a brother.'

'What shall we call him?' I asked.

'What about Derek for your father?' Laura said.

I was so moved by the thought behind the suggestion that I didn't stop to think if it would be a blessing or a curse to name a child after a man who had experienced so little joy in his life.

Laura and Derek stayed in the hospital for ten days. Because Derek was premature, they wanted to monitor him and check his weight. Like all new babies, he lost almost a pound before he started putting on any weight but, medically, he seemed to be sound. It gave Laura the chance to regain her strength before she had to think about the juggling act that lay ahead of her. I returned to work, keen to be there for her when she and Derek came home. Andrea had an extended holiday with her grandmother but I visited her every day. All the talk of hospitals had confused her but she was perfectly happy once she had seen that her mother was well. She was uninterested in the new baby, unable to understand why another child was needed when her mother already had her. Her pout asked the question that she didn't know how to put into words: 'Wasn't I enough?'

Chapter Forty

'Shall we give him back now?' Andrea enquired after Laura and Derek had been home for a couple of days.

'Andrea, why don't you give your brother a nice kiss on his cheek?' Laura tried to encourage her. Andrea reluctantly bent down over him, grabbed his body and pecked him on the side of his head, pulling away as quickly as she could. 'Gently now! He's only little.'

'Will Daddy be coming to see Derek soon?' Andrea asked suddenly, this new thought lighting up her eyes.

Laura and I looked at each other. We hadn't even got to grips with the issue of how to refer to my relationship with Derek, let alone our new relationship.

'Darling, Daddy can't come home right now. He's very busy.'

'Why?'

'He has to work very hard.'

'Don't you have to work very hard, Uncle Pete?'

'Sometimes I have to work very hard. You remember when I was away from home for all those months, don't you?'

Laura had only been home for two days when she woke during the night with a fever. She shook me awake. 'Something's wrong,' she kept on repeating.

I propped myself up on my elbows and turned the bedside light on. She was feverish but shivering and I could see that the colour had drained from her face. 'I'm going hot and cold.'

'Shall I get you something? A drink, maybe,' I offered feebly.

'Pete, I'm not thirsty. I think I need to go to hospital.'

There's nothing like the 'h' word to make you wake up.

'I'll get dressed,' I said, pulling back the blankets. 'Do you want to put some clothes on?' As I turned to cover her again, I saw a large bloodstain on the sheets and more wet blood on my own pyjama bottoms. 'You're bleeding.'

'Call for an ambulance,' she said calmly and without surprise. 'Get the children up. You can drop them off at my mother's and then follow.'

'Should I . . . ?'

'Now, Pete,' she said firmly.

'Right.' I rushed to the phone and dialled 999. They used the word haemorrhaging when I described the bleeding and asked me if I knew her blood type in case she needed a transfusion.

'I don't know,' I stumbled, the seriousness of the situation dawning on me.

'Stay with her,' I was instructed. 'We'll be with you as soon as we can.'

I woke Andrea who was groggy with sleep and got her into her dressing gown and slippers, telling her that there was no need to be scared but that Mummy was not well and an ambulance would be coming to take her to hospital. I asked her to go and look out of the window and shout as soon as she saw it coming. I didn't want to frighten her but I couldn't risk her rushing to her mother's side and panicking at the sight of blood. With Derek slung over one shoulder howling, I went to see how Laura was faring, intending to help her into some clean clothes. She was barely conscious and murmuring. Not even Derek's cries roused her.

'Stay with me, Laura, they're on their way.' I tried to keep on talking to her, keeping the panic at bay, just as I had been instructed. 'Not long now. They'll have you fixed in no time.' Five minutes passed. Six. I was torn between watching for the ambulance myself and staying with her. I paced the room, patting little Derek's back, while keeping an eye on the figure in the bed who seemed to be fading. 'Any minute now,' I told her, checking my watch, each minute seeming like an eternity.

'They're here!' I heard Andrea shouting.

'That's a good girl.' I hurried down the stairs to open the front door. 'You stay there in the warm, then we'll go to Nana's in the car. Upstairs,' I told the ambulance crew as they pushed past me. 'First door on the left.'

I followed them up to find the first, a man, giving instructions for oxygen and a stretcher to be brought in. I could read little from his expression.

'How long ago was the baby born?' he asked.

'Twelve days.'

'First child?'

'Second child.'

'Any complications after the first?'

'None that I know of.'

'Maybe if you grab some clean clothes and wash things,' a lady suggested, although I got the distinct impression that she was giving me a job to keep me busy. 'Are you coming in the ambulance, Mr Albury?' She had assumed that I was Laura's husband.

'I'll follow in the car after I've dropped off the children at their grandmother's.'

'We'll move her now. Can you go downstairs and make sure there's nothing blocking our way. It'll be St Theresa's. We'll get her checked in right away, so she may have gone down to surgery when you arrive. She's lost a lot of blood.'

They were so quick and efficient that there was little for me to do. As I walked out to look at her in the back of the ambulance, they already had a drip in place. The doors were slammed shut and the driver turned the siren on.

'Right,' I said to myself, walking back to the front door, my mind a blank. 'Andrea! Are you ready to go?'

'Is Mummy all right?' She looked so small and frightened that my heart went out to her.

'Mummy's going to be fine, but she needs to go to hospital for some rest,' I told her. 'It's very hard work looking after a new baby. Have you got teddy with you?' I tried to distract her. She shook her head, wide-eyed.

318

'Well, run upstairs and get him and then we'll be off.'

I picked up the phone to Mrs Albury, judging that she might prefer to be warned of our imminent arrival. I didn't want to be outside in the middle of the night hammering on her front door with two children in tow. It rang for some time before she answered, 'Four-seven-three-six.'

'It's Peter Churcher,' I stumbled. 'Laura's had to go to hospital. I wondered if I could bring the children over.'

'Now?' she asked, half asleep.

'Now.'

'Is it serious?'

'She's haemorrhaging and has a fever,' I told her. 'They think she might need a blood transfusion. I don't know any more than that at the moment.'

'My poor Laura!' she exclaimed. 'You'd better come right over.'

'We're on our way.'

It was only once I had dropped the children off at their grandmother's, depositing Derek in Mrs Albury's arms, that I allowed myself a moment to cry. There was shock and a feeling of utter helplessness. The joy of the last few days had disintegrated. I didn't want to let my mind wander, but already my prayers were following the lines that I would be prepared to give up my son if only Laura could be all right. Although I had been over-whelmed by my feelings for Derek, I would have done anything in my power to help Laura. At that point in time it was only a prayer. The mere idea filled me with dread, but praying gave me strength and purpose. I felt that I had an element of control over the situation, no matter how small. It was enough to enable me to switch the engine on and drive.

There was another restless night of waiting before I was able to see Laura again and then she was only half conscious and delirious, hooked up to tubes and machinery.

'Are you her husband?' the nurse asked while checking the chart at the foot of her bed. 'She's been asking for Tom. "Find Tom," she keeps on saying. "Find Tom."'

I sat by her side. 'I'm here now, Laura. You're in good hands.' To the nurse, I explained, 'I'm Peter Churcher. How long will it be before she comes round?'

'That's a good question,' she said in the sort of kindly tone reserved for bad news. 'It's early days yet. She has an infection that is causing the fever. We'll know in the next twenty-four hours if the antibiotics are doing their job. But she's very weak from the loss of blood. I'll be keeping an extremely close eye on her.'

'Should I be worried?' I asked. 'What news should I tell her mother?'

'It's serious, my dear. Tell her to come and see her daughter.' She patted my arm gently. 'And I'd go and find this Tom if I were you.'

Chapter Forty-one

I knocked at Mrs Fellows's front door, determined but already on the defensive. I could hear her heavy footsteps as she came down the stairs.

'Oh, for God's sake,' she muttered with distaste as she opened the door a crack and then closed it. Through the frosted-glass panel, I could still see her shadowy outline, so I knew that she had not retreated far.

'Mrs Fellows, I really need to find Tom,' I called through the letter box. 'Laura is seriously ill in hospital and she's asking for him.'

'It's a bit late for that now,' she replied.

'I know how you must feel but please don't turn me away,' I begged her. 'I don't know if Laura's going to make it or not.' It was as if the situation became more real when I said those words out loud. I was still bent over and leaning against the door when it opened inwards.

'I don't know if Tom's going to make it or not,' she said softly. 'You'd better come in.'

Over a cup of tea, she told me that Tom had suffered

what she could only describe as a complete nervous breakdown. It didn't make comfortable listening. Even if she had insisted, 'Peter, you're not to blame,' I wouldn't have believed her. She did no such thing. There was anger in her voice as she told me that some weeks earlier, Tom had been delivered home by a man who called himself Surly. Surly was a publican who had heard Tom busking on a couple of occasions, recognized his talent and hired him. When he found out that Tom was sleeping rough, he gave him a room over the pub as part of his salary. In a matter of weeks, Tom reversed the flagging fortunes of the business. It was a large Victorian building near Clapham Common, too large for the few locals who enjoyed a quick pint on their way home from work. Tom pulled in a young crowd who had money to spend and stayed all night. As they thought they got to know him, they started to ask for requests. They wanted cover versions rather than Tom's music. 'We Are the Champions' by Queen, 'Hotel California' by the Eagles, 'Wonderful Tonight' by Eric Clapton, 'Dancing in the Moonlight' by Thin Lizzy. He gave them what they wanted but his heart wasn't in it. The landlord noticed the change in him. Apparently Tom got abusive when he thought that the requests turned into mickey taking. Surly had to step in once when some clown asked for 'Angelo' by the Brotherhood of Man and things turned nasty. Instead of putting the crowds off, Tom's reputation grew. Everybody wanted to see this unpredictable talent – and unfortunately everyone wanted to bait him to see what would push him over the edge. Surly became concerned by his mood swings. Even though he hadn't known Tom for long, he thought that he had the measure of him and knew it was out of character. Then, for days, Tom wouldn't get out of bed at all. Surly tried unsuccessfully to persuade him to eat. He offered to call him a doctor. He was a reasonable man but he was no saint. He knew that he had a liability on his hands. Tom could have had a serious drug problem for all he knew and that was something he couldn't have going on under his roof. He had his licence to think of. To him, it seemed obvious why his discovery had been busking down the Underground and sleeping under bridges. Even after he had paid him, Tom never seemed to have any money. Of course, I knew that he had been sending whatever he earned home to Laura and Andrea, but I could understand how it must have appeared. To top it all, a man in a suit started to turn up week after week looking for him and wouldn't take no for an answer. When Tom asked Surly to lie for him, he thought that Tom was in serious trouble. He did the only thing he knew how to do; he moved the problem to someone else's doorstep. He drove Tom all the way home to his mother, who was now living in fear of every knock on the door.

'There won't be a knock at the door,' I said. 'The man in the suit was me.'

'You?' she asked disbelievingly.

'I spent weeks trying to find him. I thought I might be able to persuade him to come home.'

'Wasn't it a bit late for that?'

'I owed him that much.' I shook my head. 'Has he said anything?'

'Nothing I can make any sense of. He won't even let me call a doctor. Says he'll disappear again if I try. But I don't know how long I can watch him go on like this.'

We sat in silence for a short while, both staring at our mugs of tea.

Eventually Mrs Fellows said, 'He told me once that he stole Laura away from you and that he didn't deserve you as a friend. Well, the tables have well and truly turned now. You've got a lot of making up to do.'

I nodded. 'Is he here?'

'Not in the house.' She shook her head. 'He didn't want to risk being seen. He's been living in the shed these last few weeks.'

'Can I see him?'

'Don't expect too much,' she sighed. 'He's a changed man. If you're lucky, he might not even recognize you.'

We walked in silence down the long garden, Mrs Fellows leading with a torch. As we approached, I could see a glow through the window and hear guitar chords. Not the expert playing that I had been used to, but random chords. It sounded as if the instrument was under attack.

'Tom!' Mrs Fellows called out in an overly cheerful voice. 'You've got a visitor. Pete's here to see you.'

The playing stopped and there was a scuffling movement inside.

'Be my guest,' she said to me, gesturing inside. 'You're on your own from here.'

The band's van was still parked at the side of the garage, just as it had always been. There were signs of life. Plates and cups littered the workbenches. An ashtray. The sofa was draped with clothes. It was not an uncomfortable living space and an obvious hideaway. I was surprised that I hadn't thought to look here before. Where else would Tom have gone? I sat on the sofa and waited, looking towards the doors at the back of the van. Whenever it was not in use, the van had always had a double mattress in the back. It had seen an extraordinary amount of use when we had been in our early twenties. It was now Tom's bedroom. I heard the occasional small movement, enough to make me think that he was listening. It was easier to explain why I had come to see him without having to look him in the eye.

'I know you don't want to see me, Tom,' I started, without knowing if he could actually understand me. 'But I had to find you. Laura's in hospital. She's very unwell and she's asking for you. I know this is a bad time for you, but I wouldn't be able to forgive myself if I didn't try.'

There was silence.

'I don't know if she's going to make it, Tom. Will you come with me to see her?'

Still no reply. I tried a different approach.

'Andrea's fine, Tom. She's with Laura's mum. She's missing you so much. Keeps asking when you'll be home. She needs you too.'

I heard some more movement and then the opening chords of 'Andrea's Song', unmistakable but played clumsily, as if he was having difficulty remembering the tune.

'Laura had a baby boy twelve days ago. He was premature. We called him Derek.' Silence again. I didn't know if he was listening or covering his ears to block out the words. 'They had only been home for two days when she was taken ill. There was a lot of blood. She was barely conscious. I had to call an ambulance. I watched them take her away. I couldn't leave the children. They rushed her straight into surgery.'

There was no reaction.

'Are you getting all this?' I was suddenly angry. 'I tried to find you, Tom. I tried to find you for weeks. We didn't want it to be like this . . .' I ran out of steam.

'What makes you think I wanted to see you?' a small voice said.

I stood up, almost laughing with joy. He was looking out of one of the two square windows in the doors at the back of the van. I couldn't see him very clearly in the dark, but I could see the outline of his head and whites of his eyes. The most obvious difference was that his silhouette was altered. He had shaved his head.

'I'm pretty sure you don't want to see me, but Laura wants to see you. Even when she's unconscious and doesn't know what she's saying, it's you that she's asking for. She was never in love with me.' Suddenly, it struck me that I was telling the truth. Laura loved me but she was never in love with me. It hurt to say it out loud. 'It was always supposed to be you and her.'

'I was never enough for her. She always wanted something more.'

'No, Tom! Laura's just in love with life. She gets one thing and she's on to the next. It's hard to keep up at times, I'll admit. Come and see her, Tom. She'll put up a fight once she knows you're there.'

'I can't cope with the baby.'

'You won't have to.'

'I can't do that.' His voice was small and child-like, but he was adamant. 'I don't want him near me.'

'I give you my word.' I still have no idea what I was thinking of when I said that. At the time, I just wanted Tom to agree to come with me to see Laura. What would happen after that was too much to think about.

I heard the rattle of the door and he appeared, legs first. If he had looked gaunt when he was studying late into the night, he now looked almost skeletal, his shirt and jeans hanging off him. With his head shaven and hunched over his shoulders, he also looked shorter. As he came closer, I noticed the dark circles under his hollow eyes against the paleness of his skin. His head had been shaved unevenly at the sides and back, as if he had done it himself. He shivered visibly, although it was not particularly cold.

'When's the last time you've been outside?' I asked, looking round for something warmer for him to wear. I found his leather jacket on the sofa, the Spearheads' slogan on the back. 'Here. Put this on.' I held it out to him, but I had to help him into it. It seemed to weigh him down and swamp him, making him look smaller still. One thing was for sure. If Laura saw him and wanted him to stay, it wouldn't be for his looks.

'Are you ready?' I asked him and turned in the direction of the house.

'Not that way,' he said, grabbing my arm with remarkable strength. 'Not through the house. You remember the way.'

We walked along the alley that led around the back of the houses in the darkness.

'Like the old days,' he said, his hands buried deep in his jacket pockets.

'Just like the old days,' I repeated, feeling older by the minute.

We drove to the hospital in silence. I was aware of Tom flinching at car headlights, squinting to avoid the glare. I felt his animal presence, his unpredictability. He was like Tom, but also far removed from the Tom that I had known. I wondered if Laura would recognize him if she woke up or if she would be frightened at the sight of this stranger.

I parked and put the handbrake on.

'We're here,' I said.

'It's just us?' he asked, looking full of doubt. 'No one else is going to be there?'

'Just us.'

It was still very early and the hospital was silent. As we walked along the maze of antiseptic corridors, my footsteps echoing, Tom's brushing as he dragged his feet, I had a growing sense of unreality. All of the elation of the last couple of weeks, the shock of the previous night and the mixed emotions at finding Tom warred against each other.

Here was the woman that I loved, lying unconscious in a hospital bed, linked up to numerous machines that flashed and bleeped, administering the medicines that might save her, pumping the clean blood around her body. A clear tube protruded from her nose. A needle was inserted in her hand, held in place by tape. A cold flannel was placed over her forehead, her blonde hair dulled by the dampness.

Here was the man that she loved – that we both loved – moved to tears by the sight of her, leaning over her, stroking her hair, talking to her softly, changed and yet the same.

'What have you done to yourself?' he asked.

There were so many questions I wanted to know the answer to. What had Laura done to herself? What had we all done to ourselves? What on earth had we done to each other? What had I put Tom through?

A nurse asked, 'Are you the husband?'

Tom looked confused and turned to me for an answer.

'Are you Tom Fellows?' she tried again.

Tom nodded, not letting go of Laura's hand.

'No wonder,' the nurse whispered to me, putting her hand on my shoulder, thinking that she understood everything, before she left the room.

'Is she any better?' I asked.

'She's stable. Early days yet. Don't expect too much.'

329

I understood nothing, other than the desire to make everything all right. To take us back to a time when everything was simple and there was everything to look forward to. It seemed very clear that this was up to me. Although I had no faith to speak of, I repeated my prayer that, if only Laura would live, I would do whatever was necessary to make things right. Then I went to telephone the only person in the world who I knew would understand how I was feeling: my old adversary, Faye.

'What time of the morning do you call this?' she snapped down the phone, even before she knew it was me.

'Faye!' I said with relief at the sound of her familiar voice.

'I might have known it would be you, Peter Churcher. Just because you're up all night with the new baby doesn't mean the rest of us don't like our sleep.'

I tried to sound calm. 'Faye, you need to come home.'

'I've told you already. You may find Derek fascinating, but I'll wait until he can do something a bit more interesting than eat, sleep and scream before I come to see him.'

'It's not Derek you need to see. It's Laura. She's in hospital.'

'Laura? What's wrong with her?'

I explained to her about the trip to hospital and the uncertain prognosis. About finding Tom. I told her about Tom's breakdown. I told her that I had left Tom with Laura and that it would all get a lot more complicated in the next few hours once we knew if she was going to make it. I asked her for help. No, I begged her for help to make things right again.

'Have a bit of sensitivity, for goodness' sake, that's my sister you're talking about. Give me a few minutes at least to catch up. Have you really thought this through? Aren't you getting a bit ahead of yourself?'

'I don't think so. Believe me, I wouldn't even be considering this if I didn't think it was necessary. You come and see for yourself and tell me that you don't think Tom'll walk unless I make it possible for him to stay. He left once before. I think he'll do it again.'

'One step at a time. I'm going to get dressed and then I'll get on a train. I'll come straight to the hospital to see Laura, but it will be lunchtime at least, maybe later. Keep an eye on her for me until then. And, Peter Churcher . . .' she said.

'What's that?'

'Don't you dare screw things up before I get there.'

Chapter Forty-two

Tom,' I said quietly, 'I'm going to see Laura's mother and the children now.'

'I'm staying,' he replied, not moving his gaze from her face.

I envied him the luxury of not having to deal with other people.

'Shall I tell your mother where you are?' I asked.

There was no reply.

'I'll go and see your mother on the way.'

I looked at Laura over his shoulder and heard myself breathe inwards and outwards loudly. I wanted to say something to her or to touch her hair but I felt awkward in front of Tom. Every time I said goodbye, there was a possibility that it was for the last time. Instead I put one hand on his shoulder. 'There will be other people here later,' I told him. 'I won't be able to keep Mrs Albury away and Faye is on her way from London.'

'I'm staying,' he repeated, not taking his eyes off Laura for one moment.

I drove to see Mrs Fellows first. Strange as it might

seem, I thought that she would be the more worried of the two mothers. For Tom to disappear in his condition would have alarmed her and I was concerned that she might have called the police. I was right. She had found that he was missing when she went to take him breakfast and was already distressed.

'How's Laura?' she asked for the first time after I had assured her of his safety.

'I'm sure that having Tom there will make all the difference,' I said, only then aware that I was placing a great deal of confidence in his ability to bring her round. 'I'll bring him home when he's ready.'

'I must go and see her,' she said suddenly, as if she had only just realized that she should. I was sure that what she wanted to do was keep an eye on her own son as he watched over his wife.

Mrs Fellows grabbed my arm as I turned to leave. 'How did he seem to you?' She was desperate for another opinion.

'He's still Tom,' I replied, not sure what to else to say. 'He's still in there.'

Mrs Fellow seemed satisfied with this. 'Yes, he is,' she said.

Mrs Albury, on the other hand, was less than satisfied with my report about her daughter's condition. She wanted facts and figures and I had none to give her.

'When will they know?' she demanded.

'They say it's too early to say more.'

'And you were happy with that?' she spat at me, wasting no time in buttoning her coat and readying herself to leave. 'Mark my words, I'll get more out of them than that. You stay here with the children,' she commanded unnecessarily. 'I'll be back later.' It was clear that she now thought that their place was with her. I was the babysitter rather than the father-figure. It was only after she'd left that I realized I had not warned her about Tom. The thought of the scene that would follow cheered me up immensely. I put the kettle on and went to rouse the children. After her night-time adventure, Andrea had slept later than usual and was tearful to find that she was not at home with her mother and all of her things.

'I want Mummy,' she wailed.

'Me too.' I kissed her, mixing her tears with my own. 'Me too.' She suited my mood; she could express all the injustice that I felt. I gathered her up in the bedclothes from her makeshift bed and deposited her on the sofa in the living room, where we sat and clung to each other like lost souls until Derek made his presence known.

'Shall we get him up?' I asked her, her face close by.

'No.' She shook her head, pouting.

'Don't you like having a little brother?'

She shook her head again, fiercely. 'No.'

'Do you think you might get to like him?'

More shaking followed.

'Is that because you like having your mummy all to yourself?'

'Yes!' she declared, covering her head with blankets and grinning at last.

I left her and went to find Derek. The wailing led me

to Mrs Albury's room, where he was lying in a drawer that had been pulled out of a chest, wrapped in woollens.

'What has the nasty old lady done to you?' I laughed at the sight of him fighting fiercely with the sleeve of a cardigan. I picked him up and held him as I sat on the bed, tears welling up in my eyes. 'It seems like nobody wants you,' I told him. 'Shall we run away together, you and me? Hey? Shall we go somewhere no one can find us?' As attractive as this prospect sounded, I knew that it was the one option I couldn't consider. So I sang to him the only childhood song I could think of: 'Row, row, row your boat, gently down the stream. Merrily, merrily, merrily, merrily, life is but a dream.'

Part Twelve

Andrea's Story

Chapter Forty-three

'There's something I need to tell you,' Nana said busily as she bustled past me into the hallway, looking behind her for fear that she might have been followed. 'We might not have much time. She's not going to stop me this time.'

'Hello, Nana. Are you on your own?' I asked, looking out of the door for clues: Aunty Faye's car; a waiting taxi perhaps? Nothing.

'Shut the door, child!' she commanded, already in the kitchen and putting the kettle on. 'Sit yourself down.'

I did as I was told. She sat too and held on to both of my hands, looking me straight in the eyes. It was what she used to do when I was little and she wanted me to listen. She had tried to teach my mother the same trick. It was her opinion that I needed to be made to sit still and concentrate if there was something important to be said, otherwise there was a distinct danger that it could go straight in one ear and out of the other.

'I'm listening, Nana,' I said, trying to stifle my growing amusement in the face of her seriousness.

'I know you are,' she said. 'I'm still trying to work out where to begin. You see, you think that you're all alone in the world, but you need to know that you're not. This is going to come as a shock, but Laura and Tom weren't your biological parents.'

'They were the only parents that were ever important to me.' I smiled back at her, unflinching.

'You know?' She looked shocked at my lack of surprise. 'How could you know?'

I went to a drawer in the kitchen and took out the results of my scribblings, placing them in front of her. I had been able to bring myself to write my name back into the picture under an entry for Faye Albury and Peter Churcher. The page was covered with crossings out and arrows. It was messy, it was complicated and the result was as confused as I felt. In that way, it was an accurate reflection of my family. I made no apologies for it. 'I started looking into our family tree a few weeks ago and this is what I found. I suppose it's been staring me in the face all these years, but I didn't see it.'

She pushed her glasses up her nose and studied the end result, nodding, then she sat back in her chair. 'Well, if you know, why the devil haven't you done anything about it? This is family we're talking about, for goodness' sake! We've got to stick together. Especially at a time like this.'

'Nana, what is there to be done?' I tried to stay calm in the face of her outrage. 'I'm fairly sure that Uncle Pete had absolutely no idea about it. At least not until recently. And if that's the case, then Aunty Faye must

340

have had a very good reason for not telling him. Maybe there comes a point when it's just too late to tell someone something like that. "Peter, I've been meaning to bring this up for the last twenty-five years, but Andrea's your daughter." '

'So, you think that your Uncle Peter knows?'

'I think that he started to suspect at round about the same time as I did, but I have no idea if he knows for certain. When did you find out?'

'Me? I've known from the very beginning. From the moment I first held you in my arms. You were the spitting image of Faye as a baby. I did the maths. And Laura just wasn't as natural with you as she should have been. It was obvious.'

'And Uncle Pete?'

'You have his chin.' She touched my face. 'Faye wasn't one to admit it but she always had a soft spot for him. It seemed unfair that Laura had so many admirers when Faye was so stylish and intelligent and downright feisty.' She said this with some pride. 'I think she frightened men off. Too much of a challenge by half! I always liked Peter myself. He looked out for my girls and he never shirked from his responsibilities. That's how I knew that he didn't know about you. He would have married Faye if she had told him. It's obvious that she didn't tell him because she didn't want him to.'

'What did my parents tell you about me?'

'Tell me?' She laughed bitterly. 'Do you think they told me anything? They took me for a fool. We did what all good families do. We told each other nice lies and played our parts well. Apart from Faye. She struggled. I never asked Faye why she didn't come home for years after you were born because I didn't have to. It was obvious that it was just too painful for her. She was never going to be able to slip into the role of your aunt very easily. I waited for her to come to talk to me about it. I waited for years. I've had to watch her punishing herself, wasting half of her life. And for what? To keep a secret that it seems everyone knows. I don't know why they made the decisions they did about you. In the end they probably chose the most difficult option. But I'm proud of them for looking after each other. And, unlike your brother, I'm so glad that we were able to keep you in the family. If you had been taken in by anyone else, I might never have got to know you. But if the girls had asked for my advice at the time, it's not what I would have recommended. So, there you go. What does that tell you? Your nana's not always right.'

I thought about the perception that Laura was Nana's favourite daughter, the one she understood the most. It wasn't true. Nana had been waiting to help her younger daughter. It's hard to help someone when they don't think they need you.

And I thought about the idea of what is right. Often, there is no right. There is just a decision that needs to be made and then we all have to make it work or live with the consequences.

'So, what are you going to do about it?' she demanded.

'I'm not going to suddenly start calling them Mum and Dad. I had the most fantastic parents I could have asked for. Now they're gone, and I don't want to replace them.'

'You think you're all grown up and you won't need parents any more? You wait until you've got a family of your own. You'll need all the help you can get. You can't rely on me being around then.' She shook her head and folded her arms. 'Oh no! I'm on my last legs as it is.'

'I only said I don't want to replace them!' I raised my voice unintentionally. 'I know I've got family around me. And there's nothing wrong with your legs. In fact there's not a lot wrong with you at all, is there?'

'That's the spirit!' she said.

What I couldn't tell Nana with her stiff-upper-lip, the-truth-will-set-us-free attitude is that I had a very strong sense that both of my parents – my biological parents – were just about holding together the threads of their lives. If confronted, I worried that the delicate balance would be destroyed. I was no more ready to stop being Andrea Fellows than I had been to stop being my daddy's little girl. I told myself that I must learn to let other people be who they are, to give them time and space. I thought that Uncle Pete and I would be able to adjust to our new relationship, but I was more worried about my aunt. I couldn't have that conversation until I knew if I could deal with her rejecting me for a second time. Because that was also a possibility. I wanted to hear my story – and theirs too – but by the same token I worried that it would change me. I tried to convince myself that I would be more than content to be part of an extraordinary extended family.

'I suppose I should tell you about Uncle Pete's plan,' I said exasperatedly. 'I'm not supposed to yet, but maybe you'll understand why I'm not in as much of a rush as you.'

'The little devil!' she said after I had finished, her eyes bright. 'So I can come home?'

I nodded. 'Do you think we should agree to go ahead before we know if Aunty Faye and Uncle Pete have had it out? Isn't it possible that they might never speak again?'

'Have you no faith in me?' She twinkled at me. 'I won't let that happen. They're adults, and as adults we all have to face difficult truths sometimes. Mark my words, we'll find a way of making this work.'

As she was leaving she turned to me, almost as an afterthought, and held my hands in hers once again. I looked at her raised veins and the loose skin around her fragile wrists, mottled with liver spots. She might not have been on her last legs, but she was getting older. I could understand her desire to make things right with her family, so that they would all look after each other when she was gone. 'And what about your little brother? Have you managed to find anything out about him?'

It was then that her earlier words struck me. *Unlike your brother.* Did she think that he might be alive too?

'Not yet, Nana. I'm still working on it. Is there anything you can tell me that might help?'

'They told me he died,' she said.

'He was stillborn,' I repeated what I had been told.

'Not stillborn, no. He was premature. I was told that he died when he was about two weeks old. I didn't see the body. That was my choice, I admit, but I never quite believed that he was dead. And more and more over the years I've had this feeling that he's out there. It's probably just the foolish thoughts of an old woman.' Nana smiled and put her hand to my face. 'You're my beautiful girl and you've got a good head on your shoulders. Don't forget it. If you've inherited that much from my two girls, you'll do well in the world.'

Part Thirteen

Faye's Story

Chapter Forty-four

After Peter Churcher's dawn call and my initial decisive-
ness, the journey home gave me time to reflect. Peter
could be very persuasive; that was his job for goodness'
sake. He was an expert in the art of making you think
exactly how he wanted you to and he had a very strong
conviction that he thought he knew what was best for
everyone concerned. His plan involved removing himself and Derek from the picture completely so that
everything could return to 'normal'. In my opinion, this
seemed naive at best. What was 'normal'? From what
Laura had told me, I wasn't sure that there had ever
been a time when there hadn't been a third person in
her marriage. It also assumed that it was possible to turn
back the clocks and that everyone could conveniently
forget. And yet, at the same time, there was some sense
to it. Peter was motivated by the need to make things
right by Tom and, in doing so, he thought he could put
the family back together. I would understand, he told
me, when I saw Tom for myself. But, of course, Peter had
no idea what he was asking of me. He didn't know

when he asked me to help him deceive my sister that I had given away my own daughter – his daughter – and was already living a lie. He didn't know about my recent misgivings after Laura had told me of Peter's desire to be a father. And he couldn't have known that I didn't want him to bring up Andrea in Tom's place. I was aware that part of this feeling was born out of a childish and selfish sense of injustice. 'If I can't have her then you're not going to.' But I believe that we ignore these feelings at our peril. I had no doubt that if Laura and Peter were together in the long term, I would have had to cut off my relationship with both my sister and my daughter altogether. When Peter told me that I was a good sister, under the impression I wanted to protect Laura and her family, he had no idea what he was saying. I felt I was being anything but a good sister. There was a part of me, however small, that would have liked to say to Laura, 'There! We have both lost a child. Now you might understand how I feel!' Who was it who said that there are no unselfish acts in this world?

I suppose it was the one opportunity that I have had over the years to come clean with Peter and tell him that he is Andrea's father. Although his belief in Tom was such that he refused to accept the possibility that Laura might die, I wondered if we should have waited to see if Laura would pull through. With Tom so ill and no formal adoption ever having taken place, it would have fallen quite naturally on Peter to take care of Andrea and then it would have been possible to keep the children together. Part of me had this romantic notion that I might have had a role to play. But how would Peter react to the news that he had been lied to for four years by the people that he thought of as his closest friends? It seemed possible that he would want nothing to do with the lot of us, which, I suppose, would have been a solution in itself. And possibly one that might have cost him less in terms of sacrifice. And did I really want to change my life so dramatically or did I just like the idea of having a family of my own? And so I took the coward's option of keeping quiet. Just as I would probably have taken the coward's option and told Laura none of this if I had had the opportunity to see her one last time. The question that bothers me now is the same question that bothered me then. Would I have been forgiven? And not knowing is one of the things that makes it so difficult for me to grieve for Laura now. We were not the close sisters that everyone thought we were. We were not even as close as she thought we were. I deliberately dipped in and out of her life. In a way, I dipped in and out of my own life. I see that now. Maybe the question that I actually need to ask is can I forgive myself?

I found solace in the fact that Peter Churcher, who had loved my sister from the start, found himself capable of so great a deception. Although he had convinced himself that it was the right thing to do, it involved breaking the law and lying. Perhaps the only difference for him was that he then intended to remove himself from the situation permanently, a luxury that family members cannot lay claim to. Although my own motives were not entirely pure, I had no doubt that his were.

I simply asked, 'Have you really thought this through?'

'I've racked my brains and this is the answer I keep coming back to. It's the only way.' I could hear how painful it was for him.

'If you honestly believe that, I'll help you. Do you think we can pull it off?'

'Oh, yes,' he said sadly, almost as if he would have liked to be caught out, 'everything's in place. You don't need to worry on that count.'

'I take it the less I know the better.'

'You're a good sister, Faye.'

'Let's not go that far. And, Peter Churcher, don't you dare screw things up before I get there.'

Part Fourteen

Peter's Story

Chapter Forty-five

It was the hardest thing I've ever had to do. Far harder than learning to understand my father. Far harder than admitting to the woman you love that you have slept with her sister. Harder than giving Laura away on her wedding day and pretending to be happy for Tom. Harder even than leaving. Some things are made easier by the knowledge that what you are doing is right. Not this. I'm sure that some people would consider me very cruel. Watching Tom sit by Laura's bed, patchy stubble growing back (his hair would never grow back as it was before), his face unshaven, his eyes blinking under the hospital lights, I knew what had to be done. I had to put the family that I had pulled apart back together. It was to be a painful process for all of us.

In my line of business, I've met the good, the bad and the downright nasty. I called in a few favours. And quickly – I had no time to waste. Faye owed me no such favours, but despite her absence in recent years, she was as close to Laura as any two sisters are. What we were about to do was not the sort of thing that you could admit to after the event. I had taken a huge gamble by asking her. If she hadn't agreed to help me, I'm not sure that I could have relied on her discretion. With the help of some of the keenest craftsmen in the land and their imaginative paperwork, I prepared to give Derek up for adoption, with Faye posing as an unmarried Laura and skilfully forging her signature. Laura was so recognizable in her home town that I chose an adoption agency in Newcastle where, up until a few short weeks beforehand, I had been resident, nurturing a reputation as a solicitor who could be trusted. My instincts led me to an agency that professed to have a strong Christian ethos. Even though I had no strong beliefs, I wanted to ensure that Derek ended up in the safest possible hands. Whilst there were no guarantees, I felt comforted by the idea that he would be placed with a couple with strong family values.

We were required to appear before the adoption board, one of whom had consulted my firm on a family matter and recognized me on sight. He was joined by a white-haired lady whose spectacles kept on sliding down her nose, giving her an appearance of disapproval. The final member of the board was a younger lady with a more kindly looking disposition.

'Mr Churcher.' The gentleman greeted me with a curt handshake. 'We've met before.'

'I hope this doesn't place you in a difficult situation,' I said.

'Perhaps you'll both be so good as to take a seat while I check with my colleagues.'

They huddled outside the door and spoke in low tones. Their body language was neutral. I glanced at Faye and saw her exhale deliberately, trying to keep her nerves at bay. I wiped the palms of my hands on my suit trousers.

'Sorry to have kept you,' he said on his return as they took their seats opposite us. 'I've explained how we know each other and we can't see any reason not to proceed.'

Maybe there was less checking of paperwork than there might have been otherwise. I can't say, never having been in that situation before.

'Perhaps you can tell us what brings you here today?' the lady in spectacles asked, looking from one of us to the other.

Faye cleared her throat. 'Derek was the result of a one-night stand,' she said frostily. 'We hadn't met before and there is no relationship between us to speak of. I hadn't planned to be a mother and I'm in no position to bring up a child on my own.'

'Financially?'

'Financially, emotionally. You name it, really.' Her arms were folded tightly over her chest, but it wasn't enough to contain her shaking.

'There's no going back once you've taken this step,' the younger lady said. 'It's important that you realize that. You will leave here without Derek today and you won't be allowed contact with him again.'

I avoided looking at my son. I couldn't trust myself. I tried not to think about all of those uncertain couples who would have caved in at that stage in the process.

For a while, there seemed to be concern that we had not decided to have Derek adopted until after his birth. This was quite unusual in their experience. There was whispered conferring and an exchange of notes as Faye described how, early in the pregnancy, I persuaded her that she would have my full support if she had the child, but that I seemed to change my mind after she felt it was too late to consider the alternatives.

'He had a change of heart when reality hit him,' she said. 'I had let myself believe that things would change when I saw the baby. But he didn't even get in contact after I wrote to him to tell him that Derek had been born. Can you imagine not wanting to see your own son?' She brought her hand up to her mouth and stifled a sob. 'I'm sorry,' she faltered and the younger lady stepped forward offering a box of tissues. I tried to fix my face in the type of stare that I thought would suggest that I was being subjected to emotional blackmail.

'I offered an appropriate level of financial support,' I cut in. 'You chose to have the baby. It was your decision. I made my feelings on the subject perfectly clear, but you only heard what you wanted to hear.'

When Faye spoke again it was to the board and not to me. 'It's not just a question of financial support. He can't give me what I need. The truth is,' she blurted out, 'he won't tell you this, but he's been in love with someone else all along. He doesn't want to jeopardize that, so he will never admit publicly to being Derek's father.'

All the while I avoided the direct gaze of my client, but I could feel his eyes on me as if to question how I was qualified to deal with issues of family law.

'No!' Faye commanded herself to maintain an element of control. 'Although I thank God that I chose to have Derek, I feel foolish to have been taken in by that man and his promises. I've always believed in family and Derek is entitled to one of his own. A real family. I'm not in a position to give him the home and the life that he deserves. I hope that you can see that I want what's best for him.'

She was so good that I found myself wanting to tell her that I would make a greater effort and do more to help. Instead I fixed my expression in an angry gaze. The panel reached the conclusion that our relationship was so strained that, even though my income would allow Faye and Derek to live comfortably, it would create an unhealthy atmosphere for a child. It was clear that we could not get on. Papers were drawn up and signed. I gave away my son. The only son I am ever likely to have. When we were asked if we wanted to say goodbye to Derek for the last time, Faye agreed and clung to him tearfully, telling him how he would have a better life than she could ever offer him. I declined and left the two of them without a single word, under the harsh gaze of my client who clearly thought I was unfeeling. I heard one of the women say to Faye, 'You've done the right thing. The boy will go to a family who desperately want a child. He'll have a new name, a new start. It's for the best.' I prayed to God that it was so.

Faye was still crying when she left the building. We held each other for a moment.

'You were very convincing in there,' I told her.

'Yes, well, it looks as if I succeeded in convincing myself.' She shuddered. 'Those acting classes must have been better than I thought. Is that it?'

Yes, I thought to myself, that really is it. Derek was gone and my reputation in ruins. It seemed fitting that I should receive some form of divine retribution for deceiving the well-meaning folks of the adoption board. If my career was to suffer, so be it. Work was very low on my list of priorities. Many times since, it has struck me that if I had had the opportunity to cross-examine us, I would have asked some far more probing questions and given us a much harder time. But more than that: I have to ask what did they see in the two of us that made them decide we would be unsuitable parents?

With a falsified death certificate, we then broke the news to Mrs Albury. I had no problem putting on a convincing act myself. The pain, the tears and the grief were real. The explanation I gave was cot death. I have found from experience that people do not ask too many questions when a baby dies, particularly one who was premature. They jump to their own conclusions.

'It wasn't meant to be,' Mrs Albury repeated over and over again, patting my back. 'The poor little mite.' But I could tell that she was distracted, presumably by the thought of how we would break the news to Laura when she woke, and how this would affect her recovery.

'Do you think that I should wait before making the arrangements until . . . ?' I asked Laura's mother.

'No, dear,' she replied, her eyes full. 'You go ahead. We have no idea how Laura's going to be when she comes round. I hope you won't mind if I give it a miss. The girls don't know this, but I lost a child at a similar age the year between them. We chose not to have a service. But you must do what you think is best.'

I was both surprised and relieved. Although I had researched how to stage a fake funeral, it was the part that I would have been least comfortable with. It seemed strangely out of character for Mrs Albury, who liked to be in charge of every aspect of her family's lives. I could only presume that her focus was on the living and that she felt there was nothing more she could do for poor Derek. The Alburys were not a religious family and it seemed that she considered a funeral to be a formality that she could take or leave. My parents certainly would have felt they had a duty to go, putting personal feelings aside. There was no one else I had to consider. Although there was relief, it also dawned on me how alone I was. Other than Laura and Tom, and with my mother unable to leave the Home, I had no close friends or family. They were my whole life.

I went through the motions of selecting a small plot in a memorial garden and having a small granite stone engraved, hoping that this might bring Laura some comfort in the years to come and, at the same time, praying that it would not bring Derek bad luck. I was sufficiently superstitious that I took care not to lie when choosing the wording, referring not to his death, but the joy he brought us – however brief.

'No dates?' the stonemason asked. 'It's customary to have the dates.'

'No dates.' I was adamant.

In keeping with the other children's plots, I placed some of the toys that we had bought him there. Weeks later, when I took Mrs Albury and Faye to show them the plot, it was the sight of those damp and faded toys that Mrs Albury seemed to find the most distressing. I have visited many times over the years when I think of Derek as I find that I feel closest to him there.

Despite Andrea's reluctance to accept a little brother, I was surprised by her lack of questions at his disappearance. Her verdict was that now that the baby who had been so much hard work had gone, her mummy could get better and come home. There was some logic in this, however warped it might seem to an adult mind, and I clung to the hope that she was right.

The three of us took turns to stand sentry at Laura's bedside in eight-hour shifts, Mrs Albury, Faye and I. At the first shift after my return from Newcastle, I told the staff nurse in Tom's hearing that we had lost Derek. Outwardly, Tom seemed to react very little, although he blinked several times rapidly and his eyes darted about. The nurse, still confused about the relationship between Laura, Tom and me, reached out to both of us with a heavy hand, unsure which of us to offer her condolences to.

'Well then, we'll have to make sure we look after this

one for you. But it's going to come as quite a blow to her when she comes to. Are you going to tell her?' She addressed her question to me and I nodded my response.

'Telling's always hard. I've had to do it as part of my job for years and it never gets any easier. But you'll find the right words when the time comes.'

Mrs Albury had decided that Andrea should not see her mother as she was too young to understand what was happening. I question if this was the right decision, as to have your father then your mother disappear must have been confusing enough. At least if she had seen her mother in hospital she would have known that she hadn't been abandoned completely. To have three new parental figures thrust upon her must have been difficult. Two, if you think that Faye took over after her bedtime and left as she was getting up, claiming that she wasn't good with children. I disagreed. Once or twice, I caught Faye looking at Andrea and I could tell that she longed to go and pick her up, but just didn't know how. Maybe she, too, had been plagued with doubt after her experience with the adoption board.

'Children are just like dogs,' I tried to joke with her, misjudging her mood. 'They can smell your fear.'

'Two weeks and you're suddenly the expert,' she fired back at me, obviously unaware of the times when Laura had brought Andrea to stay. I had learned by watching Tom with Andrea. Faye had very rarely seen Andrea, let alone with family members. I saw that she regretted being short with me immediately after her outburst, but

Faye being Faye couldn't bring herself to say anything. We were bound together by our conspiracy, although it wasn't a bond that would bring us closer together. Whilst Faye didn't express regret, her role in the deception had obviously left her feeling vulnerable and she seemed to be angry with me for involving her. Coupled with her fears for her sister, I wondered how far I could rely on her and felt constantly sick with nerves that we would be found out.

Tom was the only constant at Laura's bedside. Mrs Albury and Faye were shocked by his altered appearance. I have no idea what passed between them as they sat and waited for words of hope, but they remarked on it when we saw each other briefly between visits. I found myself the recipient of Mrs Albury's steely gaze on several occasions. She said very little, but little needed to be said. I wasn't sure exactly what Laura had told her mother about what led to Tom's disappearance, but it didn't take a genius to put two and two together. The main concern that Mrs Albury voiced was whether Andrea would recognize her father, but Tom had yet to ask to see Andrea. His focus was on Laura alone.

The hospital staff took a shine to this strange figure and decided that he qualified for a bed. It was while he was there that he started the treatment that would set him on the road to recovery, barely realizing that he too was a patient.

Laura was kept heavily sedated for eight days. Each time the poisoned blood circulated around her body there was danger of damage to her major organs. She received a number of blood transfusions until the antibiotics performed their magic, her fever subsided and she was declared clean.

When she opened her eyes and looked at Tom, she asked simply, 'What happened to your mane?' It was as if he had nipped out for a quick haircut rather than been missing for several months.

Despite the fact that I was in the room, her gaze was entirely on him. She was clearly groggy and I had no idea what she remembered, if she knew where she was or why she was there. She didn't ask for Derek.

'I'm sorry,' she mouthed at Tom after a while, her eyes filling.

With his back to me, I could not see if he made a response, but his head dropped forwards.

'Welcome back.' The nurse bustled past to check Laura's pulse. 'You gave us quite a scare. Out of the way, boys. I need to run some checks.' She ushered us out of the room, pulling the curtains around the bed. We sat on chairs in the corridor. I recognized both disbelief and relief in Tom's expression. He rubbed the tufts of hair on his head as if surprised not to find curls.

'She made it,' I said to him. 'You brought her round. She's going to be all right.'

He stood up and wandered off in the direction of the exit.

'Where are you going?' I asked him.

'Home.' He shrugged, as if I had asked a very obvious question.

'Don't you want to wait and talk to Laura?'

365

'I've been talking to her non-stop for the past week.'

'What shall I tell her?'

'That's your business. You know where to find me when you're finished.'

Satisfied that he was not leaving altogether, I let him go. He must have been exhausted. I waited my turn, dreading what I should say. In the end, I didn't need to use words.

'Pete?' Laura asked, a mix of hope and regret.

I sat by her side and took both of her hands in mine. Before I could speak, I was overwhelmed by tears and I shook my head, unable to look her in the eyes.

It was as if I had only confirmed her own thoughts. 'I knew, I knew. When did it happen?'

'Five days ago.'

She bit her lip. 'It was as if I could have woken up, but I didn't want to open my eyes. I almost didn't want to come back. He was so small. He was just too small.'

We cried for a long time for the loss of Derek, not knowing where to go with the conversation next. Periodically, Laura would say, 'I didn't get to say good-bye,' or, 'Were you all on your own?' or, 'Does Andrea know yet?'

Eventually, she sighed, 'They said I can go home the day after tomorrow.'

I tried to smile. 'That's good news.'

'Do you know what I said to the nurse? I said, "I have no idea where home is any more." ' She looked away, her face crumpling again. We both knew that, as well as the loss of Derek – which was terrible in itself – this was the end of the road for us.

I tried to say the words I had practised in my head with as little emotion as possible: 'Tom needs you.'

'You're letting me off the hook.' She looked at me with a large degree of affection diluted with a small amount of pity.

'I'm afraid they think he's had a complete nervous breakdown,' I explained to her. 'It will be a slow road to recovery. Your mother wants you all to move in with her. She thinks that Andrea is settled there now and shouldn't be asked to move again. You're going to need her help.'

'Oh God, she's right again, isn't she? And what about you?'

'I'll think I'll go back to my own place tonight. It's going to be quite crowded now that Faye's back as well.'

'Faye came home?' Her eyes filled again.

'She's been so worried about you.'

'Pete . . .' she began, but I stopped her.

'Don't say anything else. You just concentrate on getting well. Everything else will fall into place.' I got up and did my best to say cheerfully, 'I should go and tell the good news to your folks. There's a little girl who will be wanting to see her mummy.'

'I don't deserve you. I never have.'

For just one second I wanted to tell her what I had done. What had I done? Instead, I turned and left. 'Get some rest,' is all I could trust myself to say. I never was any good at saying goodbye to Laura.

Understandably, I wasn't there for the full family reunion. Faye reported that Andrea accepted Tom's reappearance without question, but said to him what no one else had dared say, 'You're too thin, Daddy. You're no good for sitting on any more and I don't like your hair.' This made Faye howl as she told the story standing in my hallway. At the time, she said, jaws had dropped and everyone had been speechless.

'That's my girl,' I said with some pride, noting Faye's frown and wondering what I had done to cause offence. I changed tack: 'Does Laura talk about Derek?'

'Not once. How could she? I don't think she ever will. She's treating Tom like the child she's lost, if you ask me. It's going to be very slow progress with him. We don't know if he'll ever recover fully, let alone work again. I don't envy her one bit.'

'Have you been sent to spy on me?' I asked as she loitered, looking around. It was her first visit to the house.

'Of course I have.' Her caustic tone returned instantly. 'You're a very poor host and I'm certainly not here for the company. You haven't even invited me in.'

'You make me nervous,' I admitted.

'Have you got anything to drink?' She removed her coat from her shoulders slowly and let it drop to the floor, watching my look of horror. Then she pulled at her polo neck jumper lightly and said mockingly, 'Unlucky this time.'

I apologized and showed her into the living room where we sat awkwardly at opposite ends of the sofa, pretending to relax, a whisky glass in front of each of us and the open bottle on the table. I was drinking far too much at the time, seeking solace in my work and at the bottom of a bottle. I felt that I had suffered four losses and the fact that those people were still alive didn't make them any easier to bear. I finally had to admit to myself that I had lost Laura, the love of my life, I had lost my only son and I had lost Andrea, whom I had known for all of her life and had been looking forward to bringing up as my own daughter. And, finally, I had lost Tom, who was without a doubt the best friend I have ever had.

'Did we do the right thing?' I asked the question that would always be on the tip of my tongue.

'We did what we did and there was nothing else we could have done. You put a family back together. Mind you, you owed them that. You're not going to find my name on the petition nominating you for sainthood, if that's what you're asking.'

'That's not what I was asking.'

'And don't forget that I've got to live with myself as well. You dragged me into this.'

'I haven't forgotten.'

'And I hate the fact that you're the only person I can talk to about it because I don't want to be so reliant on you. But I do need to talk to someone. I'm not sure I can keep it all bottled up. Do you understand what I'm saying?'

I nodded.

'Of course you do.' I thought she was being dismissive

of me, but it seemed that she was correcting herself, because she continued, 'For what it's worth, I think it's a damned shame. It pains me to admit it but from what I've seen of you and children, I have strong suspicions that you would have made an excellent father.' Through the long history of our acquaintance, Faye has never ceased to shock and surprise me, but that was quite possibly the most surprising thing she has ever said to me. She seemed to struggle with the words as she cleared her throat: 'I don't suppose you considered just taking Derek and disappearing?'

'I thought about it. If only that would have worked. But how could I have left before I knew if Laura would pull through? And what mother would have let that happen? She would have spent her days trying to find us. It would always have come between Laura and Tom. Even if Tom eventually accepted Derek, he would have been a constant reminder.'

'What about you?'

'Me?' I shrugged, pouring myself another large whisky. 'I will celebrate being a bachelor by buying myself a very expensive and impractical sports car.'

She tapped her empty glass, a reminder that I was not being a good host. When I had rectified the situation, she clinked my glass. 'That's the first really sensible thing you've said so far. I'll drink to that.'

'And you?'

'What about me?' She seemed defensive.

'Will you slope off back to London?'

'Have you seen the price of train fares lately? I

couldn't afford a return. No, now that I've made it back, I'm thinking of staying and keeping an eye on things. I thought that I'd outgrown this place and I hate the idea of everyone knowing everyone else's business, but it still has this magnetic pull. It's like a bad habit that you can't give up. And there's something else. I didn't agree with what you said when you came to see me, but after you left I looked around the flat and realized it had always felt temporary. I hadn't really settled there. It wasn't home. Have you ever thought of moving away for good?'

'Every day. Do you think it's any easier elsewhere?'

'No. It still sucks. Plus the rent's higher.'

'Then I may as well be miserable here in the comfort of my own home.'

'I thought that you were planning to sell up.'

'I moved all the way to Newcastle and it wasn't far enough,' I said. 'No, this is more of a mental removal rather than a physical one.'

'If we're going to be living in the same town, I think it's important that you know that I haven't forgiven you yet and I probably never will.'

'I wouldn't expect you to.'

'I like to bear a grudge for a very long time. It's one of my few pleasures in life.'

'You are perfectly entitled.'

'So would you prefer to pretend to be friends for the sake of appearances or shall we be arch enemies?'

'My arch enemies rarely drop round and drink copious quantities of my best whisky.'

'It is very good whisky.' She rolled it around in her glass, as if giving the matter careful consideration. 'We'll have to pretend to be friends then.'

I made a toast. 'To appearances.'

'For the sake of the family!'

Chapter Forty-six

A slow period of recovery followed with Mrs Albury at the helm and Andrea at the heart of it. Laura's physical recovery was swift, but she suffered the grief of losing Derek silently and without complaint. The burden of seeing Tom's mental and physical condition weighed heavily on her and was a visual reminder of our affair. She over-compensated for both of those things by mothering him.

Although Laura did not lose her looks at the age of thirty as she had predicted, she made great efforts not to draw so much attention to them. You could never have called her 'matronly', but the platinum-blonde hair that I had assumed was natural (it had been white-blonde when we first met) was replaced by a softer honey colour, and the clothes that she made herself were altogether less fitted.

It was clear that Tom would not be able to work for some time and Laura became the breadwinner, returning to work as a secretary in an office. Although Tom gradually gained weight, his looks were permanently changed. His hair never grew back entirely and it became clear that it had been shaved in the first place because it had started to fall out in clumps. At a time when a shaven head was a sure sign of trouble, Tom stood out like a sore thumb. He took to wearing a baseball cap, which in some ways made him look younger than his years. Most of the skills he had lost, he relearned with Andrea. He spent his days with her, seeing the world through her eyes and taking a great deal of joy in her discoveries. One of my greatest sadnesses was to learn from Faye that he had given up his music. His guitar, which was so much a part of him, was consigned to the loft. He very rarely sang, not even to Andrea, but Faye reported that he had taken to whistling. It was driving everyone mad. Like a demented parrot, he would get stuck on one line of a tune, forgetting what came next.

When Andrea started school, he was at a complete loss. It was Mrs Albury who, after a brainwave, bought an ancient 'rust bucket' for him to work on. Far from coming between Laura and Tom, she had become a lifeline.

'Mark my words, it'll give him the focus he needs,' she assured Laura, who was convinced that he might be a danger to himself.

Although it took him many months of tinkering away, he surprised even her by how complete a restoration job he eventually made. He sold the car for a substantial amount of money to a passing collector who knocked at the door and made a cash offer on the spot.

This enabled him to repay Mrs Albury and buy the next desirable wreck from a salvage yard. Andrea assisted him with these, the most important decisions that he was faced with.

'I'd like to introduce you to my business consultant, Andrea Fellows,' he told the man in charge of the yard, who shook her hand seriously. 'She will be making the final choice today.'

'And what are we looking for?' The man addressed his question to Andrea.

'We need a blue one, please,' she said.

'Blue?' He nodded approval. 'I think you'll be impressed with the selection of blue cars we have to show you.'

Tom always considered his work tinkering with cars as a hobby, but it became quite a lucrative one and helped him to regain his confidence as it took him back into the outside world. Eventually, he recognized that it was important for him to get a full-time job, his first, as part of the recovery process. Not wanting to overstretch himself, he took an administrative role in an office. Sadly, it used none of his many talents, which he seemed content to let go to waste in return for a little normality. He later told me that being able to provide for his family brought him a level of contentment that he had not previously experienced. It was not the life that he had originally wanted, but it was a good life and he was grateful for his lot.

While all this happened, I kept my distance. Faye was the one who kept me updated with the family news.

Despite her return, she seemed to remain a permanent outsider. She didn't say that she blamed me in so many words, but I always felt that she could never be as close to Laura after I had involved her in the deception about Derek. She settled into a pattern of working that allowed her to travel for months at a time. It was as if she needed time away on a regular basis, even though she couldn't settle anywhere else.

It was Andrea who orchestrated my return to favour. It was one Saturday morning while I was alone reading the papers that Tom knocked at the door with a seven-year-old Andrea. I couldn't take my eyes off her.

'Andrea Fellows has requested the company of her godfather to take her to the park,' Tom announced formally, touching his hand to the peak of his cap.

'Yes! Yes!' Andrea giggled.

They were both dressed in jeans, trainers and T-shirts. I still had my dressing gown on.

'I don't think I'm quite dressed for the occasion. You'd better come in.'

Apparently they had been walking past and Andrea had recognized my house.

'Can I see my old room?' she asked, running straight up the stairs.

'I'm afraid it's an office now,' I called after her.

Tom and I were left in the hallway. There was a moment's awkwardness.

'You look well,' I said.

He removed his baseball cap to reveal what was left of his hair and raised his eyebrows.

'I never thought I'd end up with more hair than you,' I remarked.

'Congratulations,' he replied, not unpleasantly. It was a start.

'I can't believe how much Andrea's grown. She's so tall.'

'Laura's fine.' He looked me in the eye.

'I didn't ask . . .'

'I thought you'd like to know,' he said. 'She'd never say so to me, but she misses you. Were you ever going to come round and see us again?'

'I thought it best . . .'

'You're supposed to be her best friend. You told her everything would fall into place.'

'It did,' I said. 'You're a family again. And you're both well.'

'You said everything. She thought that included you.'

'No. It could never be the same again.' I shook my head apologetically. 'Tell her I'm sorry . . .'

'You should tell her yourself.'

Andrea bounded down the stairs, looking a little disappointed.

'Did you ever find Mr Rabbit, Uncle Pete?' she asked. 'I think I left him here.'

'Was he yours?' I asked, knowing full well that it was part of a box of toys that I had taken to a charity shop. 'I'm afraid he found a new home.'

'That's OK.' She took her daddy's hand and looked at him. 'Are we going to the park now?'

'Uncle Pete has just remembered that he's busy this

morning,' Tom said, 'but he's going to come over to tea tomorrow evening and you can play with him then.' He looked at me. 'We'll be having Andrea's favourite. I hope you like fish fingers.'

'Oh, I do,' I stumbled.

Andrea clapped her hands. 'With baked beans.'

Tom opened the door and turned back: 'Six o'clock on the dot. Don't be late.'

I don't know who was more surprised to see me, Laura or Mrs Albury. Andrea and Tom had decided to keep my visit a secret, but had both pretended they were very hungry and persuaded Laura to cook twice the usual amount of food. Tom clearly found the whole thing highly entertaining. Laura barely spoke while I babbled away hysterically, wishing the whole thing was over. After Andrea had gone to bed, Tom announced that we were going for a drink. By Laura's reaction, it was clearly something that he hadn't done for a long time.

'I said I was going for *a* drink,' he said. 'It won't kill me.'

'But . . .'

'You're very welcome to join us,' he offered. 'I'm sure that your mother will be quite happy to stay with Andrea.'

'No, you go,' she said reluctantly.

He kissed her cheek. 'Back in an hour.'

Once we were outside, his attitude was that of a naughty schoolboy who had pulled a prank and got away with it.

'Got to let her know who's boss again. "Be assertive," they told me. How am I doing?'

'I think you're doing very well. You certainly told me.'

'I was practising on you,' he said. 'I've spent days building up to that. You have no idea how long it's been since I set foot in a pub.' He inhaled the smoke and the smell of hops as if the blend was a luxurious perfume. 'Buy me a beer,' he added. 'I forgot to ask for any pocket money.'

It became a weekly event, repeated at first only because I was humbled by Tom's capacity for forgiveness. I can only think that facing me was part of his recovery process and that it was something he needed to do. I thought about all of those things that drew me to Tom in the early days of our friendship – his lifestyle, his talent, his self-belief and his ability to turn his hand to anything. What I had forgotten was that he was simply great company. Even without those things, he was still Tom. I grew to admire him more than I would have done if he had appeared on *Top of the Pops*.

Gradually, contact with Laura became easier, but she remained deliberately distant. It was a long time before we were comfortable in each other's company again. Part of this, I'm sure, was for Tom's benefit. Part of it was for her mother's benefit. And part of it was because neither of us could allow ourselves to talk about the thing that we most wanted to. To observers, I was Tom Fellows's friend, but in the silences and between the gaps in everyday conversation, Laura and I exchanged glances and we both knew that, although everything was different, some things remained the same.

Part Fifteen

Andrea's Story

Chapter Forty-seven

The purchase of 42 Westbrook Road was pushed through by Uncle Pete's firm, but he struggled with the architect's design to convert the two houses into flats.

'We're a room short.' He fretted over the drawings, turning them this way and that as if more space would miraculously appear. 'Flat 4 doesn't have its own bathroom.'

'I can share with Nana,' I offered, but he wouldn't hear of it, ignoring the fact that I had shared a bathroom with my parents and Nana for my entire life, apart from a brief respite when I had shared his bathroom, and three years at university when I shared with five other students. What did it matter if we were a room short? I was still waiting for my aunt and my godfather to ask to talk to me when the contracts were exchanged, still waiting when the date of completion came and we had what was referred to as a 'family celebration' in the lounge of the new house. Still waiting as the designs were drawn up. Still waiting as the four of us chose which of the flats we wanted. Sod that room! It was the thought of everything that could blow up around us that gave me sleepless nights.

'It's too late for me to say anything now,' I mourned to Lydia.

'It's not, love. It's just that the timing's got to be right and that moment hasn't arrived yet.'

'It's getting to the stage when the waiting is worse than anything anyone can tell me.'

'Then your head's getting sorted. That's a good milestone to have reached.'

'Ma!' Kevin shouted from the living room. 'Ah can't find the last piece!'

'Scuse me, love,' she said. 'He's doing one of those thousand-piece jigsaw puzzles. I buy them from Oxfam because he only does them the once, but this happens every time.' She slapped her thighs and pushed herself to standing. 'We'd better go and sort him out.'

The puzzle covered most of the available floor space and Kevin was kneeling by it, clearly exasperated. There was a small piece of patterned carpet showing through near the middle.

Lydia grabbed the empty box. 'He's been working on this all day.' She shook her head.

'Five hours wasted!' Kevin muttered.

Lydia beamed rays of sympathy at him. 'I'm sorry, love.'

'Is that a picture of baked beans?' I asked. 'It must have been really difficult.'

'Aye, he's good at puzzles, this one. He can solve anything, given a bit of time.'

'I don't suppose you'd take a look at the floor plans for the flats?' I joked, but then it struck me that Kevin might see something we hadn't.

He shrugged. 'May as well do it now, seeing as Ah can't finish this.'

'Right.' I was used to people who made promises and then put things off for another day. 'I'll get them, shall I?'

'I'll put the kettle on, then,' Lydia offered. 'The brain always works better with a cup of tea.'

Sitting round the kitchen table I explained the problem to Kevin. 'We need two flats in each house. Every flat is supposed to have a living room, a bedroom, a kitchen and a bathroom, and Uncle's Pete will have an office in the loft extension. The problem is that the upstairs flats have these big landings in the middle and these' – I pointed to bold lines – 'are the supporting walls.'

'Let's have some paper, Ma.' He took charge and quickly sketched near perfect copies of the drawings.

'So, that one's got ter stay?' He pointed to one of the bold walls.

I nodded and pointed. 'And that one.'

'Shame,' he said, sketching in some new lines, 'because this would have made the best room of the space.'

'I don't think they even thought of that one!' I was impressed with his initial thoughts.

'Is the flat for you?' he asked, scratching his head.

'Yes.'

'Are you set on having a separate kitchen an' living room?'

I shrugged. 'Not necessarily.'

'There's ernly two options,' he said. 'You make a larger living room an' put the kitchen in it, like this.' He drew another sketch, and let me take it in. 'Or, we could swap round these two like this, but you ernly end up with a shower room.'

He passed the plans back to me, as if he was ready for the next challenge of the day.

'That's brilliant!' I was genuinely impressed, not only by the speed of the solution, but by the drawings themselves. 'I think I could live with both of them. Have you ever thought of going in for design?'

'Oh,' Lydia nodded, 'you'd be ever so good at it.'

'It's just like a jigsaw puzzle, really.' It was his turn to shrug. 'Nothing to it.'

'Do you think you could come next door to explain it to Uncle Pete, like you did to me?'

Lydia folded her arms and raised her eyebrows. Kevin looked unsure, as if the thought of leaving the house pained him.

'Go on, love!' she said. 'It won't take a mo'.'

'You might have some more ideas when you see the house,' I encouraged.

'Just for a few minutes.' He gathered up the papers reluctantly.

'Uncle Pete!' I yelled, opening the front door.

'Through here!' came the reply.

'Kevin's solved all your problems for you. Come in,

386

Kevin.' I beckoned him over to the table where Uncle Pete was still struggling with the paperwork, one pencil in his hand and another behind an ear.

'Good to meet you.' He stood and leaned over the table to offer his hand, which Kevin held rather than shook. 'If that's the case, you're a better man than me. I don't have a head for these things at all. Spread yourself out on the table and let's take a look.'

Kevin walked around the back of the table and laid his plans out, and started talking Uncle Pete through them. As always, he kept to the point, short and simple, like all good technical explanations should be – unless you're trying to bamboozle your audience. Leaning forwards from the waist, Uncle Pete supported his weight on his hands. After he had glanced at the papers in front of him, I realized that he was looking at Kevin rather than the plans. As Uncle Pete quizzed him about details of plumbing and doors, I thought that he must have seen a flaw.

'Do you mind if I run these by my architect?' Uncle Pete asked, rolling them up and tapping his other palm with them.

'Ah've got no use for them,' Kevin said dismissively.

'Can I ask what line of business you're in?'

'Ah work for Morrisons,' Kevin replied.

'Do you design their stores? That must be very rewarding.'

'Ah stack the shelves.'

'They don't know what they're missing out on. I'm very grateful to you.' He held out a hand to

Kevin again who took it uncertainly. 'Very grateful.'

'Ahm good at my job.' Kevin seemed to be under the impression that he had been criticized.

'I dare say you are.'

Kevin turned to me. 'Can Ah go now?'

'I'll show you out.' I smiled and walked him to the door. 'See you soon. And thank you.'

'Well?' I said, returning to find Uncle Pete sitting and staring in front of him. 'You obviously saw a problem with them.'

'Not at all. They're quite brilliant. Simple but brilliant. I can't believe I didn't see it myself. Who *is* that boy?'

'That's Lydia's son, Kevin. They'll be your new neighbours.'

'He's not from round here, is he? There's a hint of something in his accent.'

'Lydia's from round here, but Kevin was brought up in Sunderland. He's adopted.'

'Adopted,' he repeated, nodding, his usually ruddy face pale.

'Are you all right, Uncle Pete?' I asked. 'You look like you've seen a ghost.'

'Not a ghost, Andrea,' he said. 'I think you'd better sit down. I've got something I need to tell you.'

He got up and opened the drinks cabinet, taking out two glasses and a bottle of expensive brandy.

'No, thank you,' I said as he poured two large measures, ignoring me.

'Can't stand brandy myself. It's purely medicinal. You

388

might need it,' he said. Then he sat and seemed reluctant to speak, covering his mouth with one hand and sighing.

'We don't have to do this now,' I said after a short while. 'It's still too early for both of us. I know what you're going to say.'

'No, Andrea,' he insisted gently, shaking his head, 'I'm afraid you don't. I'm still struggling to work out how the story fits together. And now the two people who could have given me the answers are gone, so I can only tell you my part. You see, it has always seemed as if the people who are missing from my life have been as important as those who are part of it. And as you get older, I'm afraid the list of missing people starts to grow. But for now, let me tell you about just two of those people.' He topped up his own glass. 'Stay right there for a minute. First of all, there's something that I need.' I heard his heavy footsteps retreating upstairs and then returning. He appeared with a framed photograph, which he set down carefully on the table and then turned towards me. I saw an ageing sepia print of a young man in uniform, grinning at the camera. 'I'd like you to meet my Uncle Jonathan. He was my father's identical twin. I know his face better than I know my own. He would have been twenty-one when that picture was taken. It was a month before he was killed. How old would you say Kevin is?'

I picked up the photograph by the frame and studied the face more closely, looking from Uncle Pete back to the print. There was only a slight family resemblance between them. 'He was twenty-one earlier this year,' I said, but I knew what I was holding in my hands. It was another piece of the jigsaw puzzle.

He nodded. 'Four years younger than you.'

And then he began his story.

Chapter Forty-eight

I approached Lydia's front door in a similar state of nerves to the one that she had been in on her return from London. Stowed away in my handbag was Uncle Jonathan's framed photograph. Uncle Pete had been reluctant to let it out of his sight, but I had insisted that I needed a prop.

'We're going to need two of your strongest cups of tea,' I said, heady with brandy and churning thoughts.

'Don't tell me,' she said as she headed for the kitchen, 'you've won the lottery.'

'Not quite.'

'Well, something's up, I can tell. Let's sit us down so I can give you my undivided attention.' She fussed about with teacups and the teapot, and then joined me. 'I could do with a break. I'm dead on my feet.'

I found myself mirroring Uncle Pete's stance earlier.

'Oh, Lordy,' said Lydia, bringing one hand to her own mouth and using the other to cover the one of mine that was resting on the table. 'You've had the talk. How did it go?'

'I think we've found my brother,' I said.

'Oh, that's marvellous!' She brought the hand that had been resting on mine to join its partner by her mouth.

'Yes, it is.' I nodded, reaching for the photograph and placing it carefully in front of her.

'Well, that's not him.' She had only looked at the age of the photograph rather than the detail.

'Look closely,' I told her, my eyes on her face rather than the picture. I watched as her expression changed from shock to confusion, then I poured her a cup of tea.

'Who is this?' she asked, her voice no more than a whisper.

'This is my Uncle Pete's uncle. His father's identical twin. He was killed in the second world war when he was only twenty-one.'

'Uncle Pete thinks that Kevin's his son,' she said.

'You've got to admit they're very alike.'

'But who's his mother?'

'It's beginning to look like Kevin is my half-brother.'

'The photos of the baby that you found! That was my Kevin?' she said. 'So, your Uncle Pete wasn't just visiting your mother in hospital.'

I had already gone through this stage of shock only hours earlier. The camera never lies. The question that I still couldn't quite understand was how the three of them had all managed to stay friends.

'There weren't any Fellows family photographs because he wasn't a Fellows,' I explained. 'I don't know how he did it, but Kevin may not have been so far off

392

the mark after all. Lydia, I need you to ask Kevin to open the envelope.'

She recoiled. 'It'll finish him!'

'No, it won't,' I said. 'It might come a shock, but he should have a choice whether to get to know his father. And he's never had a sister before.'

'But don't you see? There isn't any choice when the man's living next door. It's not like finding out that your father lives several miles away and you can visit if you want to.'

'Uncle Pete would never force himself on Kevin. He just wants to do the right thing by him.'

'Who we talkin' about?' Kevin ambled in, taking an apple from the fruit bowl and biting into it noisily.

Lydia and I looked at each other.

It was Lydia who said at last, 'Sit down, love. There's something we need to show you.' He sat and she placed the photograph in front of him. 'We think we've found your father.'

He sat there in silence for some time. Then, without taking his eyes from Uncle Jonathan's photograph, he said, 'Ma, please can you get me envelope.'

We waited in the living room holding hands while he faced his truth alone in the kitchen.

'Do you know?' Lydia said nervously. 'If Kevin's your brother, then we're almost related. I always wanted a daughter and I couldn't think of a better one than you.'

'Ma!' Kevin called from the kitchen. 'You there?'

'Yes, love!' She squeezed my hand. 'That's our cue.' We both stood and walked to the kitchen.

'Hello, Andrea,' he said. It was only two words, but it meant so much more. After so much loss, I had found my brother.

'Hello, Kevin.'

'Ah'd like ter be called Derek from now on,' he announced.

And it would prove to be about as liberating an experience as a twenty-one-year old is capable of.

Chapter Forty-nine

My history no longer fits neatly on to a family tree. If I have to explain who I am and my place in what I now refer to as my extended family, I follow my father's suggestion and draw a Venn diagram. I have experimented with putting a variety of people at the centre. Nana, the matriarch, who rules over her family with a rod of iron and a heart of gold. My mother, Laura Albury, who thought that her looks defined her, but discovered that she was defined by whom she loved. Tom Fellows, father, musician, engineer, mechanic, artist, all-round good guy, who regained his strength despite losing his hair. My Uncle Pete (and I still find it difficult to call him by any other name), who was responsible for bringing my parents together not once but twice. My Aunty Faye, well travelled, independent, feisty, a sister who was so close that she gave away what she thought she didn't need in her life and lived to regret it. Me, the child who so many people showered with affection to make up for their other losses, an unwitting referee in so many relationships. Derek, the child whose absence was so keenly felt that I now realize it was as much a part of the make-up of our family as I was. Even Lydia, whose ears we pour our stories into, whose ample shoulders we all cry on, whose endless pots of tea without which we would all die of thirst. She is the cement that holds our little neighbourhood together. Our keeper of secrets. Ironically, if our new family has a mother figure, it is her.

There is nothing that I enjoy more than to spy on Uncle Pete and Derek as they sit out on their front steps, separated by a fence but by less than a foot. From the movement of the net curtains in a parallel room two doors away, I know I am not the only onlooker. The men exchange only a few words, but the lengthy gaps between sentences are not awkward. Derek feels that gaps between words are an essential part of conversation. How can we possibly find the meaning of what is being said if hundreds of words tumble out unrestrained one after another? How can we enjoy conversation if we don't take the time to appreciate what the other has just said? To you and me, a comment like, 'Isn't it a lovely evening?' might sound like a throwaway exchange. To Derek, it is something miraculous to contemplate. He will consider the temperature, how the breeze feels as it touches his skin, how the streetlight reflects in puddles in the pavement. On clear nights he will be mesmerized by the number of stars in the sky, captivated by the cycle of the moon. On a cloudy night, he will observe how the moon is partly obscured and the resulting ethereal glow. He might enjoy the silence, or the whoosh of tyres on a wet road, the rumble of a distant train, the roar of a motorbike, or the bark of a dog. He carefully considers the company that he is in, and what impact it has on the whole experience. It might be a good quarter of an hour before he replies, 'Aye, it is at that.'

Uncle Pete, I'm sure, enjoys the welcome escape from the women in his life. I suspect there are moments when he regrets the loss of his bachelor pad, when he would gladly go back to the days when he was not expected to understand the inner workings of a washing machine simply because of his gender.

Uncle Pete and Derek are slowly adjusting to their new relationship. Bill will always be his da, but it is also hard for Derek to give up on the idea that he is Tom Fellows's son. He virtually modelled himself on him. It is certainly where he thought he inherited his practical talents from.

'It can't be genetic,' Uncle Pete says. 'He certainly didn't get that from me.'

It seems obvious to me whom they came from. My mother had always designed and made her own clothes, and turned old garments into new ones for me. They are forgetting that my father wasn't the only person who could fix things in our house.

Derek has no doubt spent many years contemplating the meaning of the word 'father', and Uncle Pete is right to tread gently. If anyone other than Bill announced that he was his dad, I suspect that after a long silence, Derek's response would be: 'No, you're not,' because that man hadn't been there to teach Derek how to play football or to buy him his first bike; it hadn't been his loose tobacco that was Derek's favourite smell; he hadn't been there to tuck Derek in at night or to read his school reports, or to watch his first school play. Uncle Pete is keenly aware of each of these missed opportunities and feels each one as a loss. At the same time, Derek doesn't bear him a grudge for not being there. He is too grateful for the opportunity that he had to have Lydia and Bill as his parents. And, now, just when he needs one, he has someone who is willing to be a father figure in his life – if he wants one. If not, Uncle Pete has made it clear that he is happy to settle for being a neighbour. As long as he can be a good neighbour.

At least when Uncle Pete claims that he wasn't there for the main events of my life, I can remind him that, actually, he was present for most of them. I still have the bear that he gave me for my first birthday. He still has an autographed portrait that I drew of him just after I had learned to write my name. After I remarked that, other than a two-year gap, there isn't a part of my life that he hasn't been there for, he came next door with three beautifully wrapped presents.

'What are these?' I asked him, laughing.

'These are your fourth, fifth and sixth birthday presents.'

'But you've given me too much already.'

Gifts come in all shapes and sizes. When I was a baby, he gave me and my mother a home. When I was three he gave me my daddy back. And when I was twenty-five he put my family back together once again, and gave Nana and me security when we most needed it.

Everyone thought that the shock of finding her grandson living down the same road as her would be the end of Nana, but when Uncle Peter told her, all she said was, 'I knew it!' She was more surprised to find that she is related to Derek, who she had always declared to be a little soft in the head, but she managed to come up with numerous explanations of what she actually meant when she called him 'simple'.

Aunty Faye has taken to referring to Uncle Pete as the 'man of the house'. It's a slight improvement on 'that dreadful man'. The days when she and Uncle Pete tiptoed around each other were short-lived and they now fight like cats and dogs one minute and make up over a bottle of his best malt whisky the next. Nana and I are glad of the wall that divides us, although you can probably guess what her verdict is.

'Mark my words,' she confides to Lydia and me, 'one of these days . . .'

But I disagree. It is their history that binds them together and it is the same history that pushes them apart. They have settled on a way to divert the mud-slinging. When one of them strikes out with a maliciously aimed home truth, the other will shrug and say, 'Nobody's perfect.' Because, at the end of the day, that is the only truth we can be certain of. None of us is. Sometimes, we do terrible things to each other in the name of love. If we're lucky, we get the chance to make up for them.

Nana now refers to Uncle Pete as the family solicitor. And although we have agreed that I shouldn't call him Dad, I have consented in principle to drop the 'Uncle', but it's hard to change the habit of a lifetime. There are some words that just go together. Bucket and spade, Tom and Laura, Uncle and Pete. No, if I am confused about what to call people, I am no longer confused about who they are. To me, Peter Churcher will always be my godfather. When I tell you that I have taken a leaf out of Derek's book, I hope you realize that I don't use that term lightly.

THE END